STEALING CHANCES

ALSO BY
Molly McAdams

The Secrets in L.A. Series

Passion

Love

Fame

The Brewed Series

Fix

Whiskey

Glow

Fire

The Rebel Series

Lyric

Lock

Limit

Linger (coming soon)

The Redemption Series

Blackbird

Firefly

Nightshade

STEALING CHANCES

Molly McAdams

New York Times Bestselling Author

Molly McAdams
www.mollysmcadams.com
Cover Design by RBA Designs
Photo by © Stocksy

The characters and events in this book are fictitious. Names, characters,
places, and plots are a product of the author's imagination. Any similarity to
real persons, living or dead, is coincidental and not intended by the author.

Print ISBN: 978-1-950048-09-0
eBook ISBN: 978-1-950048-08-3

For every single person who wished for something different in
Taking Chances and Stealing Harper . . .
Here is the alternate reality you've all begged for.

AUTHOR'S NOTE

This is an alternate reality version of Taking Chances and
Stealing Harper. So, keep in mind that in changing one thing,
there is always a ripple effect.
Enter at your own risk and enjoy.

PROLOGUE

CHASE

P ain.
 It seared my veins and licked up my spine.

My eyelids snapped open to harsh, fluorescent lights as a strangled cry burst from my chest.

"Hey there," an unfamiliar voice said before a scrub-clad man filled my blurred vision, his voice composed when he continued. "Try to stay calm. You're in the emergency room—you've been in an accident."

"Wha—" I sucked in air through my teeth as a wave of pain slammed into me just before the world went black.

Everything came back slowly that time, my vision and hearing not quite right. Dulled and warped. As if I was trying to see and hear everyone through murky water. But their urgency . . . I sensed that. The movement beneath me . . . I felt that too.

The lights above me raced quickly by, seeming to blur together, before I was brought to a jarring halt in a room. The world continued dipping in and out, and panic began unfurling in my chest when my shirt was cut away from my body as the nurse entered my line of sight again.

"We've got you," he said, firm and determined. "You just keep fighting."

But that pain was consuming.

My lungs felt constricted in a way that warned and had that panic flaring.

And everything around me was going so, so dark.

ONE

CHASE

Harper.

A gasp tore through me and shifted into a hiss when pain raced down my side. My chest heaved with shallow breaths as I tried to draw in oxygen, but each movement had that pain increasing.

Each breath was sharper than the last, even as I tried to calm and control them.

"Chase?"

My brow furrowed at the unfamiliar voice, and I tried to open my eyes to see who it belonged to. To see the girl behind the relief and worry.

But I was so focused on trying to breathe around the pain—trying to figure out *why* there was pain.

Harper . . .

The accident . . .

Shit.

"Oh God, Chase!" A hiccupped sob left the girl. "You're okay, you're okay," she said softly. "Just try to slow your breathing. Try to—"

Quick steps sounded before a man asked, "He's awake?" just as a hand slipped into mine in a way that shouted familiarity when I didn't know either of the voices in the room.

I tried to move my hand away.

Tried so damn hard to open my eyes.

But all I managed was a raspy, wheezed curse as I took a semi-decent breath.

"Yeah," that same girl said, the word sounding like a cry wrapped in laughter. "He hasn't opened his eyes yet though."

"He will," the man said, closer to me now. His voice gentle and clinical as he continued. "Welcome back to us, Mr. Grayson. You're in the hospital. You were in an accident and gave us a few scares, but you're doing fantastic, all things considered. Just continue working on leveling out your breathing for me, and let's see if we can open those eyes."

I tried.

But this new pain threatening to pull me under? It was different.

Because I was having flashes of the days and minutes leading up to the accident. The absolutely fucking *bliss* of being with Harper and planning out our future with our baby she was carrying.

Then waking up to a nightmare that I still couldn't wrap my head around.

Another woman in my bed, even though I'd never considered touching anyone else after Harper had come into my life. Harper finding us there. Leaving with Brandon so she could escape what was right in front of her.

And then leaving *me*.

After waiting for her for so long—after watching her with

my best friend—I finally had her. I finally got to hold her and love her. And I *lost* her.

Harper, I'm sorry.

I'm so fucking sorry.

I was so lost in the memories playing on a loop, fueling my need to fix what I'd unintentionally ruined, that I couldn't focus on what the people in the room were saying to each other.

I was so weighed down by my grief and my need to see Harper that when lips pressed to my forehead and that same hand slipped into mine again, my movements were delayed when I tried pulling away.

"Need—" I rasped, my head slanting slightly and sending another shock of pain. "Need to see her. Harper."

The man hummed in understanding. "Is Harper your girl-friend?" When a weak grunt left me, he said, "She's notifying your family that you're awake and giving us time to run some tests. I've dimmed the lights so they won't be too hard on your eyes when you open them, but I need you to try to open them. Until then, can you tell me your full name?"

"Chase." I stumbled over my name and tried to swallow. But my throat felt raw. Like I'd scrubbed it with steel wool. "Chase Austin Grayson," I finally managed.

"Good," the man said. "Do you know what day your accident was?"

"Saturday," I said confidently. "I—fuck," I rasped as my dry, scratchy eyelids finally opened. "Graduation . . . I graduate tomorrow."

My bleary gaze narrowed on the doctor beside me in time to see him glance at me before writing something down.

"Let's check those eyes now that they're open," he said

instead of responding and pulled out a pen that ended up being a flashlight.

I tried looking around the room once he was done with his tests, but only the two of us were in there. "Did I miss graduation?"

"Graduate from where, Mr. Grayson?"

Something about the way he phrased the question had my stomach twisting and my heart beating a little harder. But each beat had that physical pain pulsing and growing.

I ground my jaw against it and asked, "Where's Harper?" instead.

"Harper's your girlfriend . . . correct?" he asked curiously, then lowered his clipboard to study me before repeating his earlier words. "She just left to notify your family and give us time for these tests."

My eyebrows drew close as I tried to remember the girl's voice. But it had been completely unfamiliar.

"San Diego State," I finally answered, voice somehow hoarser than before. "That's where I'm graduating from."

Affirmation sounded in his chest as he wrote. "Congratulations, Mr. Grayson." But when he focused on me, his careful expression had that twisting in my stomach coming to an all-time high. "Can you tell me when your birthday is?"

And that's how it went. On and on.

Asking mundane things and repeating them as two other nurses came and went until I felt like I was going to lose my damn mind.

"Do you know—"

"When can I go?" I rasped over the doctor, then hurried to apologize. "I'm sorry. I'm sorry, but I can't be here. I need . . ."

I needed to see Harper. I needed to fix things with her.

"Mr. Grayson, you were incredibly lucky," he began with a heavy sigh. "The accident you were involved in . . . most people wouldn't make it out alive. But you're here, you have full use of your body, and you didn't have any internal bleeding."

He was giving good news. I understood that.

But the bad news had to be coming.

I could see it in his eyes and hear it in his voice.

"We lost you a couple times, but you came back. You started breathing on your own after the first day and were able to be taken off the ventilator soon after that. Since then, we've just been waiting for *this*."

"How long?" The words clawed up my throat as I watched the way he was studying me, seeming to expect something, even as he continued.

"Minor cuts and scrapes. Broken ribs and collarbone—which you're probably feeling. Severe concussion. But . . . you're lucky."

"How long?" I repeated.

"Since the accident?" he asked in clarification, but I just watched him, unable to nod or move. "Less than seventy-two hours." He lowered the clipboard and drew in a steeling breath. "And you'll probably be here for about that much longer."

I waited for what he wasn't telling me, but he just turned toward the door when it started cracking open and held up a hand to stop whoever was on the other side.

"We'll have some more tests to run, Mr. Grayson," he went on, "but I'll allow your family in here in the meantime. However, the best thing you can do for yourself is to rest."

My gaze shifted to the door.

Worry and anxiousness twisted through me as I wondered if

she'd be there. As my mind raced back to the hand that had slipped into mine and the lips that had pressed to my forehead.

I tried remembering the voice of the girl who'd been speaking to me. Tried connecting it to the voice I knew.

But then my parents were spilling into the room, and my mom was a fucking mess. And for a second, my full attention was on her. On the way she was looking at me as if she'd been afraid she'd never get the opportunity again.

But only for a second.

Because the doctor was pulling them aside, revealing my sister and her boyfriend. And my sister looked . . .

An uneasy laugh worked from my lungs, sending another shock of that pain through me. "Did you cut your hair?" I asked, then shot a quick glance to the doctor before focusing on my sister again as I lifted a hand to my head.

To the dull headache forming there.

To vainly attempt to steady the way it felt like the entire room shifted for a split second.

"What?" Breanna asked, the word part laughter and part sob as she and Konrad came to stand near the side of my bed. "That's seriously the first thing you say after you escape death? You freaking punk."

I guessed when she put it like that . . .

Then again, the first words I'd spoken had been about Harper. Because I needed to see her. To talk to her. To fix everything I'd inadvertently fucked up.

"You just . . . you look . . ." Different. She looked different.

Not just her hair. Everything about her.

But before I could ask again how long it'd been since the accident—or how and where Harper was—a slender hand slipped into mine, pulling my gaze to the other side of the bed.

But just as the slightest hint of relief began washing over me, confusion blasted through me when I saw the stranger standing there.

"Who the hell are you?" I asked as I jerked my hand away.

Her expression shifted into a stunned sort of horror, but I just looked to my sister again when her soft gasp slammed into me with the force of a sledgehammer.

"*Chase*," Bree whispered, my name a mixture of disapproval, dread, and worry.

"Where's Harper?"

Bree's mouth had been opened to keep talking, but at my question, her head shifted back and she looked at the other people filling the room until my panicked, "Where the fuck is Harper?" bled free.

"Harper . . . my best friend, Harper?" she clarified slowly as she met my stare again.

Dread spread through me like thick tar as that last day replayed, amplifying the building headache.

"Best friend," I murmured, head slowly shaking. "Is that all she is now?"

"I'm confused," Bree said under her breath, and her boyfriend muttered a curse before pulling her close and whispering in her ear.

"Chase," the girl on my other side said softly, her voice breaking.

I watched my sister and Konrad for a second longer before looking at the strange girl. "Who—" I pulled my arm away when she reached for me again. "Look, I'm having enough issues because a girl somehow ended up in my bed. So, if you could stop touching me, I'd appreciate it."

The physical impact my words had on her was immediate

and evident. Her chest caved and tears slipped down her cheeks, but she just stood there. Staring at me as if her world was crashing down around her when the last thing I remembered, it had been my world that was being destroyed.

"Chase, that's Scarlet," Bree said, words slow and unsure, even with the hardened edge to them.

"Okay?" I said, twisting the word so it sounded like a question. "Why won't anyone tell me where—"

"Mr. Grayson, I'm sorry," the doctor said as he stepped toward the foot of the hospital bed.

I curled my hand into a fist so I wouldn't yell for someone to just answer me as he continued speaking.

"I was incorrect in my earlier assumption when you woke, considering this woman has been here nearly the entire time you have." He gestured to the stranger at my side, then released a steadying breath and gave me a placating smile.

And just like that, my earlier worry was back.

Because that bad news I'd been waiting for was here.

"Mr. Grayson, it seems you may be suffering from amnesia," he went on. "Retrograde amnesia, to be exact. And from what I'm gathering, you might be experiencing some confusion."

I tried to laugh but ended up sucking in a pained breath through my teeth instead.

He was wrong.

This had to be a joke.

"Is that common?" my mom asked, the question coming out soft as she leaned against my dad for support.

"It isn't unheard of," he said to my parents as if I wasn't laying right there. "More common when the amnesia is caused by certain events. But it happens—false memories that the subconscious has completely made up or others that are truly from the past, but at very different times than the patient remembers."

"What memories?" I asked through clenched teeth and fought the urge to continue reaching for my fiercely pounding head.

"Your graduation was the day after your accident?" my dad asked after a shared look with my mom. "Is that what you told the doctor?"

I looked between him and the doctor a couple times and even looked at that girl for some reason. That girl who now could no longer look at me.

She was just staring at the edge of the bed I was lying on, silently crying.

"Why?" I asked cautiously.

"Chase, you already graduated," he said carefully. His eyes darted over my face, taking in my reaction. "Two-and-a-half years ago. Bree and Konrad just started their senior year at San Diego State."

No.

No, because . . . if any of that were true, then that meant Harper had our son *years* ago. And they weren't *here*.

"Harper . . . where's Harper?"

The girl next to me released a pained breath and staggered back a step before falling into the chair there.

"Why do you keep asking about her?" Bree began, but my mom hurried to hush her.

"Are you fucking kidding?" I asked through clenched teeth.

"Chase," Mom muttered disapprovingly.

"They're on their way," Dad finally answered. "We called them as soon as we found out you'd woken."

"They're on their way."

The words replayed again and again as my eyelids closed and relief barreled through me.

Wasn't sure I'd taken a full breath before then. I'd gladly take the pain that came with it if it meant she would be here soon.

They would.

"We should talk before they get here," Dad continued. "Because from what the doctor said, some of your confusion seems to revolve around her."

I just needed a chance to talk to her. To fix things.

Then again . . . if that day was years ago . . . no, it couldn't have been. It just *happened. I remember it all so damn clearly.*

"Chase, who do you think Harper is?" my dad asked slowly, a whisper of worry weaving through his words.

Forcing my eyelids open again, I took in the curious and concerned looks of the people in the room as my eyebrows drew close in confusion. "My girlfriend."

"*What?*" Bree said on a breath, sounding wholly confused.

Before I could respond or fully comprehend that shock was mixing with everyone's concern, the door opened, and my heart took off.

Slamming against my broken ribs when she entered my line of sight, looking more beautiful than the last time I'd seen her.

"Harper." Her name was a breath wrapped in gratitude—

What the fuck?

The frantic beating of my heart.

The relief.

Everything disappeared when my best friend, Brandon, stepped in behind her and curled his arm around her waist in a move that shouted possession.

A move I'd been forced to watch him do with her so many times before I'd finally gotten the chance to make her mine.

"Hey," Harper said a little hesitantly, gaze drifting around the room before landing on my sister and narrowing in confusion. "Is something wrong?" At that, her gray eyes snapped to me, then my parents and the doctor.

Brandon wrapped his other arm around her, pulling her close as he leaned against the wall. Nothing but relief on his face as he said, "Man, you scared the shit out of us. Glad you're awake. Glad you're *here*."

I'd been breaking before the accident.

Drowning under the realization that I'd been losing Harper over something I knew I couldn't have done. Because touching someone else when I had her? That . . . that I wouldn't do.

But we'd been through so much bullshit just to be together, and I'd known it couldn't end like that. I'd known I'd do anything to fix it.

But she was on the opposite side of the room instead of at my side. In Brandon's arms, once again. And no one in my family seemed to think anything was wrong with this nightmare of a scenario.

"What are you doing?" I asked Harper, words straining around the betrayal and heartache overwhelming every other physical pain. "You're just gonna stand there with him after everything?"

"Chase," my dad said in hesitant warning, but I didn't look away from Harper as her eyes widened and Brandon's head slanted in question.

"Yeah, we should go talk," Konrad murmured, stepping toward them.

"Harper, don't do this to us," I begged and watched as she sent a confused glance around the room.

"*Us*," Brandon echoed in a low, dull tone.

"Man, you should've known I wouldn't give her up that easily," I ground out against the wave of vertigo that crashed into me.

"Wait, what?" Harper asked with a stunned laugh as Bree crouched next to me and softly pled, "Chase, stop talking."

"Really, let's go talk," Konrad said to Harper and Brandon again.

"I think that's a great idea," the doctor said when I started refuting the idea. "Let's everyone give Mr. Grayson time to rest, and we can talk in the hall."

"Harper, wait—" I began when she and Brandon turned for the door, but Bree grabbed my hand and hissed, "Chase, *stop*."

"The fuck is wrong with you?" I demanded, narrowing my eyes on where it looked like she was fighting tears.

"Bree," Konrad said from the doorway as everyone began filing out of the room.

She looked at him and then back to me, her brow furrowing with indecision. "I don't know what you think you're remembering, but Harper isn't your girlfriend," she said gently.

"Don't," I whispered, maybe begged. Because I didn't want to be in a world where I'd truly lost Harper.

But her next words had my world tilting.

Spinning.

Shaking everything I knew.

"She's never been your anything."

TWO

SCARLET

Given his reaction, you would've thought someone had torn Chase's world out from underneath him at Bree's hushed words.

No longer frustrated or aggravated . . . he just shut down. Face paled and eyes widened as he stared at his sister, not seeming to see her or anything in the room.

And that was what made it worse.

Chase would fight anything to the death in that way of his, all passion and obnoxious arrogance that I'd fallen in love with. But when he was truly hurt—truly stunned—he gave. Withdrew in on himself as if inspecting the emotional damage.

Bree's words had *hurt* him, and they shouldn't have.

Funny that it only made my confusion and pain for myself greater when I'd expected to feel nothing but relief and gratitude in this moment.

Bree glanced at me, her face pinching with sorrow and apology. When Konrad said her name again, she hesitated for a second before hurrying to where everyone else had already left.

But I couldn't seem to move from the chair I'd spent so

many hours in, praying for the first time in my life. Waiting for Chase to pull out of the coma he'd slipped into.

Only for him to wake up and ask who I was . . .

"You don't know me." My voice was hoarse as it scraped past the shards of glass in my throat. And even though I tried to *ask* the words, it came out as a statement.

Chase slowly turned his head. Those shocking blue eyes looking at me in a way I wasn't sure they ever had.

Even from that first day, there had been a spark of interest and mischief that had lit them as they'd slowly taken me in.

This? There was nothing except a hint of resentment.

"Am I supposed to?" he asked as my building tears slipped down my cheeks. The cold, unfamiliarity in his question forcing a knife into my chest.

"I'm Scarlet."

"Yeah, I heard."

I forced back the building sob and said, "We've been together for a little over two years." That knife twisted deeper, and the pain burned hotter when denial and irritation fell over his expression. "We're getting married in a few months."

"No."

Just *no*.

One word that had me wrapping an arm around my waist in an attempt to alleviate the churning in my stomach.

"Chase—"

"Stop saying my name like you know me," he snapped, then dragged a hand over his face. "This is all some fucked-up joke. Some prank my family's playing on me because of what happened—what they think I did to Harper. But I wouldn't . . . I never would've cheated on her."

Funny how I'd never once been jealous of the girl who was

practically family to the Graysons. Until today. Probably because she'd been there before I had. Always there for family days and holidays—a permanent fixture.

Then again, I'd never worried about women in general with Chase because he'd treated me like the world revolved around me from the beginning.

And now he was breaking my heart and making me question everything over memories his subconscious had created.

"Chase, none of that . . . it's like Bree said. Harper isn't your girlfriend. She's *never*—"

"Stop," he demanded on a twisted plea.

I hurried to swipe at the relentless tears and tried to steady my breathing, but my body stilled at his next cold words.

"Take that off."

I slowly looked at where his enraged stare was locked on my hand, then followed his line of sight to my engagement ring.

My heart skipped before painfully forcing another beat and then another. "What?"

"How the hell did you get that?"

"Chase . . ."

"I said *take it off.*"

"No," I said through the pain and unknowns and worry.

"That isn't yours," he said through gritted teeth. "I was going to propose to Harper tomor—the day after the accident. With *that* ring."

I couldn't make sense of the chaos of emotions storming my body and gripping my heart.

The denial. The medical understanding of it all. The heartbreak from his coldness and unfamiliarity. The jealousy I knew I shouldn't be feeling . . .

Right?

I twisted the ring on my finger before protectively curling my right hand around it. "You bought me—"

"No."

A hushed sob broke from me. "Chase, you gave me this ring. We're getting married."

"Why are you doing this?" The obvious hurt lacing his frustration kept me from responding. He pressed his fingers to his temple, his eyelids squeezing tight for a moment, but the discomfort remained on his face when he asked, "Why are all of you doing this?"

"We're not—"

"Miss?"

I glanced over my shoulder at where the doctor stood just inside the room, my shoulders sagging at his discernable expression.

"Mr. Grayson needs to rest."

Hesitation wove through me, but I still stood. Stepping in that direction as my attention pulled back to Chase.

To where my heart had lain for the past three days.

But he was staring straight ahead, eyes unfocused, expression full of doubt and frustration.

I wanted to tell him I loved him. I wanted to tell him I'd be back. But the pain lancing my body prevented me from saying anything else as I unsteadily walked from the room. Hands gripping my chest and stomach, vainly trying to hold myself together when it felt like I was falling apart.

"Scarlet . . ."

I looked up and then around at the sound of my name, my chest heaving when I saw the Graysons watching me with varying looks of worry.

But my feet continued carrying me away from them. Away from the room I'd spent hours and days waiting and praying for him to come back to me. Stumbling down the halls and breaking into a run until I was outside.

Shaking.

Desperately trying to breathe.

Falling to a crouch with my head in my hands.

My sobs finally breaking free when arms wrapped around me and pulled me close.

"It'll be okay," Bree whispered as she held me. "It's going to be okay."

"He doesn't know me," I said through the tears straining my throat.

"He will," she said after a delay. "The doctor said the pieces of our memory we lose in these kinds of traumatic events often come back—and *soon*."

"He thinks he's with Harper," I choked out, then twisted so I could look at the girl who had come to mean so much to me. "He thinks he's *proposing* to Harper. He told me to take my engagement ring off."

Bree's expression fell.

"He was horrified when he saw it on my hand."

Her head shook for a moment before she unevenly said, "He's confused."

"But why would he think he has an entire life with her? Has there ever been anything—"

"No," Bree hurried to assure me. "Trust me, Harper was just as confused when we told her what Chase said."

I considered her words, but the damaging thought that had been plaguing me spilled past my lips. "But has something been lingering on his end? Something that manifested into a reality because of whatever memories the doctor was talking about?"

Bree pressed her lips firmly together. Her expression clearly shouted that she wanted to deny it, but there was no real way to *know*. "He loves you," she finally said. "You're his world."

I pushed to standing and wiped at the tears clinging to my cheeks before wrapping my arms around my waist.

Trying to hold in the pain.

Trying to ward off the bone-deep chill slowly crawling through me.

"I'd thought the phone call about his accident was the worst thing I would ever experience," I said, tone dulling as I stared out at the busy parking lot in front of us. That morning and that call replaying like a nightmare I hadn't been able to shake off for the past three days. "Then having them tell us that he kept coding . . ."

My jaw trembled and my head moved in jerky shakes as I turned to look at the girl whose blonde hair and blue eyes so closely matched her brother's. "He pulled through, he's awake, he's *here* . . . so why does it feel worse?" I asked through the newly building tears. "How can I be so relieved and thankful and *broken*?"

"I don't know," she whispered, her voice dipping with emotion. "I don't know, but it's temporary. The doctor said he could have his memories back within twenty-four hours."

"And the confusion? Does that go away?" My shoulders jerked in a hasty shrug. "Do I just pretend that she won't always be in the back of my mind now?"

Before Bree could respond, the sliding doors opened next to us, revealing her family.

"There you are," her mom said as she hurried over to us, opening her arms and pulling us both into a hug as she fought her own tears. "He's awake. He's going to be okay."

I nodded at her hushed words, my eyelids squeezing tight when I could no longer see through my blurry gaze.

"Can we go back in?" Bree asked, sounding at once hopeful and hesitant.

When no one responded, I pulled from Claire's hold and glanced between her and her husband, Robert.

"The doctor asked that we give him today," Robert began, then cleared his throat. His stare flashed to me before falling to the ground. "But he won't see any of us anyway."

"Because he thinks we're playing a prank on him?" I asked, recalling what Chase said.

Robert's head listed, his face scrunching on one side in a way that looked so like Chase. All hesitation and unease.

"He only wants to talk to Harper," Claire finally answered, giving me a remorseful look.

But it was clear in their tones and expressions that none of them understood this. None of them had known—if there had ever been anything at all.

My gaze slid past our small group to where Bree's boyfriend was talking to Harper and her husband, Brandon . . . Chase's best friend.

I had a feeling my expression closely matched theirs. Drawn. Bemused. So fucking lost. And full of doubt.

Except I was sure I was the only one whose doubts included Harper.

As if she could feel me watching her, Harper's head turned and her eyes met mine. Chagrin and guilt swept across her features before she forced her stare away, her chest heaving as if the action had taken effort.

Then again, if Brandon woke up from a coma and thought he was in love with me, I'd be uncomfortable facing her too.

"I need to get out of here," I said before I could do something stupid . . . like ask Harper if there was any truth behind the memories.

"Scarlet, wait," Bree hurried to say when I took a step back just as Claire reached for me, looking more apologetic for me than concerned for her son.

I squeezed my eyes shut, needing to escape all those looks that made this new reality *real*. Needing to go back an hour to when I'd been waiting and praying for Chase to just *wake up*.

"Why don't you come home with Konrad and me?" Bree continued. "You shouldn't be alone."

"I'm fine," I hurried to assure her as I focused on the concrete beneath my feet. "I just . . . I just need to go."

I needed to run. To clear my head.

I needed to erase from my mind the way he'd looked at me like I was a stranger.

I needed this not to be happening.

I hurried through my goodbyes, then rushed to my car. But instead of going home, I just drove.

For hours and hours, I drove aimlessly until I ended up on a random beach at dawn. My torn heart shattering and stitching back together as I hurled pebbles and shells into the ocean, screaming at the water and any god listening.

Thanking them for this second chance.

Damning them all for this new nightmare I was trapped in.

THREE

CHASE

She was there.

She'd *been* there.

Most of the day yesterday and for hours already today, even though I'd told her repeatedly I didn't want her there. That I didn't want to see anyone until I'd had a chance to talk to Harper.

"I know," was all she'd said each time.

Scarlet . . .

She didn't try talking to me. She didn't try feeding me the same bullshit she had when I'd woken.

She just sat there, staring at nothing or reading or doing whatever she did on her laptop. Her silent presence grating on me simply because she was still there.

Still wearing the ring that wasn't meant for her.

A near-constant reminder that my family was trying to hurt me for what I'd apparently done.

I rubbed a hand over my face, wincing when I roughed over the bruising and cuts without a thought. "There has to be somewhere else you can be," I said irritably. "A job. School. Somewhere."

"The doctor assured us this wouldn't cause mood or personality changes, but you've never been this much of an asshole," she muttered before her midnight eyes met mine. "And I do have a job. I've been rearranging or rescheduling so I could be here."

"I don't want you here," I said on an aggravated laugh.

"I'm aware," she said tightly.

"Then why are you?"

"Because if I was the one lying there, you would be sitting right here," she said unquestionably.

"God," I said on a groan, an irritated smile pulling at my mouth. "Don't you think it's gone on long enough?" When her eyebrows drew close in question, I gestured to her. "We don't know each other. We aren't engaged. This act was pointless two days ago. It's fucking old now."

Her jaw wavered but she just held my stare a little longer before looking at her laptop again.

And I fought back my aggravation as we fell into the same silence we'd been in the past two days. With her seeming to wait for something from me. With me waiting for her to *go*.

"I understand you're unable to access the last two years," she said a handful of minutes later, voice soft and shaky and drawing my attention back to her. "I'm *trying* to understand that the same injury that took away your memories of us gave you memories of a life with someone else. But the thing is that you don't need to be able to access those memories to know that I'm not some *act*. That I'm not some *prank* to make you miserable." She hurried to brush away the tears that quickly formed and raced down her cheeks. "You already have the proof you need."

Something about the ache in Scarlet's voice pulled at me. Made my fingers twitch, almost as if I'd been about to reach out toward her.

But I curled them into a fist. Ignored the stinging in my chest. Played it off as a result of making a woman cry. Of being such an asshole to her, as she'd said. It wasn't her fault my family had roped her into this.

Then again, she'd agreed to it.

Before I could think to respond to her, the door opened, and a breath rushed from my lungs on a pained wheeze. "Harper."

She paused in the doorway, hesitation warring on her face as she glanced between Scarlet and me, before continuing inside—

With Brandon right behind her.

Jesus Christ.

"What, are you guarding her now?" The question ripped from me on a growl and had Brandon's eyebrows lifting.

"Chase, this is awkward as hell," he began, voice edged with warning, even though he sounded like he was trying to be placating, "but I'm here for you just as much as I'm here for her."

"And I asked him to come with me," Harper added as she came to a stop at the foot of the bed I was propped up in. "Why do you need to talk to me before you'll talk to Mom and Dad?" she asked, using the affectionate name she'd always used for my parents.

"Because you're who I need to see—to talk to. You're who I need to figure shit out with." I tossed my hand in Scarlet's direction as she put her laptop away. "And all anyone's doing is lying to me to give me shit for what happened."

Two lines formed between Harper's eyebrows as she studied Scarlet. "And what do you think happened?" she asked before meeting my stare again.

"You think I cheated on you," I said with a harsh laugh that held no humor. "With Trish, of all fucking people."

Shock colored Harper's expression, but I continued before she could say anything.

"I don't know what happened. I just woke up, and she was there. I can barely remember half the party, but I wasn't even drinking that night."

"Chase . . ." Harper looked around at the people in the room again, her voice soft and uneasy. "Chase, all this, whatever you're worried I think, none of it happened."

My stomach twisted and fell. "Don't . . ."

"We aren't together," she said gently as my head shook. "We've never been together."

"Why are all of you doing this?" I snapped. "Harper, I'm sorry. I'm so fucking sorry for hurting you. But we—Jesus, do the two of you have to be here?" I asked, looking from Brandon to Scarlet.

But Scarlet just looked at me through glassy eyes before her stare fell to her lap, and Brandon mumbled, "Not sure this is fun for either of us, but yeah . . . think we have to."

I ignored his weighted tone and focused on the girl in front of me.

The girl I'd spent days and nights learning and cherishing and worshiping.

Gray eyes wide and unsure as she looked just past me.

Auburn hair falling to her waist—*shit, was her hair different too?*

"Whatever, man, sorry to do this to you again," I said under my breath, not bothering to look at Brandon as I did. "Harper, we've already tortured ourselves for months of trying to stay away from each other while you were with Brandon. Then staying apart after the two of you broke up because of what we'd done. Because there was so much guilt and miscommunication. But I'm not letting you do this again. I'm not giving you up because of another fucking miscommunication. I'm not letting you take our baby from me."

A heavy exhale punched from Harper as Brandon said, "Excuse me?"

"This . . ." Harper's head slanted as her hand fell to her stomach. Her *flat* stomach.

What the fuck, what the fuck, what the fuck?

"Chase, this isn't your baby," she said slowly, evenly.

My gaze snapped to hers and narrowed. "Harper—"

"No, you need to hear this," she said firmly.

"Why are you doing this?"

"Because it's true."

"It isn't fucking true," I yelled over her. "We're having a baby—a boy. We just found out it's a boy. I was going to propose to you before everything fell apart the day I got in the wreck. With *that* ring she won't take off," I snapped, gesturing to where Harper's engagement ring stood out like a beacon on Scarlet's hand.

"Jesus," Brandon breathed as he rubbed at his jaw.

Harper just looked at Scarlet like she felt *sorry* for her before finally turning to me again. "Something happened to your memories when you were in a coma, Chase."

"No," I said as she went on, already knowing where she was going with this.

"We have never been together. We've never done *anything*."

"Harper—"

"Brandon and I *just* found out we're expecting a couple weeks ago."

My head pressed back against the pillows at the news that felt like a crucial blow. But that was wrong. It had to be wrong.

"I have nearly a year's worth of heartbreak and absolute fucking bliss that says you're lying," I ground out. "That says *you're all* lying." Harper's lips parted to deny it, so I hurried over her. "Sundays were my days with you when you were still with him. Everything changed when we kissed on New Year's Eve. I finally gave you your lilies, and days later, that tension between us snapped. *We* snapped, even though you were still with Brandon at the time."

"As much as I love listening to you talk about how you think my wife cheated on me with you, I'd like it if you stopped."

Betrayal pushed through me so quickly at Brandon's words that it stole my next breath.

I looked between them and then down to Harper's left hand, only then noticing the rings on her and Brandon's fingers.

"Wife?" The word fell like ash from my tongue as my stare dragged back to hers.

"A few months ago. You were Brandon's best man," she informed me softly. "Chase, I can see how much this is hurting you, and I'm sorry. But none of that ever happened."

I was so stunned by his claim and the way she'd effortlessly confirmed it that I wasn't able to deny what she was saying. Wasn't able to call them out for continuing this fucked-up prank by pretending to be married.

And as much as I wanted to maintain that everything had *just* happened days ago, the subtle differences in everyone's appearances now seemed glaring. Because I just realized Harper wasn't looking at me the way she always had.

Even when I'd aggravated her or wrecked her heart, there had always been an unmistakable desire in her eyes. A love that had kept me close. That had drawn us together, even when we should've kept our distance.

And that was gone.

For a moment, I wondered if I really was missing years. If I really had dreamt up everything.

But my need for Harper refuted that as quickly as she about broke my fucking heart all over again.

"First, you and I have never kissed," she said resolutely. "Second, Brandon and I have never broken up, and I've never cheated on him. And third, I have no idea what lilies have to do with anything—you mean the flower?"

"Yes," Scarlet said from my side.

"Okay?" Harper said as if lilies weren't her favorite flower. "Regardless, as sorry as I am that you're in this situation and that this is hurting you, you're putting doubt in your relationship and mine when there shouldn't be any."

My head moved slowly before stopping as a thought occurred to me. "Show me," I demanded softly. "Show me your lilies, and then tell me none of that happened."

Because I remembered drawing them up. I remembered

preparing for that moment with her—giving Harper her first tattoo. Four large orange lilies wrapping around her left hip to her stomach because they were her favorite, and I'd known there was no way to give her flowers without risking Brandon's wrath all over again.

I remembered the torture of touching her and being so close to her. Her soft gasps and the way I'd had to constantly stop her from moving as if I didn't want to *make* her move beneath me.

I remembered the way she'd crushed her mouth to mine when she'd first seen what I'd done. The way I'd passed my mouth across hers again as I'd finished covering it . . . and the way she'd taken those hours and shattered me all over again when she'd answered the call from Brandon when I'd still been inches from her lips.

"What lilies?" Harper asked as Scarlet whispered, "She can't."

I sent a frustrated look Scarlet's way before focusing on Harper again. "Your tattoo. The tattoo I gave you."

"She can't," Scarlet repeated.

Harper looked between us before hesitantly adding, "I don't have any tattoos."

It was odd to know you were on a solid surface and to feel like you were falling. To feel like you were no longer tethered to the earth.

The vertigo that had been lessening over the past two days came back in an instant, making me feel off-balanced. The sudden ringing in my ears was deafening as I tried to understand what she was saying.

"You're lying." But for the first time, I sounded unsure.

"I assure you, she isn't," Brandon argued.

My gaze pulled to the side, hesitation warring as I studied

Scarlet. Wondering exactly *how* she'd known Harper wouldn't be able to show me the lilies before Harper had.

With a hard shake that only amplified the lightheadedness, I looked at Harper. "Left hip. Four of them. I know they're there."

Regret marred her expression. "Chase—"

"Harper, I know you," I said through clenched teeth. "You can't tell me we weren't real. I can feel you. Taste you."

"Fuck, enough," Brandon snapped. "That's my wife, and can't you see you're hurting Scarlet?"

"I don't even know who she is!"

"She's your fiancée," he shot back.

"Except, she isn't."

"Chase," Harper breathed, her horrified stare going to the girl next to me. With a determined huff, Harper stormed around to my other side, her voice dropping low. "I can't imagine why she's still in here, taking everything you're saying, other than because she loves you and knows you're confused. But my heart is breaking for her—*you* are *breaking* her heart."

Again, that flicker of pain in my chest.

That twitch of my fingers before I could control it.

But all of it was overwhelmed by how I felt blindsided by everything Harper and Brandon were trying to make me believe. By how I was *starting* to and how it was wrecking me.

"Chase, I love you," Harper went on. "But it isn't in a way you're expecting me to. You're family to me. Nothing more."

"You can't say that and mean it."

"But I can," she said gently, then released a long sigh. "Years ago, when a frustratingly stubborn stranger literally *tossed* me in his bed and forced me to sleep there because he thought he was protecting me from his housemates, I might've gone so far as to say a reluctant crush formed."

My heart raced as I remembered that night.

The first moment I'd ever seen her. This wild contradiction of a girl who'd made me want to wrap her up and protect her and had me falling for her in the span of a breath.

But Harper's mouth just twitched in amusement when she looked over her shoulder at where Brandon stood and added, "For about a week."

"Because you met Brandon," I said in understanding, not that it meant anything. I still remembered her warring feelings after their meeting. Remembered the way she would look at me as if she hated that she was falling in love with me *too*.

She slanted her head in acknowledgment. "It was over for me then. But even if I hadn't met him, that *very* reluctant crush had been something I'd imagined and romanticized over a week where I hadn't seen you. Because the next time I did, you were just Bree's brother." She lifted a hand before letting it fall to the bed.

"You were funny and irritating and slightly nauseating because you really didn't know how to keep it in your pants. Sorry, Scarlet," Harper muttered, briefly glancing to the side. "And you were super protective of me when it came to my relationship with Brandon, but in an annoying older brother kind of way."

Brandon grunted in agreement as my head shook.

"No. No, we fought constantly," I argued, looking at Brandon. "We *physically* fought over her. All the guys in the house were involved because they were always pulling us off each other."

A hushed breath eased from him. "Never once fought you unless it was for training at the gym."

What the hell was happening?

How could they look and sound so confident when I could distinctly feel every pain and pleasure of the past year with Harper?

Or—fuck, however long ago it was.

How could I know in my gut what was real and still have this feeling like my world was being shifted? Like I was falling because I didn't know which way was up.

"Harper, I—"

"You're going to get these last couple of years back," she said softly, assuredly. "And this memory your mind created will fade. Hopefully." She playfully rolled her eyes, making my chest ache. "Then I'll just be Harper again. Your friend and the girl you view as a sister, and this will become a *super* awkward story."

"You're everything," I maintained.

She made a face as if she hated having to hurt me, then shook her head.

When her lips parted, I whispered, "You're my *Princess*. You're *everything*."

Confusion stole across her face when I held out my arm to show her the piece that had the word 'Princess' hidden within it, but her stare just darted between the tattoos and me a few times before she hesitantly asked, "Chase, do you know what you're showing me?"

"Something I should have a long time ago."

Her head moved subtly as she tapped the spot on my forearm. "I think *you* should look at it."

I knew what was there.

One of my closest friends and coworkers had done the tattoo for me while giving me so much shit because of the hidden word.

But Harper's tone had me afraid to look.

Afraid that my world was about to shift all over again.

Slowly, I pulled my arm back and turned it to look at the spot I'd just shown her. My stomach dropped and the bed disappeared from beneath me when the word I'd expected to see wasn't there. In its place was a four-letter word.

A *name*.

Scar.

It felt like an eternity passed before I finally forced myself to look at the girl sitting next to me. Same as she had been for days.

Looking destroyed. Lost.

Looking like she refused to run no matter what I threw at her.

Curses and denials gathered on my tongue even as her earlier words replayed in my mind. *"But the thing is that you don't need to be able to access those memories to know that I'm not some* act. *That I'm not some* prank *to make you miserable. You already have the proof you need."*

Jesus, how could everything I knew be a lie?

How was I supposed to trust my thoughts anymore?

Because this was that *proof* she'd talked about, and my mind was still screaming it was wrong.

My heart was violently thrashing, begging me to continue fighting for the girl on my left because the one on my right was a stranger.

With one last glance between the three of them, I let my head fall to the pillows and released a sigh as my year with

Harper flashed through my mind in bits and pieces. Faster and faster until it came to a crashing end.

And that devastation I'd been wrapped in since I'd woken exploded until it felt like I was suffocating. Drowning in the heartache and the fear that I wouldn't get Harper back—that I'd pushed her away for good . . .

Because none of it had been real.

FOUR

SCARLET

He hadn't spoken.

Ever since he'd noticed my name on his arm two days ago, Chase had sat there. Staring blankly ahead, even as people came and went. Looking like we'd all betrayed him. Like *he'd* betrayed himself.

And I'd been there as much as I could. Waiting for him to regain any piece of his memory. Waiting for him to talk to me. Waiting for him to just *look* at me.

But he hadn't, and my heart had slowly broken a little more.

And I knew I should've been more excited for him to be released from the hospital and come home, but as I'd cleaned and shopped for groceries for the first time in over a week, the unknowns and worries had plagued me.

Because even though he'd only been awake four days, I'd realized my hope that his memory would come back *the next day* was already beginning to fade while my suspicions grew.

Whether or not he'd harbored feelings for Harper all these years, I wasn't sure. But at least *some* of his 'created' memories with her were actually his memories with me. And he'd been terrified that he'd lost her because he'd woken with another woman in his bed . . .

He'd been desperate to make her know he hadn't cheated on her . . .

As soon as he'd mentioned the lilies that he'd tattooed on me, my worries had formed. When he'd tried showing her the tattoo on his arm that was my name and not hers, they'd begun spreading through my veins like a disease that had only grown over the past couple of days.

I'd never worried about my relationship with him. But what if these created memories were actually his fears with me come to life?

What if he'd confessed his sins without realizing what he was doing?

"That's insane," Bree said when I told her as much.

I grabbed our coffees and mumbled a *thank you* to the barista before turning toward her, my voice hushed as we walked to the front doors of our favorite shop. "Bree, there's something you don't know."

Her steps faltered as she looked at me, and after a delay, she took her drink from my hand. "Okay, let me take a sip before you tell me whatever this is because, clearly, it's heavy."

A weighted breath tumbled from my lips, my eyebrows lifting in agreement.

"Judgment-free zone," she said once she'd taken a long drink of her iced coffee.

I gave her an affectionate look, then pushed on the door so we could slip outside. "I was with someone when I met your brother. Chase knew," I hurried to add.

Her eyes widened, but she lifted her cup. "Still a judgment-free zone," she said quickly before taking another drink.

"You're such a dork," I said as a soft laugh eased from me, but I didn't feel any lighter.

If anything, that weight on my chest and in my stomach felt heavier.

"I should've broken up with him immediately because Chase was . . . well, I fell for him that first night," I finally went on. "But I didn't, and I know that's terrible. But I'd been with my boyfriend for years, and I tried telling myself Chase was just an intriguing stranger. Then I got trapped until I was hurting them both."

"And Chase knew the entire time?" Bree asked from where we stood outside my car.

My head moved in a jerky nod. "He was never okay with it, and I *really* hurt him by taking so long to decide, but we couldn't stay away from each other."

"How long did this go on?"

"About two months," I said regretfully.

"Okay, well, I thought that was going to be more dramatic, like a year, or something," she said, then slanted her head. "Still bad—*no judgment*!"

"I should've broken up with my boyfriend the night I met Chase," I said unquestionably as I reached for the handle of my door and slipped into the driver's seat.

"But you didn't," Bree said once she was sliding into the passenger seat of the car, "and that was years ago. So, what does this have to do with Chase's weird memories of Harper?"

My tongue darted out to wet my lips as those suspicions wound deeper and deeper until I felt sick with them. "He thought Harper had been with Brandon," I informed her softly as if someone might be listening. "That they'd gotten together *when* she was still with Brandon before she finally left Brandon for Chase."

Bree's expression fell. "Oh."

"And he told Brandon they physically fought over Harper."

"Okay!" Bree said as if that were a piece in the Chase Mind Puzzle in my favor. "Chase probably never even met your ex, right?"

I made a contradictory sound as I reversed out of the parking spot. "My ex had had his suspicions for a few weeks, but when I broke up with him and told him everything, he went to the tattoo shop. Chase let him get a hit in before Brian and another artist had to pull them off each other."

"Shit."

A laugh left me that held no humor because there was nothing funny about this. "And with everything else?" My shoulders lifted before heavily falling. "It's us. These memories have been us, just twisted so he thinks it's Harper."

"But maybe not everything," Bree argued gently. "He's so in love with you, Scarlet. He wouldn't hurt you."

I focused only on driving for a while before murmuring, "That's what I'd thought. That's what I *want* to believe."

"Maybe you have it wrong," she said a few minutes later, sounding hopeful as she turned in her seat to face me. "Instead of being your relationship twisted around, maybe the memories really are just randomly created events with little added twists of the two of you."

"Maybe," I muttered, but doubt fueled the word and filled the car as we fell into silence.

And I knew from the way Bree sat there the rest of the way,

just holding her drink, that all my suspicions were no longer 'insane' theories.

There were too many similarities for them to be.

When we pulled up to the house, Bree rested her hand on my arm to keep me from leaving the car. "I know you've heard stories about him, but you didn't know how Chase was in college. He was . . . well, honestly, I'm surprised he doesn't have dozens of kids or a disease."

"Thanks, Breanna," I mumbled dryly.

"Sorry." She scrunched her face apologetically before leaning closer, her blue eyes clashing with worry and resolve. "That stopped when he met you. Immediately. He wouldn't cheat on you."

"Yeah," I breathed. "Yeah, you're right." I tried to force a smile and rambled, "It's just this week. The exhaustion and fear and heartache from it. I'm letting it get to me and trying to create solutions that only cause more pain."

"It's going to be okay," she said confidently. "I can't imagine how difficult this is for you, but he will come back to you."

Before I could respond, my attention caught on the car slowing down on the street and turning into the driveway.

Claire's car.

"They're here," I said quickly.

"What—already?" Bree asked, looking over her shoulder as I reached for my coffee and the door handle at the same time. Forgetting completely about my seatbelt until I tried to get out of the car and got caught on it.

I needed to slow down.

I needed to breathe.

But I was trembling when, just seconds ago, I'd been fine.

The doctor had said going about his normal life might help with the retrieval of those lost memories. But this was Chase's first look at our life together, and I felt anxious over it. Because what if he hated our life and broke my heart even more? What if this didn't work?

But what if it *did*?

I drew in a shuddering breath as I finally managed to step out of the car and tried desperately to cling to that hope as I watched their doors open. My feet automatically taking me to the man my heart called for as he stiffly and awkwardly got out of the car, only to falter at the warning look he sent my way.

"What are you doing here?" he asked as he adjusted the sling his arm was in.

I looked to the house as if I somehow might've driven to the wrong one, then gave his parents a hesitant look. "I live here too."

"With Bree?" he asked doubtingly, then looked to his sister and back to me just as Bree came bouncing to my side and announced, "Konrad will be here in a minute."

My stare swept to his parents again before locking on Chase. "With you."

His eyebrows shot up as he looked at the house.

"We said we were taking you home," Claire said as she came up beside him.

"Yeah, I—" He dragged his free hand through his hair, his head subtly shaking. "I thought this must be Bree's new place when we pulled up. What happened to my house?" When his mom started gesturing to the house just past us, he said, "No, *my* house. The one on—"

"Where you lived with Brandon and all the guys?" Bree

asked, then hurried to explain, "You stopped renting it after you graduated."

Chase nodded slowly as he took in the house. "So, this is where I live." He didn't phrase it as a question, so I didn't bother answering. I wasn't sure I could without correcting the 'I' to 'we.'

"Well, let's get inside," Robert suggested when a heavy awkwardness fell over us.

"Right," I said, hurrying away from Chase and everyone else so they wouldn't see how I was struggling to hold on to my waning composure.

Once I had the door unlocked, I burst inside, my gaze touching on everything as if the house might have fallen into chaos in the time it'd taken Bree and me to run and grab coffee.

But it was how we'd left it.

It was how it usually looked.

And suddenly, it didn't seem like enough.

Oh God, please work.

"Anything?" Claire asked hopefully as soon as they'd all entered, and Bree hissed, "*Mom.*"

"I'm sorry," Claire said repentantly, but she still looked at Chase expectantly.

He looked between the three of them before seeming to realize what they were waiting for. "I don't suddenly have my memories back, if that's what you're asking." He glanced around the entryway and study before muttering, "If anything, I'm now wondering if any of my memories are real."

"Of course they are," Robert assured him, but I just stood back, waiting near the kitchen, feeling like an interloper in my own home.

"Kinda would've thought I'd have something that showed I

surf," Chase said before giving a hesitant laugh. "Because I thought I did that."

"We do," I assured him, then felt everything in me shrink when his cold stare narrowed on me. My voice coming out weak when I added, "Our boards are in the garage."

"*We* surf?" he confirmed.

"Every morning."

He looked at where Bree stood beside him. "I don't surf with Brandon and Konrad and the guys?"

Bree looked at me as if she could feel the pain that burst from me at being dismissed by him. With an apologetic glance directed at me, she told him, "You do. Scarlet surfs with all of you and sometimes out-surfs you. She also could've answered that for you."

A breathless laugh left Chase as he spared a look at me before hanging his head. "Yeah, guess she could've."

And then he was gone.

Walking past me. The sound of his steps slowing in the kitchen before they moved deeper into the house. As if he was taking everything in. Trying to recognize it.

"What can we do?" Claire asked. "How can we help with this transition? Do you need food? Help taking care of him? Anything?"

"No," I murmured, then swallowed past the tightness in my throat. "No, we'll be—" I choked over the word 'fine' and stared at a spot on the floor for a moment before stammering, "I can—I-I already got everything. Thank you though."

"Of course, honey." She gripped my hand in hers and gave me a smile I was sure was meant to be reassuring. "Everything will be okay."

"Are you guys not staying?" I asked when Robert stepped toward the door, a whisper of panic weaving into my words.

I'd been alone with Chase for hours each day, but this was different.

This was unfamiliar territory to him that was *supposed* to be familiar. A place he shared with me when he wanted nothing to do with me.

"The doctor said it would be best," Robert began, then nodded behind me, even though I was sure Chase hadn't come back. "Get him back in his normal life and give him space to get used to it. Become acquainted with it again. Hopefully recognize it. *You're* his normal life."

"Right," I whispered, then glanced to my side where Chase should've been. The place he normally *would've* been whenever we were saying goodbye to people.

But the empty space felt so significant that it stole my next breath.

"Do you need us to pick up a new phone for him?" Robert asked after we'd already said our goodbyes as if he'd just remembered. "Chase asked what happened to his on the way here. Not sure he realizes just how bad the wreck was."

A chill raced down my spine at the images I was sure I'd never be able to scrub from my brain. From their paled expressions, I had a feeling his family was thinking the same.

"I already got one last night," I said thickly, gesturing behind me. "It's in the kitchen."

"Oh, thank you, honey," Claire said, reaching out to squeeze my hand one last time. "Anything at all . . . please . . ."

"I'll call," I said, knowing it was what she needed to hear.

She looked into the house one last time before Robert led

her away, and Bree wrapped me up in a tight embrace just as Konrad pulled up to the curb.

"He will come back to you," she muttered before meeting my eye, and then she was gone too.

I'd never been so afraid to be alone with Chase.

Not that I was afraid of *him*. Just afraid of his words.

Terrified of the way the smallest actions and looks seemed to slay me when they used to warm every part of my soul and light a fire inside me.

With a stuttered breath, I locked the door and turned to make my way through the house, leaving my coffee in the kitchen as I did. Worry and trepidation growing thicker the further I made it until I finally found him.

Standing in our bedroom.

Staring at the large photo of us that hung over our bed.

One I'd always loved and suddenly felt unsure of because it was beautiful and raw and utterly *us*, and he had the power to ruin it.

We'd just gotten the keys to this house and had rushed over with a few boxes, beyond excited to just stand in the home because it was *ours*. And after unceremoniously dropping the boxes in the entryway, Chase had carried me back to this room as we'd torn at each other's clothes.

The middle of the floor of this room would always be my favorite spot in the house because we'd spent hours there.

Loving each other. Laughing. Planning our future in this house.

And then he'd told me to stay.

"Stay?" I'd asked as he'd scrambled into his boxer briefs.

He'd dropped to the floor again, caging me in with his hands on either side of my head, and had captured my mouth for a slow, searing kiss. "Right here. Stay."

A contented hum had sounded in my throat. "Not going anywhere."

I'd watched as he'd jogged out of the room, listening as his steps echoed through the empty house. And seconds later, he'd been back with my purse.

"What—"

"Just wait," he'd begged as he'd rummaged around, a smirk pulling at his mouth when he'd produced a pen and let my bag fall to the floor.

And then he'd been there with me. Pressing teasing kisses and bites up my thigh and hip as he'd rolled me onto my side.

"Stay," he'd repeated, grabbing my butt teasingly as he'd removed the cap from the pen and held it just over my skin. Going back and forth as though he'd been trying to figure out where to begin.

"What are you doing?" I'd asked when the pen had continued moving without ever touching my skin.

He'd hushed me. Those blue eyes flashing to meet mine for the briefest moment, all affection and excitement before he'd focused on my hip again. "Giving you something," he'd muttered as the pen's tip had finally touched down.

The photo above our bed had been taken about an hour later, after he'd drawn my lilies on me—a couple days before tattooing them in the same place—and had claimed my body all over again.

It was wholly indecent, considering we were clearly naked,

even though nothing was showing because of the angle, and Chase's tattooed forearm was mostly covering my breasts, but it was my favorite.

Our obvious adoration and excitement. The way I'd caught the beginning of his smirk as he'd been trailing his nose along my jaw.

I loved it.

"There a guestroom here?" Chase asked, turning to look at me.

My stomach clenched when I noticed the muscle ticking in his jaw and frustration dripping from him.

Just as I began nodding, he started walking toward me— toward the door. "Then I'm staying in there."

"Chase—"

"What did you expect?" he ground out just as he'd passed me. "That I'd miraculously remember everything the second I set foot in this house? Or that I'd pretend with you because I'm supposed to be going through my day-to-day life to hopefully get those lost memories?"

"Of course not, but—"

"We supposedly have a life together, right?"

My chest heaved at the 'supposedly' he'd slipped in, and I willed the burning in my eyes to soothe. But before I could respond in any way, he went on.

Voice cold and so unlike the man I knew.

"What if you woke up tomorrow, and everyone told you your life was a *lie*? Some fucked-up joke your own mind had played on you?" His stare dragged over me before meeting my own. "Don't you think you'd be a little bitter? Broken? *Wrecked*?" His eyes rolled as he started past me again.

I pressed my hands to my chest and mouth to prevent the

cry threatening to break free, my eyelids squeezing shut and tears slipping free when he spoke near the doorway.

"It isn't that it's *you*, Scarlet. I'm sure you're a great person, and you're—Jesus, you're gorgeous. It's that I have no idea who you are, and my entire being says I'm in love with someone else."

The sob ripped from me, and my body crumpled at the crucial blow.

To my heart. My soul.

To our strained bond that used to feel indestructible.

FIVE

CHASE

I t was two-and-a-half years past when I thought it was.

Harper wasn't pregnant with our son. She was married to Brandon.

I understood that. I'd had to come to terms with that, as fucking devastating as it'd been.

Didn't mean every reminder that it was the future didn't trip me out. Didn't mean my heart didn't break all over again at every reminder that the girl I'd fought for and loved wasn't mine. That none of it was real.

Didn't mean it wasn't weird as shit to be standing there with Brandon the way we always had before Harper had come into our lives and put a strain on our friendship.

Because that strain had apparently never happened.

Our friendship had never faltered.

Seriously . . . a fucking trip.

"You keep looking at me like that," he said as he settled against the counter and folded his arms over his chest the next day. "Like you're waiting for me to do something and want to beat the shit out of me, and I can guess why."

"You can't," I said before he could continue. "You can't imagine how this feels."

He slowly dipped his head in a nod. "Never claimed to. But what do you want me to do, Chase? Avoid you until you get your memories back?" He waved a hand toward me before folding it again. "I get you think all this shit happened, and that has to be hard. But look at it from my side . . . I had to listen to you tell me how my wife cheated on me with you. I'm standing here *knowing* that you think you're in love with her. But I'm not going to abandon you. You're like my brother."

And there was my problem.

I kept waiting for him to throw a punch because I could *remember* hurting him by sleeping with Harper when they were still together. I could *remember* his hurt and betrayal when she'd left him, and we'd gotten together.

At the same time, it took constantly reminding myself that none of it was real to not be the one to swing first because he had her. He'd *married* her.

Felt like I was going insane.

"I don't know what I want," I finally answered just as footsteps sounded in the far hall.

I slanted my head but didn't look over my shoulder, listening as they faltered until Brandon called out, "Hey, Scarlet."

"Hey," Scarlet replied hesitantly.

"You okay after this morning?"

My gaze snapped back to him and narrowed as a hushed, uneasy laugh sounded from the living room.

"She got worked," Brandon explained. The words came out teasing, but I had a feeling it was for Scarlet's benefit because the look he gave me said it'd been bad.

"Surfing? She really goes with everyone?" I asked as she entered the kitchen, running her fingers through her short, relaxed, bleach-blonde hair.

It was the first time she hadn't had it styled closely to her head since I'd woken from the accident, and it completely transformed her features. Made her look a little more innocent, even though her full lips and the seductive shape of her eyes still shouted wicked temptation.

Scarlet hummed in acknowledgment but didn't meet my stare. She hadn't since yesterday, not that I blamed her.

I knew I'd hurt her. That I'd *been* hurting her.

"Yeah, but we hadn't gone since—" She choked on what she'd been saying, her dark eyes shifting around quickly as she cleared her throat and swept her hands over her bare stomach.

Movements all nervous energy and making her look incredibly insecure when nothing about Scarlet said *insecure.*

The sports bra and leggings she wore fully displayed her inviting curves and toned body. And the placement of the tattoos decorating her brown, sun-kissed skin was meant to draw eyes the way I'd just realized they had mine.

But before I could force my gaze away, I saw it . . .

The edge of a tattoo I'd know anywhere, curling around her hip.

Fucking *lilies.*

"I probably shouldn't have gone today either; I was too distracted," she finally muttered as I dragged my stare from her body, only to lock onto her face.

Jesus, why am I looking at her?

I ground my jaw as I finally forced my attention away from Scarlet. Feeling so damn confused and hating that it felt like I was betraying the girl I loved because I'd gotten caught up in appreciating the beauty of a girl who was apparently my fiancée.

Absolutely going insane.

"Thing was massive, and the sets we'd been getting weren't clean," Brandon said in Scarlet's defense. "We were surprised she didn't bail."

"Distracted," she reminded him.

"Regardless," he said with a patient sigh, "you good?"

"Not the first time it's happened. Won't be the last." She shrugged, then looked at me before quickly glancing away. Her delicate throat worked and her head slanted as she stammered, "Do you—I'm—um . . . Chase, do you need anything?"

"No."

Her head moved in quick, subtle nods as she turned. "I'll be in the garage if you do."

"Damn," Brandon whispered when Scarlet stole through the kitchen and through a door that must've led to the garage.

I tried forcing away the lingering confusion and guilt and met his disappointed stare. "What?"

"Wasn't sure you could be more of a dick to her than you were at the hospital. Glad to see I was wrong," he added sarcastically.

"I didn't ask for her to be here."

"She didn't ask for you to forget her." He held up a hand to stop me from responding, tone apologetic when he said, "I shouldn't have said that. That isn't fair to you. But this—what you're doing—isn't fair to her either."

"She wants her fiancé," I said gravely. "I'm not him—not anymore. I know nothing of the life she had and is ready to continue with me." I gestured to the kitchen around us. "I don't know this house or where anything is in it. I don't know her last name. I don't know what she does for a living. I don't know how I fucking met her. I don't know *her*, Brandon."

"So ask her," he said as if I should've already thought of that.

"She—" I pressed my lips into a tight line and fought the aggravated smile I could feel forming.

Because voicing the words gathered on my tongue would only cause more discomfort. More issues. But accepting that my life was with Scarlet meant fully accepting that I wasn't actually in love with Harper.

I refused to accept that what I felt wasn't real.

And a small part of me was clinging to the chance that there was truth to my memories.

I'd accepted that Harper and Brandon were married. That Harper wasn't *mine* in the sense that I couldn't hold her and kiss her whenever I wanted. But what if our heartbreaking affair had really happened? What if Harper and I had come together when we shouldn't have? After I'd gotten engaged to Scarlet, or she'd married Brandon, or sometime in between.

What if my mind had twisted the reality of our situation and fit it into something from years ago, and I'd carelessly outed us in front of Brandon and Scarlet?

What if my fiancée wasn't the person I was in love with?

And it was that small part that kept me from asking Scarlet for details about her or our life together. Kept me from wanting to get close.

"I can see those thoughts you're warring with," Brandon said, his voice edged with warning. "Chase, I can't imagine waking up and losing years' worth of memories and having an entire year changed. But I can't stress this enough: the Chase that was standing there a little over a week ago wouldn't stomach anyone even suggesting him and Harper together."

My jaw ached from the pressure I was putting on it, but I didn't say anything. Just waited for him to continue.

"Knowing how you truly view Harper, you're going to have a hard fucking time dealing with the way you've been thinking about her when you get your memories back," he said. "Not only that,"—he gestured in the direction Scarlet had gone—"you *worship* that girl."

"I get that," I said through clenched teeth. "People keep reminding me of all that. But that isn't what I feel or what I *know*."

"In that regard . . . you can't have my wife." He shrugged. "I would say 'sorry,' but I'm not. She's mine."

Yeah, we'll see about that.

"Is that why you're here?" I asked, forcing the thought aside and nodding to the remnants of the breakfast he'd brought with him. "To remind me of that?"

A breath that bordered on a laugh bled from him. "I'm here because this is what we do. Mostly," he amended with a slant of his head. "We surf. We go home. We meet back up at the gym and then have breakfast at one of our houses."

"McGowan's?" I asked, brow furrowing as I waited for him to confirm or tear apart more of what I thought I knew.

"Yeah." He blinked quickly and scrubbed a hand over his face. "I know I need to explain things to you, but I keep expecting you to already *know*. I bought McGowan's last year—Konrad and I bought it when McGowan decided to retire."

"You own McGowan's?" I asked dully. "The boxing gym. The place—I mean, we met there, right?"

Confusion washed across his face as if he was surprised I'd even question that. "Yeah . . ."

"I don't know what in my life is or isn't real," I said harshly.

He held up a placating hand. "Sorry—yes. I met you there my freshman year. That's how we got started fighting in the Underground. Not that you fought long."

I nodded, thankful that at least something was as I'd remembered. "You still fight?"

"Hell no. Harper would kill me." He scratched at his temple, something flashing across his face. "I've taken too many hits. One of my last fights didn't end well, even though I won—you were there. Wasn't anything like what you just went through, but I apparently scared the shit out of everyone, enough that Harper warned me against fighting again."

"But you said *one of* your last fights," I said, the unspoken question clear.

His eyebrows rose in confirmation. "Yeah, well, I'm not perfect."

"Could've fooled me."

A hushed laugh him. "Shut up, man."

The corners of my mouth had been twitching in amusement before I finally realized what he'd said earlier. "How the hell did you *buy* McGowan's?"

One of his shoulders lifted. "Underground."

Surprise wove through me. "Fuck, I'm in the wrong profession."

His next laugh was sharp and loud. "That was your exact reaction when I first told you I was buying it."

"Good to know I'm still me," I muttered, then said, "Speaking of, it's nothing crazy like a business, but I need to buy a phone." I gave him a wry smirk. "I was told mine couldn't be found."

Brandon didn't respond.

Just stared at me. His face ashen and jaw working.

"What?" I asked hesitantly.

"Don't look at the pictures," he said under his breath. "Ever."

"On my phone?" The question came out slow and uncertain because that was one of the main reasons I wanted a new one.

To see what was on it.

See if it could help me confirm any of the memories I'd supposedly created, or at least piece together what was true.

"Of your truck," he said grimly. "Of the accident." His head moved in wide, slow shakes. "Chase, it's nothing short of a miracle that you're standing here. Your phone was probably destroyed with everything else."

I nodded on a delay. "Right."

"But, yeah, I'll take you to get a new one. When do you want to go?"

I cleared my throat and ignored the pain when I pushed from the spot at the counter I'd been leaning against. "Now."

"Tell Scarlet," he said when I stepped forward, freezing me in place.

"Seriously?"

He gave me a look like he was trying not to lose his patience with me. "After what happened, it will freak her out if you just disappear. Yeah, seriously. It's also something you would've done before."

I clenched my jaw so I wouldn't respond and headed in the direction she'd gone. Thankful I didn't have to try a bunch of doors to find the garage because there was only one off the small mudroom.

Opening the door, I started calling out that we were leaving but faltered when I found her in there. Moving quickly through the space that was decked out to look like a small gym, arms weighed down with battle ropes.

"What are you doing?" I asked instead.

She looked around, that insecurity surrounding her in a second when it hadn't been there just before. "Setting up."

"For what?"

"Training."

I took in the space again before looking at where Brandon stood behind me. "Are we too good for McGowan's or something?"

"Idiot," he muttered, then jerked his chin to gesture behind me. "Ask her."

"If she's too good for McGowan's?" I asked in a dull tone.

He inhaled slowly as he pinched the bridge of his nose. "Jesus. No."

I looked back to where Scarlet had returned to setting up and asked, "Training for what?"

"My clients," she answered before meeting my stare for the briefest second. "I'm a personal trainer."

"And you can't do that in a gym?"

"I would hit you if you weren't broken," Brandon muttered behind me.

But I didn't need his threat to know my tone and the question had been shitty. I'd known as soon as it left me.

I just couldn't seem to stop with her.

As fucked up and possibly incorrect as it was, all I could

see when I looked at Scarlet was that she meant I wasn't with Harper. She meant my heart would continue shattering.

And it came out in every word I said to her.

But the way that insecurity seemed to explode from her at my question had my gut twisting and my chest tugging painfully. Had my fingers twitching.

Because I knew in that second that *I* was the reason behind her insecurity.

Shit . . .

"Technically, yes," she answered as she continued setting up, turning so her back was facing me. "But I don't. Is there something you need?"

The way her tone had dipped and wavered had me shifting forward, but I forced myself to stay in the doorway.

Clearing my throat, I said, "I need a new phone. We'll be back soon."

"Counter." She glanced over her shoulder, but not enough to look at me. "Near the coffee bar. It's already set up for you except for the touch ID." Moving across the garage, she lowered her voice to add, "Let me know if you don't remember your password."

"I know my password," I said, even though it came out unsure because the password I thought I knew could've been some invented memory. When I turned to head back into the house, Brandon's glare had me breathing out a sigh and looking to where Scarlet was staring at a long wall of different weights. "Thank you."

Her dark gaze flashed my way before falling again, and I took that as the only response I would get.

But just as I started shutting the door, she called out, "You need to be wearing your sling."

I gripped the door with my good hand and drew in a slow breath before glancing over at where she was holding a bumper plate like it was her lifeline.

"Don't tell me you're fine because you aren't," she said, stopping me before those exact words could leave my tongue. "It hasn't even been a week and a half; you need to help your body while it heals."

I didn't respond. Just slipped past Brandon's shit-eating grin and walked back into the kitchen, looking for the *coffee bar*, as she'd said, and feeling like an idiot because it was very obviously exactly that.

I just hadn't been paying attention enough to notice it earlier.

Once I found the phone box nestled next to the espresso machine, I snatched it up and worked off the top. Ignoring the momentary flare of my near-constant pain and rolling my eyes when Brandon tossed the sling onto the island.

"Told you not to take that off," he said, grin widening at the reminder of our conversation when he'd first come over.

"It was irritating me."

"Tough shit."

"Are you leaving yet?" I shot back, but the question had a loud laugh breaking from him and a smile tugging at my mouth.

"I should though," he said as he looked over at the time on the oven. "I need to get back to the gym unless you need something."

"I need my truck," I said, my smile fading. "I need to be able to go to the shop. To just *leave*."

Brandon's head bobbed before shaking. "You want to go somewhere, call Konrad or me. We'll take you. Scarlet will take you. Hell, you want to go to the shop? Brian will swing by and get you on his way in. But you can't drive until the doctor clears it."

I knew all this was necessary, but I felt like a burden. Like a useless child. I felt trapped. And before I could stop them, the words "This is bullshit" fell from my lips.

"You got hit by a fucking semi, Chase," Brandon whispered, making my head jerk back. "Be thankful you're here. You'll get back to your life soon, but until then, do what Scarlet said and just heal."

"I got hit by a *what*?" I asked, voice low and careful.

Surprise slowly took over Brandon's expression. "No one told you?"

"Think that's obvious."

Brandon's shock faded until his face was that same ashy-white I'd seen earlier. His eyes glazed over until he looked sick when he confirmed, "Eighteen-wheeler. Went right through a red light and into you."

I tried to remember the accident.

Tried to remember what I'd been told about it.

But no one had given me any real information, and I didn't remember a thing.

"Thought I watched you die, man." The agony in Brandon's voice snapped me back to the present and had me going still in a way that sent a jolt of pain down my side.

"Wait, you were there?"

"Konrad and I were right behind you." He jerked his chin as if it was all playing out just past me. "We'd just left McGowan's and were going to pick up food on the way here."

"Shit, I didn't know," I muttered as I thought about how

that must've been for them. Watching it unfold right in front of them.

A breath left him that was all dulled amusement. "You shouldn't be here," he said as if I wasn't getting it. "You shouldn't be *standing* there. And you have bruises and cuts and a few broken bones—only one of which needs a goddamn *sling*. Chase, do you have any idea how lucky you are?"

I dipped my head as my stare fell to the phone in my hand.

"So, wear the sling. Help your bones heal properly. Stop being a bitter asshole because you're already restless." He leaned forward to push the sling closer to me. "And listen to Scarlet. She knows more and can help you better than most."

My stare snapped up as I grabbed the material off the island to put it back on. "What do you mean?"

He held his hands out to his sides as he stepped away and started toward the entryway. "Ask her."

"Is that going to be your response to everything with her?"

"Yeah, because you need to talk to her. You need to get to know your fiancée in case these years don't come back to you."

He'd been the first person to even hint at a chance that they wouldn't. And instead of causing me to panic over the possibility, it eased something inside me. Like the pressure on me to remember had lessened with those simple words.

"And if they don't?" I asked hesitantly.

"Then the two of you will figure out what to do from there." Brandon shrugged. "But I saw you fall in love with her once. Amnesia can't take away what you felt for her."

I didn't tell him he was wrong.

I didn't tell him it clearly *had*.

I just nodded and walked him to the door before going back to the phone. Back to the thoughts and suspicions I'd had.

Entering my password, I went to the messaging app and only felt a small hint of relief when it was full.

But after looking through the different conversations, there wasn't anything that was cause for alarm. Nothing that would've made my mind conjure up what it had. And the few messages I *did* have with Harper were always about my family.

But it was obvious from just the most recent conversation with Scarlet that she'd meant something incredibly significant to me.

Locking the screen before I could go back any further or do something worse, like go through the pictures, I left the phone on the counter and went back to the guestroom. Intent on sleeping away this searing heartache that was so much worse than the constant physical pain radiating through my body.

SIX

SCARLET

I hadn't noticed it before . . .

The big empty space above our bed.

Then again, he could've come and taken it when I'd been in the shower. But the bare space where our picture had hung just the day before was all I could see as I stood near the foot of the bed, frozen in grief and anger and pain.

Asshole.

I finally forced myself from the room and stormed through the house, my throat thick with emotion as I desperately tried to swallow back the building tears.

"Give it back," I demanded through clenched teeth as I flung open the guestroom door.

Chase's eyes snapped open from where he lay on the bed and narrowed on me, confusion and irritation covering his face in an instant. "What?"

"Give it back."

"The phone?" he asked slowly. "I left it on the counter this morning. Also thought it was mine."

"You know what I'm talking about, Chase. Don't disrespect me by pretending otherwise."

He sat up, his face creasing from the pain of the action, but that furious glare never left me. "If we're not talking about the phone, I really don't."

My head shook roughly as a traitorous sob built in my throat. "Why are you doing this?"

"I'm not doing shit."

"You're breaking my heart!" I cried out as the tears I'd been fighting filled my eyes until Chase and the room were nothing more than a blur.

My body sagged against the doorframe as I covered my face with my hands and willed the tears back. "God, you're such an asshole," I whispered as I let my hands fall.

Without looking at him again, I turned and went back to our room. Keeping my stare away from the wall as I went to the closet to grab a pair of shoes.

Once I had them on, I grabbed my phone and hurried from the room, only to come to an abrupt stop when I nearly ran into Chase as I rounded the hall.

He reached out as if he was going to steady me but dropped his arm before he could touch me. "Where are you going?" he asked as he took a step away from me.

My lips had parted to say *anywhere*, but my shoulders sagged and a defeated laugh punched from my chest. "Does it matter?"

He gave a slow nod, taking my anger. "Been called an asshole enough times in my life to know it's true—and I know I deserve it from you. But considering I have no idea what you're talking about, I'd like it if you explained *why* you're pissed at me."

"Don't do this," I said on a weak breath. "Don't play dumb. You know—"

"I fucking don't, Scarlet."

"Just give it back!"

"What?" he ground out, reclaiming that earlier step. "Give *what* back?"

"Our picture." The words came out strained as I gestured behind me. A hushed cry fell from my lips when I asked, "Why are you trying to hurt me more?"

His stare had dragged to the hall just past me but snapped back to mine at the pained question. Something like regret and sorrow flashed through his blue eyes before it disappeared when he asked, "What picture?"

My body sagged with the weighted breath that rushed from me. "Chase . . ."

"Scarlet, I don't know what we're talking about. I don't remember the last two-and-a-half years, if you forgot."

"Trust me, I'm painfully aware," I said through the glass lodged in my throat. "But you don't need these last years to know what I'm talking about." I gestured toward our room again. "You were looking at the picture when you got home yesterday—the one above our bed."

His gaze drifted that way again and his expression fell as if he finally understood what we were talking about.

"And you think I took it?" he asked as those eyes swept to me and narrowed.

"Why wouldn't I?" My face creased as I remembered the day before. "You looked *livid* when I found you studying it."

"I haven't set foot in that room since I told you I was staying in the guestroom," he said firmly, making me second guess my assumption for the first time since I'd noticed the large canvas was missing. "Did you ever think maybe it fell? Or did you just automatically assume I took it to hurt you?"

"It didn't fall," I said confidently. There was no space behind the headboard. The canvas would've been on the bed if it had somehow fallen.

Still, Chase stepped past me and headed for the room.

I didn't go with him.

I just sagged against the hallway wall and tried to soothe the intense emotions that had built so swiftly.

"I didn't touch it," Chase said when he entered the hallway again. "And Brandon never went past the kitchen this morning."

"Then who—"

"I don't know, Scarlet," he said over me as he started through the living room, only to stop. After long seconds, he met my stare. "I know I'm hurting you. But I wouldn't do *that*."

Once he was gone, I slid down the wall until I was on the floor with my knees tucked close to my chest and my face buried in my hands.

I hated that I didn't know how to believe him, even though I could hear the honesty in his voice. But there was no other practical explanation for where the photo had gone.

I hated that I didn't know how to be in a room with him and have this distance between us. Or have him look at me like I was *nothing* to him when he used to look at me like I was *everything*.

I hated that I didn't know how to handle the bitterness and resentment that bled from him and reached out to me. That I didn't feel *strong enough* to.

I hated that I still wanted to run . . .

With a shuddering exhale, I let my head rest against the wall and tried to suppress the jolt that went through me when I noticed him standing there.

Watching me.

"Thought you were coming with me," he said, voice soft. "To search the guestroom or something."

"Well, if you did take it, now I know not to look there." I tried to deliver the words on a tease, but they came out dull and lacked any humor.

Chase dipped his head in a nod but just continued standing there for a while before hesitantly asking, "You hungry?"

A saddened laugh slipped past my lips at the familiar question, and my eyes rolled as I stood. "We're not ordering Chinese," I said on a sigh. "I'll make something."

"Who said I wanted Chinese?"

I swayed when my feet became one with the floor. The pain in my chest so sudden and brutal that it felt impossible to breathe.

"I do," he said cautiously. "I was going to suggest it. I was just wondering how you knew that."

"Really?" My head had snapped to the side as he'd spoken, the smallest spark of hope blooming as I searched his expression.

But his eyes just narrowed as if he was still trying to figure out how I could've possibly known.

"It's your go-to whenever I'm mad at you," I informed him as that hope grew, my voice shaky when I added, "Because it's my favorite."

"Oh." His stare drifted to the side, and I could see he was *trying*.

Trying so hard to take what I'd said and fit it to

anything . . . but the frustration and helplessness when he looked at me again told me enough.

He didn't remember.

"It's something," I whispered encouragingly.

He lifted his good hand before letting it fall. "It's food."

My lips parted, but nothing left them as I watched him stalk away, all that defeated aggravation trailing behind him.

Swiping my hands over my stomach, I held on to that hope and followed to where he was staring into the refrigerator.

Grabbing the handle of the door he was holding, I began closing it, my movements slowing when he spoke.

"Scarlet, I don't remember."

"Not yet," I said softly. "But your subconscious gave you something that was so completely *us* because—oh, because you know how to frustrate the hell out of me, Chase Grayson." A smile curled at the edges of my mouth in response to his. "And you think food's the way to make everything better."

"Does it ever work?"

"Somehow," I admitted, my eyes rolling when a breath of a laugh left him. "But it's more the way we connect over food when we're alone. You're always right there with me. Talking to me and giving me all of you. Chinese food is just my favorite, so it's an added bonus."

He looked at me then, his brow furrowed as he studied me. "You still want to cook, or should we order?"

I shrugged, pulling my phone out of my pocket as I did.

Another hushed laugh left him when I opened the app for our favorite restaurant. "Got it," he muttered as he headed for the cabinet that held the cups.

I tried to contain the excitement and nervousness that

crashed through me. The feeling close to those addicting, dizzying highs when first falling for someone.

Ridiculous, I knew because I *knew* Chase. I was *engaged* to him.

But this was all new territory with him. Unsteady, worrying territory.

And the stranger who held my heart had smiled. He'd laughed. He'd offered an olive branch across that void separating us.

I'd take them all and cherish each piece of the Chase I'd known that only served to fuel that dangerous hope.

———

"You need to stretch," I said a little over an hour later. When Chase gave me a curious look, I gestured to him with my container of food before setting it on the end table. "I know you don't want to admit it, but you're uncomfortable. You keep making a face whenever you start relaxing into the chair, and you're not sitting the way you normally do."

"I'm fine."

"You aren't," I said firmly. "You need to stretch to make breathing and moving easier and to alleviate the strain you're putting on your neck and the rest of your injured arm."

His eyebrows rose, but he just continued watching me for a moment before he resumed chewing the bite he'd taken.

We hadn't said much other than what was necessary before the food had arrived. But once we'd settled in the living room, I'd struggled to not fall into our normal routine of teasing banter and going over our days. Of talking about *everything* because it was our time.

But then he'd asked, *"Did I do the lilies on your hip?"* and I'd been brought right back to our painful reality.

Ever since, the conversation had been strained and full of lulls, but he'd continued asking questions. He'd continued laughing.

So I was taking it.

"The doctor tell you that?" he asked as he dropped his fork into his container and set it aside.

"No."

"Brandon said something this morning," he began, voice a low murmur as he studied me. "Said I needed to listen to you because you know more and can help better than most." Lifting his head in question, he asked, "What'd he mean by that?"

"He could've meant a lot by that." I spun my engagement ring before hiding it with my right hand again. "I obviously know about our relationship. I know what you've been up to the past two years more than anyone else."

"Think he was referring to you telling me to put the sling on."

My head moved in slow nods. "That was probably because I double-majored in sports medicine and kinesiology," I replied, the words coming out soft and uneven. "I was a physical therapist when I met you. Hadn't been for long and didn't stay in the field much longer though," I added quickly and tried to ignore the chill that swept down my spine at the memory of it.

"Didn't like it?"

A hushed, frantic laugh escaped me. "Something like that."

It was odd telling Chase pieces of my life when he already knew me inside and out. Because I wasn't simply *reminding* him, and my mind kept shouting that he knew all this.

He knew *me*.

It was unsettling because he'd already taken so much of our relationship and crushed it right in front of me. And it felt like any bit of information I gave him would suffer the same fate.

It made me insecure in myself and my past when I never had been before—but he'd never judged me before. Yet everything I did and said seemed to make those eyes grow colder and more hateful.

"Do I already know?" Chase asked, drawing my attention to where he was still intently watching me. When a questioning hum sounded in my throat, he clarified, "Why you're not a physical therapist anymore."

"You know everything about me," I whispered, hating that those words were no longer true. "But it isn't important."

"It feels important."

"I told *you*," I said quickly, voice straining. "I told the man I trusted because it all happened after I'd already fallen in love with you. I'm not telling the guy who looks at me like I'm single-handedly ruining his life."

His mouth parted to speak, but a breathy laugh left him instead. "Yeah, makes sense." His head bobbed subtly as he reached for his food, only to let it fall to the table again. "I don't want to hurt you, but it's like I can't stop. Which sounds like bullshit," he muttered as his gaze flashed to me before drifting to the side. "But you're right—what you said. As unfair to you as it is, that's how it feels."

The air rushed from me on a pained wheeze at his admission.

I'd known. I'd *felt* it. But having him confirm my suspicions *hurt*.

"I feel so fucking conflicted," he went on, then gestured to me. "I get that we were together. But every thought and want—"

"God, Chase, stop," I pled as I stood from the couch, snatching the carton from the end table as I did. "I can't handle you telling me you're in love with Harper again."

A hollow of agony formed in my chest as I blindly staggered into the kitchen. The food almost slipped from my fingers when his words replayed in my mind and nearly knocked me to my knees.

"I get that we were together."

Were . . . he'd said *were*.

No, no, no. He—

This isn't real. This isn't permanent. *It can't be.*

I refused to believe this was truly the end of us.

I fought the cry begging to escape and hastily set the container on the island as I rushed for the garage door. My lungs aching and screaming by the time I made it out there before I let it go.

The pain.

The tears.

The anger.

All of it bursting from me on a soggy curse as I shakily held myself up against a wall. That hope I'd been clinging to earlier all but gone as I realized each blow to my heart hurt more than the last, and it was getting harder to believe we could make it through this.

I straightened from the wall and wiped at my cheeks when the door began opening minutes later but kept my back to him to give me that extra time to try to compose myself.

"Yeah, see, even though I don't know you, I don't like that I'm doing this to you," he began in that soft, rumbling voice that had always gotten to me. "But lying to you will only give you hope that we'll go back to however you remember us."

My eyelids slipped shut as the tears fell harder.

"And I'm sorry I'm hurting you with all this bullshit about Harper, but—" A hesitant laugh left him. "This sounds stupid, but I want to say I know how you feel. Even though I guess I don't because I was apparently never waiting for her to choose me over Brandon."

I wanted to tell him that it *had* been real. That what he was remembering had been *our* story. *Our* pain. But that void in my chest grew at the sadness and longing in his voice.

"I want to remember, Scarlet. I'm trying to. But right now, this *feels* real to me."

"You're already breaking my heart, Chase," I mumbled as I finally opened my blurred eyes. "Don't insult me by lying about *this* when you just said you wouldn't lie to me about the rest."

The silence behind me was deafening and screamed his challenge.

Turning to face him, I ignored the slight falter in his expression when he saw the tears still steadily falling and said, "You don't want to remember because then you'd have to truly accept it wasn't real with her, and it's so obvious you aren't ready for that."

His jaw twitched as he gave a firm nod.

Rocking back a step, he paused and asked, "Is this what you do when you're mad or we're fighting?" Before I could ask what he meant, he said, "You keep trying to run away."

My chest pitched with the force of my next exhale as memories danced across my vision. Fights that were all passion as we argued our sides while Chase held me close, refusing to let me go anywhere because he'd always wanted to get everything out and settled right then.

And as much as it always frustrated me in the moment, in the end, I loved that he couldn't bear to watch me walk away whenever things were tense between us. Then again, all that passion usually shifted until clothes were shed and our bodies were slick with sweat.

Kind of hard not to love our way of arguing.

"I've never walked away from you," I finally said, refusing to give him more than that. Refusing to give him those parts of our life that were so personal and could sway his mind.

Because if Chase was ever going to come back to me without his memories, I wanted it to be because he fell for me again. Not because he felt obligated to or because the memories I gave him made him *want* to.

"Then why are you now?" he asked, refusing to just let it be.

"Because this is my pain." My shoulders lifted in a weak shrug. "Even though it should be *ours*, it isn't. And as much as I want to scream at you for the things you say, I logically know I can't blame you for any of it. So, there's no point in sharing my pain with you when you can't possibly understand what you're doing to me."

If I hadn't been watching him so closely, I might've missed the regret that flashed through his surprise, but they were gone as quickly as they appeared.

"Got it," he muttered and turned to leave. But just as he reached for the doorknob to go back into the house, he stopped. Body still and head hanging as he wavered. "Stretch *how*?"

My eyebrows rose when he shifted to glance at me. "You—do you want me to show you?"

"Not if you don't want to," he said resolutely. "I was referred to a physical therapist; I'm just waiting to hear from them."

"That's a little insulting," I mumbled, earning another one of those smiles.

"I didn't know," he reminded me, the words bordering on playful before everything about him turned serious. "But you don't have to do this. I shouldn't have asked."

I walked toward him, holding his curious and patient stare. Letting my actions answer for me as I reached past him to press the garage door button to let in the cool evening air.

When I stepped back, I shrugged. "Unless you think I don't know what I'm doing . . ."

"If anything, I think you'll hurt me on purpose," he teased as he started following me.

"I'll make ice packs for you afterward," I mockingly vowed as if I had every intention of doing what he'd said.

Chase's next smile was slow and mischievous and still had the ability to stop me.

My steps. My heart. My world.

"Then do your worst, Scarlet."

SEVEN

SCARLET

"And that's it," I called out, a laugh pouring free at the relieved groans that sounded from my friends a few days later. Straightening from my position, I let a smirk shape my lips. "Oh, come on, it wasn't that bad."

"What did we do to you?" Anna asked through heaving breaths.

"I think I'm actually dying," Litany said dramatically before flopping to the ground.

"You need to stand up," I reminded her as my eyes rolled. "It wasn't anything different from our last two sessions."

"And our last two sessions were brutal," Samantha complained as she opened her bottle to chug the remainder of her water.

"She's literally trying to kill us," Litany said as she propped herself up on her elbows.

"Always the dramatic one, LT," I mumbled affectionately and blew a kiss her way when she narrowed her eyes. "Stand up."

"Ugh," she groaned as she stood, dragging it out to get a

reaction from me if her hidden smile was any indication. "Happy?"

"Extremely." The word had been a tease, and yet, it wasn't too far off from the truth.

My smiles were almost constant. My laughs were coming freely. And my movements were so much different than they'd been at my Tuesday session with them.

Lighter. Not as stiff.

It almost felt like—well . . . *before*.

Going through my days doing what I loved. Training and doing workouts. Helping the occasional person with an injury.

It made me feel alive. Gave me purpose. And it gave me the freedom to have lazy mornings with Chase and easy after-noons before he went to the shop.

Not that we'd had any of those this week since we were still on very unsteady ground. Still, he'd been different since we'd started physical therapy three nights before.

That coldness was slowly receding from those blue eyes, and his glances were lingering. Those smirks and hushed laughs that had always done crazy things to me were becoming much more frequent—as were our conversations, even though they rarely touched on anything that had to do with us.

But it was something.

More than something . . . it was *everything*.

It felt like I was falling for Chase for the first time all over again. And the swarm of wings in my stomach made it feel like I was walking on air.

I started collecting the weights, bands, and balls we'd used, taking them over to sanitize so I could prepare for my next class.

"I didn't want to say anything before," Samantha began,

voice hesitant, "but I really wasn't expecting to see you like this today."

When I looked back at her, she gestured to me with her bottle, her eyebrows drawn together in worry.

The other two girls murmured agreements as Samantha hurried to continue. "I'm loving it; I'm just surprised. And I'd like to think you're just this happy to see us," she teased, forcing a laugh from me.

"Of course I am," I said as I grabbed another medicine ball. "My best days begin with the three of you."

"Fact," Anna interjected.

"I'm sure we would've heard about this before this morning," Samantha went on, voice lowering as she glanced at the door that led to the house, "but are Chase's memories coming back?"

My smile slipped as I looked in that direction before walking over to put the medicine ball down. "No."

"Then what has you all glow-y?" Litany asked. "Because you could barely make it through a set without crying on Tuesday."

"It's seeing all of you," I said playfully, then lifted a shoulder and conceded. "It's him. I mean . . . Chase is different, and he still has no idea who I am or who we were together. But he's here, and he's talking to me. And the last couple of days were so much better than the ones before it."

"Better *how*?" Anna asked flirtatiously.

My eyes rolled. "Just *better*. He hasn't been dismissing me or looking at me like he hates me. He's been—" I sucked in a stuttered breath and shook myself when I realized I was just standing there holding weights. Walking across the garage, I set them down and then looked at the girls again. "Anna, you were there when we met. It was instant."

"Pretty sure the entire block got pregnant from the way he was looking at you," she said, a laugh bursting from her when I picked up one of the bands and flung it at her. "It's true!"

"But it stayed that way. Instant and intense. This is . . . slow and like he can't help himself, even though he clearly doesn't want to fall for me."

"Wait, what? Why?" Litany asked.

"He still thinks he's in love with Harper," Samantha said in realization, voice soft. Always my sympathetic friend. Always the worrier of the four of us.

"Yeah," I said sadly. "He *knows* it didn't happen, but he's struggling with accepting it because he's absolutely sure his feelings are real."

"Damn, friend," Anna muttered as Litany asked, "And you still think it's because he took things that really happened with your life?"

"It makes sense. It fits." And that still worried me.

His adamant claims of not cheating on Harper. His apologies for hurting her because some girl had ended up in his bed. All of it continued tormenting me at night, keeping me awake as that one piece of the puzzle eluded me.

Because I could shift and piece together every other part of Chase's confused and twisted memories. But *that* didn't fit into our lives in any way.

That I knew of.

"But the positive is that he's falling for you all over again," Samantha said. "Even if he's trying not to or doesn't want to right now because he's confused, he can't help but fall for you because the two of you are made for each other."

A saddened smile tugged at my mouth. "Maybe. I could be reading everything wrong, and he could still hate me as much as he did when he woke up a little over a week ago."

"I doubt that," Samantha said.

"The entire block," Anna repeated her earlier words, enunciating them loudly.

"I have to pee," Litany announced cheerfully.

"Of course you do," the rest of us said in unison between laughs and lighthearted groans.

Litany scoffed in mock offense as she pulled the scrunchie out of her long blonde hair. "Brats," she muttered as she re-did her bun.

"The most random timing," Anna said, telling her the same thing she always did.

"Take it up with my bladder," Litany shot back as she gathered her things and blew a kiss at me. "See you at brunch."

A soft laugh danced along my lips when I said, "Bye, friend."

"I love brunch so much more than workouts," Anna said after LT disappeared into the house and began grabbing her things as well. "Scarlet doesn't try to kill us there."

A huff left me. "Um . . . excuse me." I gestured to the makeshift gym around us. "I seem to remember *all* of this was your idea."

Anna pointed at Samantha. "Don't put this on me. Blame her too."

"Not blaming anyone," I said easily, a smile lighting my face. "Just reminding you that you're part of why I started this."

"Well, *past* me didn't realize I would hate you for kicking my ass twice a week."

I lowered my voice to an impish whisper. "Your ass looks fantastic though."

"Yeah. Not the point." Anna's eyes rolled as she put on her sunglasses, a smile of her own tugging at her mouth. "Brunch is still better."

"Always," I agreed, then looked to where Samantha was just watching the entire thing with amusement. "And I thought LT was the dramatic one."

"They're battling for the title," Samantha teased.

"No, no," Anna argued. "LT is dramatic *all* the time. I'm like a Mogwai—you can't get them wet or feed them after midnight. This is what happens when you make me work out before coffee. I turn into a Gremlin."

I pressed my lips together to suppress a laugh as Samantha mumbled, "She just stole the title."

"And on that note," I began with a soft clap, "I need to get ready for my next class."

"It won't be nearly as entertaining as ours," Anna said as she pulled me in for a quick hug.

I winked at Samantha before saying, "None of them ever are."

"Let us know if anything changes before tomorrow," Samantha whispered as she hugged me.

I just nodded, even as doubt swirled through me. "See you tomorrow."

I watched them go, my stare drifting to where Litany's car waited. A breath of a laugh leaving me because I had no doubt she was in my kitchen, making coffee for herself.

If anyone, *she* was the Gremlin. But we all adored her for it.

By the time I was sanitizing the mats and equipment, she

was calling out, "See you tomorrow," from the street, having left through the front door the way she always did.

I didn't bother responding with anything other than a wave. She wouldn't hear me anyway since she always slipped into her car as quickly as possible because she liked to pretend I didn't know about her coffee thievery.

I clearly knew.

I also didn't care, considering she always filled our kitchen with her latest baked creations.

Grabbing my phone, I switched to my favorite songs from the workout playlist and turned the music up. Letting it pour through the speakers in the garage as I went through the methodical routine of cleaning and preparing.

I was so lost in the music and routine movements that I didn't notice the Jeep pulling onto the driveway or the guys walking up until that familiar, husky voice sounded from just beside me.

Stealing my breath and sending chills across my body.

"Need help?"

My head snapped up and my eyes locked onto Chase's, getting trapped there for long seconds before I was able to pull myself together. "What? No." I cleared my throat and straightened. "No, I've got it. I'm just about done anyway."

Konrad gave a half-wave as Brandon looked between Chase and me, expression curious and guarded.

"How was breakfast?" I asked slowly, thrown off by Chase's best friend.

In an instant, the energy surrounding us shifted from slightly uncomfortable to bordering on suffocating.

When Chase's gaze fell to the floor, I looked in time to see

Brandon and Konrad share a meaningful glance before Brandon said, "It was great."

But his tone and the stiff way the three were suddenly holding themselves said *great* wasn't quite how it should've been described.

A scoff bled from Chase as he shifted away, turning for the door to the house. A whisper of remorse flashed through the cold resentment in his eyes when they met mine again, and then he was gone.

Stealing that high I'd been on all morning.

Stealing my smile.

Stealing that sliver of hope that we had any chance of recovering from this.

I gripped the gaping wound in my chest when the door shut behind him and tried to stifle the way the oxygen fled from my lungs on a rush. Tears pricked at my eyes as strong arms enveloped me, but I didn't look away from that closed door.

"What happened?" I asked through the knot in my throat when Brandon released me.

A sigh escaped him as he looked to Konrad for help, but Konrad just shook his head. Scuffing a hand over his face with a mumbled, "Jesus, dude."

"He was fine," Brandon finally said, lifting his hands like he was at a loss. "Then we got to my house, and when he found out it was *my* house, he immediately wanted to know if Harper was there."

"Fucking took off for the front door," Konrad added.

"But he's been—" I pressed my lips together as my head moved in firm shakes.

That hollow in my chest was opening so wide and so deep,

I was sure that even if we made it through this, my heart wouldn't survive unscathed.

"What happened?" I repeated. "Was she home?"

"She has an early class," Brandon said. "But Chase lost it when he saw a picture of us from our wedding. Started yelling all this shit about what I took from him." He cut another look at Konrad and blew out a sharp breath before studying me like he was trying to figure out how to phrase what came next, but he never attempted to go on.

"You didn't actually hit him," Konrad mumbled.

My lips parted on a strained gasp as my attention quickly darted between the two before finally landing on Brandon. "You tried to hit him?"

He lifted his hands again before placing them on his head, lacing his fingers over his buzzed hair.

"In Brandon's defense," Konrad began placatingly, "Chase pushed too far."

"He's still healing," I argued tightly.

Brandon's head bounced in faint nods before shaking. "He said his memories felt pretty real and asked if I was sure Harper hadn't been fucking him behind my back." His shoulders bunched up. "Konrad stopped me when I went for him."

I stood there for what felt like hours as I absorbed what they were telling me and tried to piece it together with the guy I'd been spending these past days with.

At the beginning of the week, I would've expected it. After these past days, I guess I'd just let myself believe that part of this nightmare was over.

I'd been stupid to.

"Do you think it's possible?" The question was full of

doubt as it poured from me, but I had to know what Brandon thought.

I knew I could connect the pieces of Chase's mind. But maybe it was only because I wanted to.

"No," he said immediately, unquestionably. "Not only would neither of them do that to us, but they definitely wouldn't with each other." He let his arms fall heavily as he explained, "The way he keeps saying all of it is just getting to me though."

"I know what you mean," I mumbled sadly.

"He loves you."

My head shook and my eyelids squeezed tight at Brandon's declaration.

When I opened them again, he and Konrad were slightly blurred. "He doesn't even know me."

"He wouldn't stop talking about you," Konrad said in encouragement. "He found a way to bring you up no matter what we were talking about."

"He apologized for the Harper comments," Brandon began, words slow and hesitant. "Said he couldn't stop hurting you either because he's been so torn and confused. Then he said, 'This is gonna hurt Scarlet.'"

"Right after that, he asked if we knew how frustrating you were and launched into a list of things you do that irritate him," Konrad said with a small smirk.

"But he kept smiling during the entire rant," Brandon added. "He loves you. He's just afraid to know that."

"Because he's fighting to hold onto something that was never there," I whispered and let my stare fall when their expressions did the same. Clearing my throat, I rocked back a step and forced a shaky smile. "I really appreciate the two of you coming to see him or get him since he's stuck here. And I know he appreciates it, even if he keeps saying things he shouldn't."

"It's nothing," Konrad said assuredly.

"Our mornings have started with him for years," Brandon added. "Making a detour to keep that happening isn't a burden to us. He's family. You're family."

I nodded and offered another smile as emotion welled. "I should see if he needs anything before my next class starts showing up," I managed, voice strained as I took a step toward the door.

"See you in the morning?" Konrad asked, eyes narrowing as if he knew exactly what I was doing. As if he knew I needed a second to breathe and collect myself before I broke down in front of them.

"Of course." I forced as much of a tease into the words as that void in my chest would allow, then asked, "Who else is going to show you up out there?"

Brandon barked out a laugh as Konrad defended, "That was one wave."

"And I will never let you live it down."

"Later, Scarlet," Brandon called out as they headed back down the drive, but I just rushed into the house and hurried to shut the door behind me.

My chest heaved with a pained breath as my back settled against the wooden surface. Eyelids closed tight as I desperately tried to find that feeling I'd been surrounded in earlier.

That hope and excitement that was fueled by fluttering wings.

That bliss.

But as Brandon and Konrad's words played again and

again, my dread grew deeper and tightened its grip on my lungs. My heart. Suffocating every bright light I'd managed to find these past days.

"I said something to Brandon."

My eyes flashed open, and I looked to the side to see Chase standing just a handful of feet away, watching me carefully.

I pushed from the door and tried clearing my throat, but it felt like it was filled with jagged rocks. "I know."

"I can tell," he muttered with a soft huff. Dragging his good hand through his hair, he held it there before gesturing to me. "Told you I wouldn't lie to you."

My head slanted in question, but he continued before I could ask what he meant.

"I knew what happened this morning would get back to you one way or another, and I didn't want you to think I kept it from you. But they said it'd be best if it didn't come from me."

I played it all again. And again.

Everything from when I'd first noticed Chase beside me in the garage, to his leaving, to their words.

It felt different now, and yet . . .

"I don't want to know." The words came out on a pained wheeze as I fought the burning in my eyes. "Chase, I don't want to know how much you think you love her. Or that you think you were in a relationship with her. Or that you think the two of you were having an affair."

"I said I wouldn't lie to you," he repeated as if it were that simple. "Keeping it from you feels like lying."

I pressed a hand to my chest as my body sagged. "I can't keep—Chase, my heart can't handle it."

"Then tell me how to do this," he demanded, his handsome face set in a mixture of frustration and desperation. "I can't win no matter what I do here, so tell me what you want from me."

"I want my life back!"

"So do I," he shot back, pulling an anguished whimper from me because I knew as soon as the words left him that he didn't mean his life with *me*.

God, would this nightmare never end?

"Shit." The curse left Chase on a breath and his expression fell to match mine. "Scarlet, I'm—fuck, I'm sorry."

"I, um . . ." My tongue darted out to wet my lips and a traitorous sob rose in my throat when he took a step toward me. "I have a class."

I reached for the handle behind me as I turned and had just started opening the door when he was suddenly there.

Chest pressed to my back.

Hand on the door.

Keeping me from walking away the way he had always done.

My body shuddered with the familiarity of it all, and I struggled to keep myself still. To keep from leaning into him.

But like everything else, the moment was ripped from me when he jerked his hand back and stepped away.

"I don't . . ." he began unsteadily, then cleared his throat. "Sorry, I don't know why I did that."

Glancing over my shoulder, I took in the way he was staring vacantly at the wall. Brows drawn close in concentration and confusion as if he was trying to make sense of the automatic response that had taken over him.

With a subtle shake of his head, his blue eyes drifted to me. "I just wanted you to know that I don't want to hurt you. I hate that I am because I can clearly see what this is doing to you.

But keeping any of this from you feels wrong, and that doesn't make sense to me either because—" A frustrated smile flashed across his face as his head slanted.

"Because you don't know me," I finished for him, already knowing what he was going to say.

"Right," he muttered, stare searching mine for long moments before he asked, "You hungry?"

A breath of a laugh left me despite the aching in my soul. "No. And you're not either. You just got home from eating."

"Chinese tonight?" he asked, refusing to back down as the beginning of a smirk tugged at the corner of his mouth.

"You can't pull that card every day and expect it to always work." My eyes rolled as I twisted the doorknob again. "I kind of wish Brandon had hit you now."

He shrugged as if he wasn't bothered by it in the least. "You're smiling."

"Only because I'm imagining your best friend knocking that smug smile off your handsome face," I lied as I swung the door open, my breaths stalling in my lungs when the tips of Chase's fingers landed on the back of my hip.

The touch was light but firm. Not enough to keep me from walking away, but the pressure and the placement of his hand went so far past strangers.

This was familiar. Intimate. Possessive.

This was *us*.

My gaze drifted from his hand to where he was intently watching me. Once again studying me like he was trying so hard to find something.

Even if it was just the extent of the pain he was causing rather than his memories, I'd take it if it gave me these moments with him.

"I am sorry," he repeated, enunciating each word to make sure I understood their depth.

"I know you are."

"But you don't understand," he said sympathetically.

My head moved in faint shakes before I admitted, "No. I don't understand this any more than you do. Just for different reasons."

His chin lowered in acceptance before he moved away, eyes slowly dragging over me. Taking me in in a way that had me grounded in place because I didn't want it to end.

But a blend of voices and someone calling out my name had Chase's eyes snapping to the open doorway before shifting to me one last time.

"See you tonight, Scar," he called out as he turned to head deeper into the house.

I watched him leave. Unable to move. Unable to speak.

My body felt alive. Felt like it was on fire. All from a look.

And my heart? It was thundering. Fighting for that hope and for *us* in that chasm of pain all because of one word. Because of a name.

Scar.

EIGHT

CHASE

I studied the boards lined up next to each other for another second before shutting the large garage door and heading into the house that weekend, already talking as I went. "When can I surf?"

A soft laugh filled the kitchen and had my mouth twitching into a smile until Scarlet said, "Few months."

"Months?" I echoed dully.

"Chase . . ." she began with a sigh, her dark eyes meeting mine from where she was getting ice packs ready for me. "I don't even know what the doctor said about the trauma to your head. But broken ribs and clavicle . . . I mean, have you seen yourself?" Her saddened stare swept my bare torso before falling away.

As if each reminder of my accident was too painful for her to linger on for long.

I didn't need to look at the major bruising taking up the side of my body. It was kind of hard to miss.

"Then when can I stop wearing the sling?"

She pressed her hands to the counter and inhaled slowly as

if I were trying her patience. Considering the amount of times I'd already tried or asked to do something far beyond what I was allowed to, I had no doubt I was.

"A few weeks," she answered.

"Scarlet—"

"Oh my God, Chase, just let me put these on you," she pled on a frantic breath, grabbing the bags of ice and bandages, and rounding the island to where I stood. "You drive me crazy."

I knew that.

The edge of my mouth tipped back up into a brief smirk as I held out my arms for her to strap the ice to me the way she liked to since I apparently did it wrong. "I can't tattoo. I can't drive. I feel trapped here with nothing to do and nowhere to go."

"You've gone out to breakfast with the guys. We're going to your parents' house tonight," she reminded me as her fingers moved over the bruising on my torso without ever touching me. "These are looking good."

A grunt rumbled in my chest, but I just studied her as she deftly secured the ice and bound my ribs, then moved to my shoulder to do the same.

Her fingers grazing my skin. Her face so close to mine.

Seeming to hold her breath the way she did every time.

And fuck me because I was pretty sure I'd started doing the same at some point. But she was *right there* and making my heart race as if it didn't belong to someone else. With those seductive eyes and full lips and that sharp, teasing attitude that kept drawing me back in no matter how hard I fought it.

It'd been like this since that first night of therapy with her. But over the last couple of days, it had only heightened.

Driving me crazy during the hours she did private and

group training sessions in the garage. Consuming my thoughts during the small breaks I took from researching amnesia or when Brandon and Konrad stopped by. Edging in on dangerous fucking territory during the evenings when Scarlet did therapy with me.

And I *hated* that I looked forward to that time with her. I hated that I couldn't look away from her and that my heart kicked up every time she smiled. Because when we separated at night, I felt like I was dying under the guilt of what I was doing to Harper.

A girl who was apparently *nothing* to me.

And it sucked to feel like I was betraying someone, only to remember she didn't love me. To remember none of it had been real. To be reminded that I wasn't going to be a father.

Every. Fucking. Day.

"Just give it time," Scarlet finally said as she finished with my shoulder, her stare meeting mine and getting trapped there when she realized how close we were.

Barely a breath apart.

And those lips that had been a constant torment this week were so damn close. The smallest shift, and I'd—*fuck.*

She cleared her throat and stepped back when I forced myself to look away, her voice shaky when she said, "I should start getting ready. We need to leave in about an hour."

"Right."

I was drowning in that guilt. Hating myself all over again. But my gaze still pulled in her direction when she started away from me, heading toward her bedroom.

Catching me watching her when she turned to add, "I know you want to do more than you can. I know you don't like having to rely on other people for things. But if you go too fast, too soon, it will hurt you more or damage the bones permanently."

"I know."

A soft smile touched the corner of her mouth, drawing my entire focus when she teased, "Then stop asking to do things you know you can't like an impatient child."

"No promises," I muttered after she'd already left, leaving me staring after her while my heart wrenched from my chest because it knew she was the wrong girl . . .

Right?

————

"I know Konrad," I said suddenly, grabbing Scarlet's arm and pulling her to a stop outside my parents' house an hour and a half later.

Her brow furrowed as her eyes shifted, taking in the excitement on my face. "Yeah," she said slowly, making the word sound like a question.

"I knew when I woke up that he was Bree's boyfriend." Just as quickly as my excitement had slammed into me, hesitation warred. "He's Bree's boyfriend, right?"

"Yeah." The word dragged from her on a hushed laugh. "You've seen plenty of evidence of that since you woke up. But he's been her boyfriend for years—longer than I've known you."

"How long?" I asked impatiently, ignoring the *evidence* comment because I really didn't want to think about what my sister did with anyone. "Because from what I remember, she met him not long after she started at San Diego State."

Scarlet's gaze drifted for a second as she nodded. "That sounds like what I've heard."

"And I remember that," I said, not realizing until I pulled her closer that I'd never released my hold on her.

In an instant, I was acutely aware of how close we were. Of how she smelled. Of the way she looked and was looking at me.

Like she'd been craving this. Like she'd been afraid she'd never have this again.

I dropped her arm and rocked back a step before I could do something insane—like let myself get lost in her a little longer. Wonder what those mesmerizing lips of hers would feel like until I gave in and found out . . .

It didn't occur to me until she lowered her head to hide the pain on her face that I already knew.

Somewhere.

Some *other* me.

I cleared my throat and swallowed the building apology, then looked to my parents' house again. "I remember Bree and Konrad—I've *remembered* that. And what I remember with Harper was from that same time," I explained instead.

Her tone was all pain and hesitation when my name fell from that goddamn mouth. "Chase . . ."

"You all can't keep telling me there isn't truth in what I remember." I slanted a warning look her way in time to see her press her lips firmly together as if forcing herself not to let her thoughts slip free. "And you know it. I can see that."

That pain cut deeper in her eyes as her head moved in fast, subtle shakes. "You don't know what you're seeing."

"Then what are you keeping from me?" I demanded when she started for the house, and she whirled on me.

"It was a coma-induced dream, Chase," she seethed, voice trembling through its severity. "You're waiting for me, or someone, to tell you you're right, but there was never anything between you and Harper."

I grabbed her hand and squeezed it before she could move. "Do you feel this?" I asked, then hurried to add, "Physically. Do you feel me touching you?" When her brow just furrowed, I took a step closer, unable to help myself. "I can still feel her. I know what she feels like against me."

"Stop," she pleaded, trying to pull her hand free and tightly closing her eyes when I went on.

"I can still smell her like I just spent a night holding her. I know what she sounds like when she's yelling at me and when she's whispering my name."

"Jesus, Chase, *stop*," Scarlet cried.

I searched her creased expression and watched as a lone tear slipped down her cheek.

And there was that terrible feeling again. Like I hated Scarlet for being the reason I'd lost my life and hated myself for hurting her. Like I would do anything if it would take her pain away.

My chest ached and my muscles twitched with the need to pull her closer.

I let her go instead. Taking a step away as I said, "You can't tell me it was a dream when I remember everything about her."

"Remember everything about who?"

I glanced to the side to see my sister and Konrad standing there. Konrad looked disappointed and worried as his gaze shifted from me to Scarlet. Breanna looked pissed off as she glared at me, hand on her hip, waiting for a response.

"You know exactly who I'm talking about," I said, daring either of them to keep up the lies after what I'd just realized.

"Kinda hope I don't," Bree shot back.

"When did the two of you start dating?"

My question brought her up short and even seemed to surprise Konrad from his stunned, "Wait, what?"

"Few weeks after my freshman year began," Bree said slowly, head listing as she studied me. "Why?"

I gave Scarlet a knowing look, but she just slowly shook her head before dropping her stare to the ground.

"Because I knew that," I finally responded before looking to Bree and Konrad again. "The first party you and Harper came to at my house . . . did one of my housemates have a blow-up doll?"

Bree's gaze shifted to the side for a moment before a bemused huff punched from her chest. "Yeah—"

"And that first winter break . . . did Harper go to Arizona with Brandon for Christmas but come home to spend New Year's Eve with us?"

"I . . . wait, that's right." Amazement and hope filled Bree's expression. "Chase—"

"And she spent every Sunday with us for family day," I said over her, more confident than before.

Bree began nodding, but I went on.

"And Harper's dad is a massive douche in the Marine Corps who doesn't talk to her."

Bree's stare shifted to Scarlet before locking on me again. "Why are you asking all these questions about Harper?"

"Because I knew all that," I repeated through clenched teeth. "How do I know all that if I supposedly dreamt that entire year with her? If I've had it all confused and twisted?"

My tone dropped and filled with all my anger as I took in their lost expressions. "Fuck you both."

"Chase!" Bree snapped as Konrad said, "The hell, man?"

But I'd already turned and was stalking away from them, past Scarlet, and toward the house.

Anger and confusion stormed my veins in a lethal combination as I shoved through the front door. Not thinking about where I was going or what I would be met with once the others followed me until I heard her.

"Hey."

That one word stopped me as if I'd run into a wall.

Just as I'd told Scarlet, I *knew* that voice.

Looking up, the oxygen rushed from my lungs on a strained breath when I saw Harper standing just outside the hall, watching me curiously.

"You okay?" she asked, her eyebrows drawing close when she looked past me. "Wait, how did you get here?"

I didn't respond.

I didn't think.

I just started toward her and didn't stop, even when I was backing her into the hall.

"Chase, what are you doing?" she hissed, hands pressed firmly to my chest as she struggled to match my steps.

"Here," I said when I brought us to a stop in the middle of the hall. "This is where we first kissed."

Her wide eyes got impossibly wider. "Where we—what?" she asked, choking over the words. "No."

"New Year's Eve."

"No," she said firmly. "Chase, we have never kissed."

"I know what I remember," I argued gently.

"You don't."

"Harper, I *know you.*"

A sound like sorrow and frustration left her. "Not the way you think you do."

My hold on her arm tightened as if I could keep her there. Keep her mine. Or maybe I could wake up from this fucked-up nightmare if I held her tight enough.

"Why do you keep doing this?" I begged through my frustration and never-ending agony.

"I don't want to hurt you, but you need to know the truth," she said. "You need to be told until you remember."

"I do remember." Her head shifted back as surprise swept across her features, but I continued speaking before she could say anything. "I remember everything from that first night I met you until the accident. Harper, I know *us.*"

Sorrow replaced everything again as her head shook. "Chase—" Her gasp filled the small space when I pulled her down another few feet and into the bathroom, then hurried to shut the door behind us. "No, no, no. We can't be in here."

"You and me," I said over her, pleading with her to give me this time. "The way we always were. Using the seconds or minutes when no one was around to argue or talk in a way that was us. In a way that was *real.* So, talk to me."

"None of that happened," she said as she pushed against me, and I realized then *just* how weak her pushes were.

Instead of taking comfort in it, it made me pause. Step back.

Because there was nothing about her feeble attempts to stop me that shouted hesitation as if she didn't truly want me to let her go.

It was as if she was afraid of physically hurting me.

And the Harper I knew wouldn't have let that stop her. She would've used that to her advantage.

"I hate that this is tormenting you—I really do," she went on as she kept a hand outstretched in case I stepped toward her again. "But you need to know that none of it was real so you can move on from it until you get your memories back."

My voice was all soft bemusement when I said, "But I remember you." I met her disappointed gaze. "I've known things about you and Bree and Konrad since I woke up. So, how can the rest of it not be real?"

Her shoulders sagged. "You think you know things."

"Bree confirmed them."

Surprise flashed across her face for a moment before her head shook. "I don't know, Chase. I don't know how any of this works. But I know what you think happened between us didn't."

"I remember tossing you on my bed that first night," I argued, reminding her of the memory she'd already confirmed for me. "I remember you threatening to cut off my dick if I touched you."

"*Lorena Bobbitt* you," she corrected as a wry smile touched the corner of her lips.

"Same thing."

"My version sounded better." A breath of a laugh left her before her expression fell into something more serious. "But you never crossed that line. Not that night or any night after, and I'm thankful you didn't."

"Harper—"

"No, Chase, you need to understand this." She gave me a pleading look that had my defense dying on my tongue. "You ruffle my hair. You talk to me about your relationship with Scarlet because you know Bree won't give helpful advice."

I might've laughed if I were having the conversation with anyone else because she was right.

Bree always gave the worst advice.

"And the only time *you* have ever kissed *me* has been when you've kissed the top of my head the way you do with Bree. It has never been romantic, and it's always been in celebration of something—like when I got engaged or married. Or when Brandon and I told everyone that we were expecting."

My head slanted and my eyelids shut as that pain crashed into me, nearly knocking me back a stop.

Because not having Harper, not being able to hold her, was a crushing sort of pain. But what she'd just said went so far past that.

Accepting the knowledge that I wasn't going to be a dad, that she and Brandon were having a baby, was incapacitating.

"I don't know what else to say to make you believe me, but we're a product of twisted memories," she said resolutely. "Nothing more."

"I've heard you," I said, the words scraping up my throat as I focused on her again. "I've heard you and I've seen the truth written all over you. But it doesn't change that when all those memories slam back into me, they feel more real than anything has in my life."

Sadness swirled in her gray eyes as she took a step to close some of the distance between us. "What if it isn't me?"

My eyebrows drew close as I studied her.

"Have you considered that these memories might feel so real to you because they happened with someone else?" When I just continued watching her, her voice dropped to a whisper when she said, "Scarlet."

"Scarlet isn't pregnant," I informed her as if that alone was all the proof I needed that it wasn't her.

But the way my heartbeat kicked up at just the mention of her was immediate. The pain and guilt that had sliced through my chest each time Harper had said her name during our conversation were impossible to ignore. The way my entire body twitched with the urge to find her, to see her, to apologize was something even Harper noticed.

And I still hated Scarlet for it—as unfounded and inane as that hatred was.

"But you'd just found out I was pregnant not long before your accident," Harper informed me. "And you'd been with Brandon right before it happened. Dreams often pull from what's been in our life recently. What if it twisted all of that with your life with Scarlet?"

My head had been shaking but stopped when my memories clashed with her implications.

My eyes narrowed on her when I asked, "Now you're saying I was in some fucked-up love triangle with the girl who's supposedly my fiancée?"

"*Is* your fiancée," she corrected firmly. "And I didn't say that. I'm just trying to help you figure it out."

"I don't want you to help me figure it out," I said through clenched teeth. "I want my life back."

But as soon as the words left me, I realized the girl in front of me wasn't the one I'd been picturing as I'd said it.

And it rocked me.

Made the floor beneath me feel unsteady.

And I hated that I couldn't know if it was real or because of how things had been between Scarlet and me this week or because of what Harper was saying.

Shaking my head, I moved for the door. "I shouldn't have come tonight."

"Chase, you'll figure it out," Harper said as I gripped the handle and flung the door open with her directly behind me—

And felt her small body slam into mine when I saw the guy waiting directly across the hall.

Arms folded across his chest as he leaned against the wall. Face impassive.

But from the way his jaw ticked every few seconds, I knew his anger was simmering just beneath the surface.

"You had to know this was coming," Harper whispered to me as she pushed around me and headed for Brandon. "We were just talking."

"I could hear," he muttered, never taking his eyes off me.

"Great," I murmured and took a step into the hall. "Guess we're done here then."

But I'd just started turning away when he grabbed my bad shoulder and slammed me back against the doorframe, forcing a hissed curse from me.

"*Brandon*," Harper snapped in blatant shock. "He's recovering!"

Brandon's hand tightened on my shoulder. "I know."

I clenched my teeth and tried to breathe through the pain because I knew I'd pushed him to this, even though I hadn't done anything to deserve it.

Well . . . not this time.

"I didn't touch her," I ground out before another wheezed, "*Fuck*," scraped up my throat when he shoved me against the frame a little harder.

"I pulled her into the bathroom," I conceded. "That's it."

"My wife," he said in a low, lethal tone.

"Yeah, I've heard you."

"I shouldn't have to keep reminding you of that." His voice dropped to a whisper. "You're like my brother, Chase. The hell are you trying to do to us with this shit?"

"I didn't touch her," I repeated, meeting his hardened stare and faltering when I realized I'd had Harper in a room and hadn't done anything.

Hadn't tried to kiss her. Hadn't tried to prove that we were something. And I'd never had the *urge* to.

I hadn't been mesmerized by her lips. I hadn't wanted to feel them. I hadn't been consumed with the need to be closer to her. I'd stepped back. I'd *left*.

"Have you considered that these memories might feel so real to you because they happened with someone else?"

Harper's words replayed again and again until I was struggling to find the denial that had been so quick to rise earlier.

"You forced her into a room to talk to you," Brandon said, and I gave a subtle shake of my head as I was brought back to the situation in the hall. "That's more than you should ever do to anyone, but especially to her. To my marriage. To your relationship. To our friendship. Understand?"

"Yeah. *Shit,*" I hissed when he shoved off me.

"Stay away from my wife," he warned as he took another step back to where Harper watched with a horrified look.

"Not sure I've caught that title yet," I said dryly, my eyes rolling as I turned. "Might need to say it a few more times." The words faded to nothing when I caught sight of the woman at the end of the hall.

Standing tall, even though it looked like she was crumpling.

Arms wrapped tightly around her waist. Face devastatingly blank, but her eyes were screaming with pain.

Fuck.

My entire body reacted.

Knees nearly giving out. Arm twitching like I could reach her from where I stood. Chest shredding and tearing open like I might have something to offer her.

Like she might own part of me.

"You don't need to explain," she began, voice thick with emotion and forcing a jagged breath from me, "I heard everything."

"Everything," Brandon echoed when Scarlet turned and left. "She was the one who made me realize why Harper hadn't come back. She was standing here with me until the end."

"Oh no," Harper whispered before hurrying in the direction Scarlet had gone, but I just stood there.

Unable to move.

Mind racing as I thought about all I'd said.

Fuck, fuck, fuck.

"Yeah," Brandon muttered as if he could hear my thoughts. "If this is your reaction to that . . . I'd give anything to make you see her pain when we got in the hall and realized the two of you were in there." He took a few steps away before glancing at me from over his shoulder. "Looked like she was drowning in it."

"I get it."

"Do you?" he shot back.

"I don't know how to do this," I snapped. "I can't figure out what's going on or what I'm feeling. I can't figure out what's real. Give me a fucking break."

He nodded for a while before shaking his head. "Not when that break means letting you destroy both our relationships."

And then he was gone.

By the time I finally left the hall, he and Harper were talking quietly in the entryway with Bree and Konrad.

I glanced in the direction of the living room and kitchen, looking for my parents and Scarlet before looking at the four of them. My body went still as dread slowly pushed through my veins when I found them watching me with careful expressions.

"What?" I asked uneasily.

Brandon took a breath, but Bree spoke before he could. "Well, you're an asshole, for one."

"Yeah, I'm aware," I mumbled as I looked for Scarlet again.

"She isn't here," Brandon said, dragging my attention back to them. With an unapologetic shrug, he explained, "Scarlet left."

Guilt and something close to fear spiked through me. My lungs ached and screamed for oxygen as I struggled to make them work as pain seared my chest.

But I just stood there in my confusing, incapacitating thoughts and pains until I could offer them an unaffected, "All right."

"Asshole," Bree snapped as I turned to walk deeper into the house.

I was that and more. But I was afraid to accept everything that was so clearly laid out in front of me. I didn't *want* to accept parts of it.

I couldn't trust my emotions after Harper had put that bull-shit in my head.

And with how painful this week and a half had already been, I didn't want to let myself fall for Scarlet. Because what if I finally got my memories back only to find out that I'd really been in love with someone else all along?

Or if the mixed memory theory was correct . . . what if there *had* been an affair? But what if Scarlet had been cheating on *me*?

NINE

SCARLET

"Someone better have ordered me something with alcohol in it because I am ready for the tea that's about to get spilled," Anna said as she plopped into one of the chairs at the restaurant.

"Who said there was tea?" Samantha asked, even as her worried eyes darted my way. Assessing. Encouraging.

"Um . . ."—Anna gestured around us—"we're at brunch. Don't get me wrong, I love brunch. Especially with my favorite girls. But it's Tuesday."

"Dramatic," Samantha muttered with a wry smile as Anna went on.

"Saturday is for brunch. Tuesdays and Fridays are for getting our asses kicked by Scarlet. So, don't tell me something didn't go down."

"I gotta pee," Litany said in way of announcing she'd arrived just before she dropped her purse onto the last remaining chair.

"Brat, tell your bladder it can wait. There's tea," Anna yelled on a whisper.

"I'll be fast," LT said defensively as she began hurrying off, only to stop and give our waiter a look that very clearly shouted she was interested. "Well, hello . . ."

"This girl." Anna gave the two of us a look she reserved for when LT irritated her before asking, "Is it an alcohol kind of morning?"

"Yep," I said before Samantha could respond.

"I knew it," Anna hissed, then looked to our waiter, who was too busy watching LT walk away, and I just tried to hold it together.

I hadn't been home.

I'd driven straight to Samantha's apartment when I'd left the Grayson's Sunday night and had stayed there.

I'd gotten dozens of calls and messages from everyone that had only increased when I hadn't shown up to surf yesterday morning or today. But I hadn't answered or responded to any of them.

I wasn't sure if it was because I didn't know what to say or if I was embarrassed by what had gone down in the few minutes we'd been at the Grayson's. Or maybe it was because I was *afraid* of what I'd say.

Because when I'd driven away and that first sob had shattered the weight pressing against me, I'd known the hope I'd continued searching for and clinging to was nothing more than a dream. And in my aching soul, I knew what came next.

I'd known.

I'd just been avoiding it. Pretending everything would get resolved one way or another.

"Okay, I'm here!" LT said as she rushed up to the table. Expression bright with excitement and mischief as she not-so-subtly looked for the waiter. "What's going on?"

"Tone it down, Susie Sunshine, and try to keep it in your pants for once," Anna said as she pushed a mimosa closer to LT. "It doesn't look like we're getting exciting news."

I inhaled shakily, but when my lips parted, nothing came out.

"We love you," Samantha whispered as she reached over to squeeze my hand. "And we're here for you."

"Oh shit," Anna mumbled. "What'd he do? I'll put him in another coma."

A strained laugh punched from my lungs as my eyes rolled. "Not necessary, but thanks for the offer."

"Always, babe," she said just as softly, her normally amused expression weighed down with worry.

"And it isn't Chase's fault," I went on. "Really, he . . . well, as much as I want to blame him, I can't."

"Well, technically . . ." Anna mumbled under her breath, earning another eye roll from me.

"I can't," I said unwaveringly. "I know it's bothering him that he's hurting me. But he's even more confused than before because of some of the *real* memories that he woke with. So, he's back to thinking we've been lying to him, and his memory hasn't changed at all. And it's just . . . it's breaking me."

My lips lifted into the briefest smile of gratitude when Samantha grabbed my hand again, offering me her strength when I struggled to continue.

"I'm calling off the wedding." The words rushed from me, thick and trembling. "I wanted to tell you before I announced it to everyone else. But I contacted the venue and photographer and everything yesterday . . . it's done."

Anna's jaw dropped, but before I could begin to explain myself, LT asked, "And?"

Anna's head jerked back before she whipped around to face LT. "What in the fuck do you mean by 'and?' Our best friend just told us she has to call off her wedding."

"I mean, *and what else*?" LT said defensively, narrowing her eyes at Anna before looking at me. "Are you and Chase staying together? Are you separating? Are you going to continue living together? And if not, who gets the house? Because your business is there."

"Oh, I-I—" I stammered, head shaking as that hollow tried to swallow me whole. Tears slipped down my cheeks before I could attempt to stop them when I said, "I don't know. I didn't think about all that."

"Do not listen to her," Anna said, holding a hand in front of LT.

"Honestly, LT," Samantha whispered from beside me.

"It was a legitimate question!" LT snapped.

"No, she's right," I said in her defense. "I should've thought about it."

"Not the time for your no-nonsense literal-ness," Anna said to LT before focusing on me. "What can we do for you? I seriously wouldn't be able to imagine having to do this under normal circumstances. But this? Babe. And what happened?" she asked before I could respond. "I thought you said things were good."

"Yeah," I whispered through my tears, my lips pulling into a sad smile. "I thought they were, but I . . ." One of my shoulders lifted in a shrug. "Well, it's like he keeps getting pulled back into these 'memories' of this life he thinks he had. Then everything falls apart between us all over again because he blames me for that life not being a reality."

"He doesn't," Anna said, looking to Samantha for backup.

But Samantha kept her lips pressed tightly together since I'd already unloaded all this onto her.

"He told me he does," I informed them, then added, "But to answer what LT asked, Chase still doesn't remember me or our relationship at all. So, he doesn't even think of us *as* together. He keeps saying things like, 'I get that we were together.' Or refers to me as the girl who was *supposedly* his fiancée." A sad laugh punched from my lungs. "He's probably relieved that I haven't been home."

"That isn't true," Samantha said quickly.

"I'm about to go knock his memories back into place if it is," Anna said unapologetically.

"He texted you," Samantha said as if reminding me, but I knew she just wanted the other girls to know. When I didn't elaborate, she looked to Anna and LT and explained, "He said he was sorry."

"But that was it," I said miserably.

"Sorry for what?" LT asked, cradling her mimosa close to her chest. Looking like she was holding her breath as she waited for one of us to explain.

And with a shaky inhale, I did.

Everything from how Chase had been all Sunday to how it'd fallen apart when we'd arrived at his parents' house that night.

"And I know he's sorry," I said once I'd finished telling them the entire thing. "I know a part of him doesn't like that he's hurting me. But that 'sorry' doesn't mean anything when the anger and betrayal he directs at me is so much stronger."

"Dude, I hate this for you," Anna said softly. "This isn't Chase. He wouldn't do this to you."

"Yeah, well," I whispered on a strangled laugh. "You know,

it's funny . . . they say soulmates find each other in every life. Love each other through anything, even death. Either we're not soulmates, or it's all just bullshit because he can barely tolerate me through lost memories."

A weighted silence surrounded our table. Drowning out the restaurant noises and chatter from the other tables and making me feel uncomfortable in my own skin.

"I need to go," I said, already standing and grabbing my purse.

The girls made objections, and Samantha reached for me, but I slipped away before I could do something like make things more uncomfortable or break down all over again.

But by the time I pushed out of the restaurant's door, Samantha was there, pulling me into a fierce hug and refusing to let me go until a shuddering breath wrenched from me.

"I know it doesn't seem like it, and I don't know how, but it will be okay," she murmured. When I nodded, she asked, "Are you coming back to my apartment?"

"Um . . . I don't know," I said as I pulled away. "I appreciate you being there for me the last couple of days, but I should probably—"

"Just get whatever you need from the house and come back."

My head bobbed for a long while as her words had my stomach sinking. "You think I should move out?"

"I just don't think Chase is the kind of guy who will give you the space you need and deserve to figure out your thoughts," she said uncertainly.

"There's nothing for me to figure out," I said adamantly. "I know what I want."

"But if this is your life now," she began gently, a grimace

tugging at her mouth, "then there's a lot of difficult things that need to be figured out—like what you're doing with your wedding."

"Right," I whispered, then took a hesitant step back. "Right. Then I'll, uh . . . I guess I'll go pack."

"Only if you want to," she offered when I took another step away. "You don't have to do anything I said; they're just suggestions. But my apartment is there for you."

I nodded and forced a smile. "Thanks, Sam," I murmured before hurrying to my car.

But during the drive home, my resolve grew weaker and weaker.

It wasn't that I was under the delusion that Chase would miraculously get his memories back today or tomorrow, or any time soon. So, our wedding needed to be called off.

I knew that.

It was that these days away from him had been excruciating. It was that the thought of a life without him crippled me. It was that I didn't know how to abandon him just because he was lost, no matter what it cost my heart in the process . . .

By the time I was standing at our front door with the key in my hand, I was torn.

Memories from before and after Chase's wreck waged a war on my heart and mind until I was absolutely sure I would walk in and fight for the man I loved, all while packing to leave.

But as soon as I set foot inside, I nearly crumpled under the weight of the battle. My lungs strained as I tried to breathe because he was in every part of that home. In every memory.

Beautiful and devastating and real and—*right in front of me.*

I stopped halfway through the entryway when he moved into my line of sight from the kitchen. Looking exhausted and relieved and frustrated as hell.

His jaw shifted irritably even as his bright eyes drifted over my body again and again as if he was making sure I was really there. But everywhere his eyes touched had my body coming alive. Everywhere they lingered felt like an open flame.

When his gaze landed on mine again, he nodded and turned away. Calling out, "Coffee?" as he did.

With a shuddering breath, I forced myself to move. To follow him. And struggled to find the courage to explain where I'd been. To explain what I'd done. "Chase—"

"I'm sorry," he said over me, then turned to lean against the counter. Tattooed arms folded over his chest and highlighting that he wasn't wearing his sling.

But now wasn't the time to get on him for that.

"You told me you never walked away from me before, and that's all I seem to make you do. I made you *leave*," he ground out. "I made you feel like you couldn't go back to the place where you live." He pressed his good hand to his chest before folding his arms again. "I'm sorry."

I wasn't sure why I expected anything else. I shouldn't have expected anything at all. And yet, his apology had my shoulders sagging. Because when I'd received that *I'm sorry* text from him yesterday morning, I'd been hoping the apology was for something else.

"That's what you're sorry for?" I asked and tried to mute the deprecating laugh that bubbled free.

His eyes narrowed, but that coldness was met with a well of remorse. "I'm sorry I hurt you."

"I know you are, Chase. But I—" I clenched my hands into

fists and stopped myself from begging him to apologize for everything he'd said to Harper and to me the other night at his parents'.

With a strained breath, I confessed instead, "You need to know the wedding's been canceled. Every—" The word hitched in my throat, but I forced myself to get out the rest without breaking down. "Everything's been taken care of."

"What wedding?"

My entire body jolted from the impact of his question.

Jesus, how could I still be so hurt by him? How could his words still crush my spirit so completely?

"Ours," I managed to say.

His eyebrows shot up. "We were getting married?"

"Chase, you know we're engaged! I *told* you we were getting married in a few months."

"When did you tell me?" he asked, the question filled with equal amounts doubt and shock.

I struggled to remember exactly when it had been, my head shaking as I sputtered, "I don't know. Right after you woke up."

"So, when I thought you were lying about who you were," he said roughly. "When I thought everyone was lying to me about everything."

A wounded sound wrenched from me. "You still think we are," I whispered as I turned to head to the bedroom.

"Scarlet, you've only told me two . . . maybe three things about our life together," he began when I'd made it only a step away. "Why is that?"

My head slanted in his direction. "What does it matter? You don't believe me anyway."

His eyelids closed as a whispered curse escaped him. But

when he focused on me again, the intensity of his stare stunned me. Seizing every part of me that had always belonged to him because that look was anger and desperation and *fear*.

"You were there when the doctor told everyone it might help if I was told and shown the memories I'd forgotten. If I was *in* the life I don't remember," he said. "But you haven't said anything about it. I want to know why."

"Before I answer, I want to know what you've tried to find out on your own with what's available to you." At the furrow of his brow, I turned fully to face him and explained, "Your phone. You have hundreds of pictures and videos of us. You have years' worth of conversations." His head began shaking and his lips parted, so I hurried to add, "Your sketchbooks."

Chase stopped moving.

Everything about him was so eerily still that it looked like he was carved from stone.

"It's there," I said softly. "*We* are there. So, what have you tried to find out?"

"Where are my sketchbooks?" he asked instead.

I gestured aimlessly. "Everywhere. You leave them everywhere."

"I haven't seen any."

I drew in a breath to respond with any number of the places where the books were always lying around and realized I couldn't remember the last time I'd seen one. "I don't know, Chase. They're literally all over the house. But you haven't answered."

His head slanted just the slightest movement, but it was enough to let me know he had no plans to. "You don't want me to."

"Because you haven't looked?" I assumed bitterly.

"Because I've only really looked through my texts with Harper."

My chin lowered in acceptance, and I struggled to swallow past the rock lodged in my throat. "You don't want to know," I said weakly, then met his hardened stare. "I haven't told you because you don't want to know about our life. I also don't want to make you feel like you *have* to love me or make you *think* you do because of stories you're told."

"Or is it because Harper's right?" he asked, words taking on a cold and cruel tone. "Is it because these memories I have are really memories with someone else? With *you*? How do I know that you weren't with someone else? That I wasn't fighting for you?"

My stomach dropped because, as much as it *had been* our life, it wasn't in the way he was thinking. It wasn't recent. "Chase—"

"But, really, you could tell me anything now, and I wouldn't know if it was real or not."

"You would've never been with me if I was the kind of person who took advantage of people that way," I snapped defensively.

"I don't know that," he said with a subtle shrug. "And what if I *was* in love with someone else?"

"No," I wheezed, even as the worry that had been plaguing me for weeks gnawed at my stomach. "No, I *know* you. I *knew* your love and your passion and every single thing you felt for me. Your life and your heart were with me, not someone else."

"But I don't know that," he repeated sharply.

"I do!"

"That doesn't mean anything to me, Scarlet," he shouted.

My head shook wildly as I battled the emotion threatening

to break free. "Tell me you don't feel it," I choked out. "I know you see a stranger when you look at me but tell me you look at me and feel *nothing*."

One second, the kitchen was heavy with our accusations and frustrations and pleas. The weight of the unknown pressing closer and closer around us and making it hard to breathe.

The next, Chase erased the distance between us with a couple large strides and reached for me.

Hand curling around my jaw and tilting my head up to meet his just as his mouth crashed against mine.

TEN

SCARLET

Hard.

Fervent.

Desperate.

Stealing the last of my air and piercing that veil of resentment in a shockwave of passion and need when Chase parted my lips . . . and then everything slowed.

The kiss.

His movements.

My frantically beating heart.

His fingers trailed down my neck as he took my bottom lip between his teeth. Gently tugging before his tongue darted out to taste the same place. And I went weak.

Legs trembling as a whimper crawled up my throat and turned into a sharp, reprimanding gasp when he lifted me onto the island. A string of hissed curses bursting from him and fanning across my lips at the stark reminder of his injuries.

"Chase—"

"Worth it," he growled as he captured my lips again.

Kissing me like he'd been holding himself back from this

very moment. Kissing me in a way that was as unfamiliar as it was familiar.

Because this was Chase. The love of my life. The man I was supposed to marry.

But this kiss? This was all new. This was that overwhelming, first kiss kind of high.

I never wanted it to end . . .

"I don't want to know you and I don't want to love you," he confessed against my lips before brushing a faint kiss across them as if he hadn't just destroyed the moment and buried my heart a little deeper. "But you're all I think about."

My stare flashed to his when he moved back enough to look at me.

"My memories feel real to me," he said as if he hadn't told me that very thing dozens of times. "And I'm afraid of what happens when I find out there's truth to them. I'm afraid of being blindsided the way I have been every fucking day. Of being blindsided by *you*. Of finding out none of what you've been saying is real."

"It was. It *is*," I said pleadingly. "Chase, we—" I pressed my lips tightly together and shook my head.

"Tell me," he begged, sliding his hand around my hip and gripping tight. "You keep telling me what *wasn't*. Tell me what *was*."

"I don't want you to fall in love with our past," I reminded him. "I don't want you to feel obligated to it. Either we are strong enough to make it through this, or we aren't. It's that simple."

His eyes searched mine for long moments before he realized, "You don't think we are."

A strained sound rose in my throat when his arm fell away

as he stepped back. "Before your accident, I would've sworn we were," I said confidently. "After? With the way you look at me and blame me for keeping you from a life you never had? With the way I can't sleep because of your desperate need to convince Harper you didn't cheat on her?"

I pressed a hand to my twisting stomach and studied the way his expression fell into that cold mask he'd worn so often lately.

"It's the one thing I can't piece together with your real life, and it terrifies me," I admitted. "If anyone is at risk of being blindsided when your memories return, it's me. It's *that*."

His head bobbed quickly before shaking. "You just tried assuring me that my heart and life were with you, not someone else."

A confirming hum built in my chest at his unspoken question. "Before you woke up from the coma and started saying everything you did, I would've bet my life that you would've never looked at another woman, let alone touched one. But everything you were saying was from our lives in one way or another."

"Like the lilies," he murmured as he began nodding again, but his movements stopped and his head listed. "Everything?"

"In one way or another," I repeated in confirmation.

The muscle in his jaw twitched. When he spoke, his words were laced with warning. "Explain the triangle."

My mouth slowly fell open as those months burst through my mind.

"I don't see how being caught up in a love triangle is going to make me feel *obligated* to our past," he ground out. "Explain."

I watched him for a while longer before nodding. "Your

family and friends didn't know," I began, then hurried to amend, "Brian did, and you'll understand why. But I just recently told Bree because of everything you were saying when you woke up."

He didn't respond in any way, just took another step back to take up his earlier position against the counter. Waiting for me to continue.

But I was *shaking*.

Absolutely trembling as I struggled with how to tell Chase something he'd already gone through. But this wasn't the same guy.

This wasn't the guy who was willing to fight for me.

This was the guy who was already suspicious of everything I said and judged nearly everything I did.

"I was dating someone when I met you," I finally began, words coming out weak and unsteady. "I'd been dating him for years."

Chase didn't say anything. Just watched me, waiting for what would come next. Waiting for the rest of the story. But it was there in his eyes . . . the frustration. The assumptions. The betrayal.

"You and I were instant," I whispered through my embarrassment and watched as his expression shifted with that anger.

"Did I know?" he asked, the question all grated steel.

"Yes. Anna and I—" I shook my head and explained, "She's one of my best friends. We'd gone to get tattoos. Brian was doing them, but you and I started talking and never stopped, even when you started tattooing someone else."

A small smile touched the edge of my mouth as I remembered that night and quickly fell when I focused on the coldness of his eyes.

"I told you from the beginning that I had a boyfriend and must've repeated it half a dozen times in an attempt to remind myself. But again . . . instant."

"What happened?" he demanded when I didn't go on.

"You told me I was with the wrong guy, and I ended up giving you my number," I said with a roll of my eyes. "When we went to leave that night, you followed us out and grabbed my hand, pulling me close to you. I was so sure you were going to kiss me, but you just held me there and looked at me like you were committing me and that night to memory before you repeated, 'You're with the wrong guy.'

"I should've broken up with him that night," I went on, "but I told myself probably a hundred times that I wouldn't hear from you. And when you called me the next morning, I told myself it was nothing. That *you* were nothing, even though I'd known from the first moment I saw you that you were unlike anyone I'd ever met."

"So, when did you leave him?" Chase asked, already guessing it'd taken me far too long.

"Two months later," I whispered. "I hurt you so much during those months and made it worse when we gave in because we couldn't stay away from each other anymore."

He rubbed at his jaw, head bobbing as that frustration poured from him. "How long into everything was that?"

"A little over a month."

"So, it took you another month to break up with him?" he asked with a sneering laugh.

I tried to keep my spine straight and shoulders back. Tried not to let his words affect me.

After all, this was *our* story. *Our* life.

But it was difficult when it felt like I was laying my sins

bare to him and receiving his disappointed judgment for the first time.

"A few weeks," I corrected, then added, "Chase, you were right there with me."

"You should've left him."

"Stop judging me for something I did years ago," I snapped shakily.

"It's happening right now for me," he reminded me.

"It doesn't change the fact that you already knew. That you were *right there with me*," I repeated through clenched teeth. "Giving in to something so powerful and unstoppable."

"If that's how it was, why didn't you leave him?" he asked, head shaking. "That first night. When we hooked up. Any time in those weeks after."

"Because I felt trapped—"

"No." The word was soft but held a depth that had the rest of my explanation dying on my tongue. "No, I want to know *why*. *Why* did you stay with him? *Why*, if we couldn't stay away from each other, was I not worth it to you?"

"That wasn't it," I choked out, but he continued.

"*Why* did you continue choosing him over me if we were supposedly *instant*, Scarlet?"

"You were worth everything," I cried out, repeating a version of the same words I'd told him years before. "I know what I did, and I know the mistake I made in taking so long to choose you when we both already knew I *would*. But it isn't fair to make me defend myself over something you already know and were a part of years ago."

"I don't know any of this."

"But you *did*," I shot back, then quickly wiped at my wet cheeks. "You knew how I felt for you. You knew I fell in love with you faster than should've been possible. You knew he wasn't just someone I'd been with for years; he was my best friend, and our parents had been best friends since high school. Not only that, less than a month before I met you, his parents had bought us a place, and his uncle had given me a job at his prestigious physical therapy clinic. And even though I worked my ass off for that degree, I knew it was only because of who I was to their family.

"So, it had nothing to do with you not being worth it," I said as my chest shook with trembling breaths. "It had everything to do with being *trapped*. It had everything to do with being terrified of hurting people who had always been family to me. Being terrified of imploding my life, my family, and my career, and then deciding none of it compared to the pain of not being with you fully."

Chase didn't respond when I finished.

Just watched me as long minutes came and went in excruciating silence.

And somehow, that silence and his masked fury terrified me. Like I was at risk of losing him because of our past. Like I hadn't already been losing him for weeks.

"That why you aren't a physical therapist anymore?" he finally asked, voice gruff. "Because of us?"

My already wrecked body nearly convulsed with the force of the chill that shot through me. "That isn't something I'm telling you. Not now. Not like this."

"But you said I know," he murmured, confirming what I'd told him last week.

"You knew."

He nodded slowly before asking, "Did your life implode? Your family?"

"For a little while," I admitted. "They were so angry with me and wanted nothing to do with you."

His eyebrows rose at that and his head slanted. "Is it still like that?"

"No, they adore you," I assured him. "They live in Fresno, but they came down those first days after your accident. They've been worried about you."

"And your ex?" The question left him on a rumbled growl. "You still talk to him?"

"No," I said sharply as that chill threatened to consume me. "You were the last one to see him."

A cruel smirk stole across his face. "And how did that go?"

"You never told me, and I never asked," I said honestly, surprising him with the answer.

And I realized at his stunned reaction that he believed me. He'd questioned my actions and morals but hadn't once questioned any of what I'd told him. For the first time, he hadn't immediately denied our past.

He'd even accepted that part of his memories was from us.

Maybe. Possibly.

"I had my assumptions, but the entire situation was . . . well, it was sensitive," I finished on a whisper, intently studying his expression.

"Clearly," he muttered, then ran a hand over his face in agitation. "My memories still feel real to me."

My shoulders sagged, but before I could respond, he continued.

"But I had Harper alone." He pushed from his place against the counter and came back to where he'd left me, muttering, "I had her right in front of me and I never wanted *this*," as he did.

Effortlessly stepping between my legs and slipping his large hand around my waist.

Eyes roaming my face and dipping over my body. Making my chest's movements become more exaggerated as his stare broke me open. Left me feeling bare and vulnerable and beautiful in this paradox of a moment.

Because, once again, this was a man who had looked at me thousands of times. Who knew every part of me intimately.

But the eyes that had been reluctantly drawn to me this week were from a stranger. The stare that was on me now was from a man who was enraptured with a woman he didn't know.

"I never had the urge to kiss her," he went on as his gaze fell to my mouth. "My heart didn't fucking race like I wasn't the one in control of it. I just kept thinking that I wanted my life back." Grabbing my hand, he lifted it to his chest and placed it over the frantic pounding of his heart. "All I think about," he whispered as his forehead fell to mine. "But those memories, Scar . . ."

"They're us."

"Maybe," he conceded. "But they tell me I'm in love with someone else."

"And this?" I asked tightly as I pressed my hand against his chest.

His head moved against mine in a subtle nod. "Looks like I'm the one who's trapped this time."

Horror rushed through me and gripped my chest when he reached for my engagement ring. "What are you doing?" I asked, then choked over my pleas when he began removing it. "What are—*no*. Chase!"

I tried clenching my hand into a fist, but he gently unfurled my fingers to continue sliding the ring off my finger.

"Stop!" I begged, the word thick with emotion and fear and grief.

"Listening to your story . . . maybe you're right," he said calmly as he placed my hand over his chest again and pressed his forehead harder to mine when hushed sobs racked my body. "Maybe everything I remember is our life twisted around."

"Why are you doing this?" I asked through the tears straining my words.

"If that's true, who knows what I did to you? Because it'd be like you said: You would be the one at risk of being hurt when my memories come back," he said as if it was as simple as that.

"But we don't know that," I tried vainly, my heart twisting and shattering under the weight of what was happening. Under the roller coaster of this fucking day. "Don't do this. Please—"

"For all we know, I don't deserve to have you wearing this," he said as he pulled me closer to him. Trying to comfort me while I was falling apart. "But as it stands, I don't know you, Scarlet. As it stands, my mind is on you and my heart is fucking wrecked because of something everyone is saying didn't happen. Until I figure my shit out, you don't deserve to have to deal with that pain."

I pressed against his chest, my head shaking as that fear gripped my lungs in an iron vice. "What are you saying? What does this mean?"

"I mean, I want to be honest with you," he said without reservations. "I want to tell you what's happening and what I remember, even if it hurts you. I want to figure out the truth for myself, and I know I would've left my entire life in sketches, but I haven't seen my books."

"They're here," I said confidently, ready to look for them if it would mean he wouldn't do what he was. But Chase seemed to sense my thoughts and gripped my waist tenderly, keeping me in place on the island.

"Then I need to look through them," he said adamantly. "And if these memories really are twisted versions of our life, then I did something to you. Or something happened. And I have a feeling there's someone who knows, and I've been subconsciously avoiding him because I knew he'd have the truth."

I was so wrapped up in my emotional spiral that it took far too long to understand who he was talking about. "Brian?"

"I tell him everything," Chase said with a subtle nod.

"Why—" A hiccupped sob broke free. "We need to call off the wedding, I know that. I did that. But we don't have to end because you're struggling with your memories."

Half of his face scrunched up in unease.

"Chase, somewhere in there, you're still my fiancé."

He lifted his other hand to curl his fingers around the back of my head. Holding me there for long seconds before he shook his head. "I'm not that guy," he whispered, forcing a sob from me. "Next time you're wearing this ring, if you ever wear it again, it's because I gave it to you."

"You already did."

He pressed his lips to mine, silencing my claims before he repeated, "It's because *I* gave it to you."

My face crumpled at the realization that Chase prepared to never get his memories back.

"Until then, I want to get to know you," he went on. "I want you with me while I figure things out, but I won't blame you for saying *no*. I won't stop you from leaving if I hurt you too much to stay." His hand fell to where mine still rested against his chest and pressed harder against the fierce pounding there. "All I think about," he muttered before releasing me and walking away.

Leaving me alone.

Leaving me a trembling, crying mess.

Leaving me broken in a whole new way when I finally understood what Chase had been doing all along—what he'd been saying. What he'd done for me.

He hadn't taken my ring to hurt me. He hadn't taken it to leave *me*.

He'd ensured I wouldn't be trapped again. He'd given me the freedom to escape the pain our situation had already caused and would inevitably continue inflicting.

As if I would ever choose a life without him.

ELEVEN

CHASE

Scarlet hadn't brought up the conversation in the kitchen or the fact that I'd been unable to stop myself from kissing her. She'd just walked into the guestroom a while after I'd left her and flung my sling at me, playfully glaring before she'd turned right back around and called out, *"Help me look for your books."*

I had.

I also hadn't been able to fight the smile that had crossed my face because that simple interaction had said so much.

She understood what I'd done. She was staying.

For now.

But after turning over the entire house and only managing to find one of my sketchbooks, I'd looked at her and asked, *"Could they have been in my truck?"*

"No, they were here." She'd gestured irritably around. *"Everywhere. You kept them everywhere because you didn't want to have to go looking for one."*

I'd nodded as worry and unfounded guilt had gripped my

stomach tighter. *"Think it's time I go to the shop and see Brian."*

"Okay, I'll take you."

"No." When hurt had flashed through her eyes, I'd hurried to add, *"Need to talk to Brandon too. I'll call him."*

But throughout texting Brandon and waiting for him to show, I'd barely been able to look at Scarlet. When I'd left, I'd simply studied her, trying so damn hard to remember things that weren't there. Trying to know what I could've done.

Because it had to be something.

"They aren't there," I said to Brandon when we were nearing the shop I'd been tattooing at for—well, shit, I didn't even know now.

College.

I think.

Brandon glanced between the street and me a few times, caught off guard by the abrupt change in our conversation. "What?"

I drew in a sharp breath and released it just as quickly. "My sketchbooks," I explained. "Scarlet and I found one, but she said I had a ton that were always lying around everywhere."

"You do," Brandon confirmed, making that worry grow thicker.

"They aren't there," I repeated. "The only one we found was hidden in a closet and was only there because it was full."

Brandon lifted his hand for a second before letting it slap onto the steering wheel. "Okay?"

"I sketched whatever was in my head," I told him. "Whatever was happening in my life, whatever was consuming my mind, it went onto paper."

"The last two years," he said in understanding.

"Everything that happened will be in there," I confirmed. "Scarlet told me something earlier—something about our life that I guess no one really knew—that made me think for the first time that everyone could be right."

"First time?" he asked dully and shot me an irritated look, even as a smirk tugged at his mouth.

"The memories feel so damn real," I defended. "But if that part of my memories was really my life with her, then the rest of it has truth somewhere. And I woke up thinking I'd hurt Harper—I was afraid I'd lost her—because a girl had been in my bed."

Brandon dipped his head after a moment. "You think you cheated on Scarlet?"

"I don't know."

"You wouldn't," he said adamantly as he pulled into one of the shop's parking spaces. "I know you wouldn't."

"But what would explain those memories?" I challenged. "Why would all my books be gone? It's like I was hiding them from her."

"Fuck," he muttered as he ran a hand over his face, then fiercely shook his head. "You worship her. Worshipped," he corrected quickly. "There's no way."

"Guess we'll find out," I said as I looked at the place that had been like a second home to me. "Because the girl that had been in my bed worked here with me."

"What?" Brandon asked, nearly choking over the word. "You fucked Marissa?"

My head snapped in his direction and expression fell, but only for a moment.

Marissa was Brian's wife. There was no way in hell I would ever think about her in that way, let alone touch her.

"Marissa? *Brian's* Riss?"

"Yeah," Brandon said with wide eyes. "She's the piercer. She's the only girl who works here."

"Fuck that. No," I said quickly. "It wasn't her. And when did she start working here?"

Brandon gestured toward the building, but his expectant look faltered. "About a year or so ago."

"Jesus." I dragged my good hand over my face and fought a shiver. "Just the thought, man."

"Few weeks ago, that would've been your reaction to Harper."

I braced myself against the onslaught of memories and forced myself to meet his patient stare. "I'm sorry for the other night."

A breath of a laugh left him. "I know you, Chase. You wouldn't be doing this unless you genuinely believed that had been your life—that we were all lying to you. I can also see how this entire thing is tearing you up, and as much as I hate you even thinking about my wife, I hate this for you." He leaned forward and lowered his voice. "I'm here for you, but I'll sure as shit let you know when you overstep."

"Good." My chest pitched with amusement even as a frown tugged at my mouth. "It's weird . . . I see it. I feel it. I feel emotionally attached *to* the memories. And everything in me is screaming to get back to that life. But it wasn't until I was in the bathroom with Harper that I realized I don't actually feel anything for *her*."

Brandon's eyebrows raised, his expression a perfect mixture of relief, amusement, and intrigue. "Maybe because the real girl in those memories has been right beside you this entire time," he said knowingly, and I listed my head.

Refusing to agree or disagree with him when my mind was still so twisted.

"Yeah, Scarlet's something," I muttered instead. "But that's why I need to talk to Brian. He'll know if I did something to her. He'll tell me the truth."

"The fuck," Brandon said with an offending huff, his next words leaving him on a teasing breath. "Good to know where I stand, asshole."

"No, it isn't that," I said quickly. "You're family. You know that. But with this?" I gestured to him. "Brandon, all of this shit revolves around us and your wife. Brian is completely removed from it. Not only that, but if everything was the way you've all said it was, I don't know if I would've told you if I cheated on Scarlet."

Brandon's eyebrows drew close in irritation and hurt, but he just waited for me to continue.

"She still goes surfing with you even though I'm not there, so she's clearly close to you. You can't tell me she wouldn't have found out." Without giving him time to argue, I continued, saying, "As ridiculous as Brian is, the guy's a fucking vault. And the memories I'm currently dealing with have me going to Brian for *everything* since it involved Harper."

"So, you think you went to him," he said in understanding.

"If it happened," I corrected. Drawing in another breath to continue, I let it free instead. Hesitating for a moment before I finally confessed, "He and Riss have been texting and calling, and I've been avoiding them, and I've had no idea why I would even want to. This might be my reason why."

Brandon nodded before whispering, "If you cheated on her . . ."

"I know," I mumbled.

"Do you?" he challenged, studying me like he was trying to figure out what exactly was going on between Scarlet and me.

"I'm starting to. I hardly know her, and I'm already racked with guilt over the thought of cheating on her." Reaching for the handle, I popped open the door and said, "Thanks for the ride."

"Chase," he called out before I could shut the door, and I turned to see him leaning over the console. "I'm here, man. Clearly," he said on a laugh. "Something happened? I'm fucking here. I would've *been there*, even though, yeah, I would've made sure Scarlet found out . . . from you."

I dipped my head in understanding and gratitude, then closed the door and turned to take in the building in front of me before finally heading inside.

Memories, real and twisted and who-the-hell-knew-what blasted me as soon as I walked through the doors, and I let them consume me for the seconds before my nickname rang out through the shop.

"Chach!" The relief and excitement in Brian's voice forced a smile to cross my face that faltered when Marissa's trembling voice echoed from the back.

"Chachi?" She barreled down the hall and nearly dropped to a crouch when she saw me standing there. "Jesus, you asshole."

A sharp breath burst from me just as Brian stepped up to me, arms spread wide.

"Scared the shit out of me and my woman," he said when he released me. "Couldn't get ahold of you. Scarlet said you made it through but weren't *you* anymore, and that's all we got."

"You talked to Scarlet?" I asked as I accepted a hug from Marissa.

"Asshole," she muttered against my chest.

"Your lady love stopped by the day after you woke up, dude," Brian said as Marissa fell into his arms, softly crying. "Last we heard about you."

"Who do you think you are trying to take you from us?" Marissa asked, glaring at me accusingly.

"Trying to make sure you remember how much you love me," I said, forcing something of a tease into my voice.

"I'd punch you if you didn't look like death warmed over," she warned, holding her fist up to stress her words.

"Don't doubt it, Riss." I glanced around the mostly empty shop, then asked, "Are any of my sketchbooks here?"

"Here?" Brian asked with a hesitant laugh. "Dude, how hard did you get hit?"

"Pretty fucking bad, the way I hear it."

He squeezed Marissa a little tighter, then said, "You don't leave your books here. Ever."

I nodded, having already known that. Well, at least, I'd thought I'd known that.

"Haven't been able to find them, thought I'd ask," I muttered, then took another sweep around the shop.

Seeing things that were so damn real.

Seeing the place where I'd done Harper's tattoo. Where I'd led her to the mirror to show her the piece once I'd finished. Where she'd kissed me.

The place at my station that had become *hers*. Where she'd sit and talk to me for a few minutes on her way from one place to another.

The place she'd been talking to—

"Does a girl named Trish work here?" I asked softly, afraid to say her name too loud.

Both Brian and Marissa just stared at me, eyebrows lifted in question and confusion.

Marissa was the first to make a sound, but it was just a hesitant noise as she looked at Brian as if she wasn't sure what to do with these questions I was asking.

"Never had a Trish work here," Brian finally answered. "Only chick that ever worked here other than my lady was gone before you started with us."

"Got it," I murmured, then said, "Riss, I love you, but I need to talk to Brian."

She straightened and folded her arms across her chest, staring me down in that way she always had. Reprimanding with just a look. "Literally every single thing you say to him will be repeated to me when we get home."

"I got that, but I need this to be just the two of us for now."

She glared for a second longer before rolling her eyes and stomping off like a child, calling out as she did, "If you leave without saying goodbye to me, I will find you and make Brian hold you down while I pierce your nose."

"Think we should just do it," Brian said with a wicked grin.

"Shut up, Bri." I rolled my eyes, then nodded in the direction of my station.

"Damn good to see you, Chach," he said solemnly. "We've been a mess, worrying about you."

"That's my fault," I said as I sank into my chair, a grimace crossing my face at the pains that had been flaring since I'd lifted Scarlet onto the island.

Still worth it.

"Well, no shit," Brian said as he fell into the client chair.

"And what's with these questions about your books and a chick named Trish? Is this what your lady meant about you not being you?"

I dragged my free hand through my hair a couple times before leaning forward and meeting his stare. "Brian, I know what Riss said, but I need to talk to you. I mean, really talk to you."

He held his arms out to the sides. "Baby, I'm a vault."

The corners of my mouth twitched into a smirk. "I know."

With a ragged breath, I sat back and told Brian everything. Every memory I'd woken up with and the ones my friends and family were telling me now. How the false ones all twisted to connect to my supposed real life and the glaring one that *didn't*.

"What in the blessed shit?" he asked when I finished.

I lifted my hand and let it slap down onto my thigh.

"This is legit? Like, I'm not stoned, you're not playing me, legit."

"Legit," I confirmed with a dip of my head. "I *just* found out Riss even worked here. I didn't know until Brandon said something."

Shock covered his face as he turned to look toward the hall that led to the back rooms, and then a laugh was tumbling from him. "Can't believe your boy hasn't beaten the shit out of you for all the things you've been saying about his wifey, my dude."

"Yeah, well," I said with a sigh. "I'm definitely pushing him to a breaking point."

"What a trip," he said, still all amusement. "You got a whole second chance at life and ended up thinking you had a second life."

"Something like that." I lifted my chin and said, "Need you to clear up things for me."

He pressed a hand to his chest in exaggeration. "I'd be honored to."

"Scarlet and me . . . is that real?"

His brows lifted. "As the air you're breathing, Chachi. The two of you?" He held his hands up a couple feet apart before smacking them together. "Absolute magnets. Nothing could keep you apart."

"Even her ex-boyfriend?"

He sucked in a breath through his teeth, shrugging as he did. "That was rough on you and rough on her, and it got dicey in here for a whole minute. But it worked out in the end, and watching the two of you together . . . fuck, man, it's beautiful. Riss always says it's like the two of you are in a dance, the way you seem to move together."

I sat.

Waited.

Let his words replay again and again, hoping it would spark something, but there was only that racing of my heart whenever I thought of Scarlet now. The girl I would've done anything to be rid of just a few days ago because the way she consumed me had pissed me off as much as it had intrigued me.

"What do you mean it got dicey in here?" I asked, slanting my head in question.

"With Scarlet's ex," Brian said as if I should've already known. When I just continued staring at him, he asked, "Didn't she just tell you about those first months when the two of you were figuring your shit out?"

"Yeah, but I don't think I know about whatever happened here," I said as I thought over my earlier conversation with

Scarlet. "She said I was the last one to see him and that she'd never asked about what happened."

"Oh, she knows," he said assuredly. "And it definitely wasn't the last time she saw him because that shit got way worse."

My eyebrows drew close over my eyes, and I readjusted in my chair. Trying to find a position where my ribs weren't screaming in pain, all while I was itching to stand. To pace.

"Explain," I said in a low demand.

"Fucking trip, man," he muttered to himself before scooting closer on the chair. "If I remember right, it was right after Scarlet ended things with the other guy. Then he comes storming in here, knowing exactly who you were and what had been going down between you and Scarlet. You were doing a piece, but you just stood up and met him in the middle of the shop. Let him get a hit in, and then you two went at it. Jeff and I had to pull the two of you off each other."

My chest pitched as flashes of fights with Brandon stormed my thoughts.

Fights he swore had never happened.

"Your lady wasn't far behind him and was a mess when she realized what happened," Brian said, pulling me back into the present.

"So, she knew about that," I confirmed softly. "And you said she saw him again after?"

A somber look stole over Brian's expression as he nodded. "Not in the way you're thinking, and it isn't for me to say what happened if she isn't telling you."

"Brian—"

"Brandon knows," he said and lifted his hands in mock surrender. "But I think if your lady love isn't telling you, then

Brandon won't tell you either. But I will tell you, your boy was with you when it all went down."

A groan raked up my throat at the frustration of it all. "Brian, I'm trying to remember what I'm missing. I'm trying to figure out what actually did and didn't happen. How can I do that if you're all keeping something from me?" I gestured toward the main doors. "Because Brandon hasn't even hinted that something might've happened with Scarlet, and Scarlet said you were the only one who knew she'd been dating someone when we met."

"Might be true," he said with a shrug. "But Brandon's your ride-or-die. Have no doubt he'd do what he did without knowing the target."

I went still. "I'm sorry?"

"All I'm saying."

I glanced around before leaning close to hiss, "Did I fucking kill someone?"

Brian's head tilted back as a sharp laugh left him. "Ah, Chach. God, I've missed you." He let out another long laugh before meeting my horrified stare. "Don't think you know how to kill anyone. Doesn't mean Scarlet's ex-man wasn't in serious agony when you were done with him. Doesn't mean he didn't deserve it."

I stared off to the side, trying to figure out what could've happened. But as each scenario came to mind, my anger only grew.

At the possibilities.

At the knowledge that no one had told me.

At the thought that I could've been so in love with someone and possibly destroyed that . . .

"Brian, I need to know if I cheated on Scarlet."

A choking sound left him. "What?"

When I reminded him of the last of my coma-induced memories, he said, "That's a big hell-fucking-no, Chachi."

"But everything else is in my life somehow."

"Scarlet's your Sun," he said unquestionably. "Your world revolves around her. You can't live without her." But just as soon as he'd finished speaking, his expression fell and his gaze drifted.

"What?" I demanded, that guilt flaring because I knew whatever he'd just remembered was what I'd been worrying over.

His stare snapped to me before falling again, and after nearly a minute, he cleared his throat. "Two . . . three days before your wreck," he began hesitantly, head bobbing faintly, "you came into work raging. Threw your chair. I wasn't here yet. Jeff told me when I got here."

"Why?" I asked through clenched teeth.

He lifted a hand. "By the time I got here, you were anxious as fuck. Knees bouncing a mile a minute and looking bad off. Riss and I thought you were on drugs. I could barely get you to talk to me, but we were slammed all night anyway. Next day, it was worse. Finally got you in the back and asked what was up. Asked if things were okay with your lady, and you snapped. Punched a wall and kept saying shit like, 'I didn't know. What the hell am I gonna do?' between cussing up a motherfucking storm."

"That's all I said?" I asked as that guilt nearly swallowed me whole because, as vague as it was, his story was all the proof I needed that I'd fucked up in a big way.

"We didn't know what to think," he said in way of confirmation. "We didn't know if something happened with Scarlet or what. Next thing we knew, you'd gotten in that wreck, and Riss and I—" He grimaced as shame stole across his expression. "Because of the way you'd been, we thought it'd been on purpose until we heard the details of how it happened."

"Jesus," I whispered as I fell back against the seat.

"But cheating on Scarlet?" he asked, head shaking. "Chach, I can say you wouldn't do that."

"But you thought I'd take my life," I said, words coming out on an irritated huff.

He raised his hands, trying to placate me. "Timing was fucked."

"I'll plan my near-death experience better next time," I said with an eye roll, then added, "You're so sure I wouldn't cheat on Scarlet, but how do you explain the similarities in my memories and what you just told me?"

"You woke up, and this Trish chick was in your bed," he began after a while. "You don't remember how she got there or what happened. Maybe . . ." He shrugged. "I don't know, man. I really don't know."

My head moved in a jumbled mess of nods and shakes as I rubbed my hand over my face. Thoughts a blur of everything Brian had told me and all those clashing memories.

Heart tripped up in the endless battle of that addicting craving to get closer to Scarlet and that desperate need to get my life back. That restless hunger whenever Scarlet entered my thoughts or line of sight and that piercing agony of having the joy of becoming a father repeatedly ripped away from me.

"Whatever happened, I clearly fucked up, and it's gonna destroy Scarlet," I muttered as I focused on him. "I need to figure out what I did."

"Don't think you got a second chance at life just to lose

your lady," Brian said. "The two of you have gotten through a lot. You can get through this too."

A muted laugh punched from my lungs. "I've already wasted my second, third, and fourth chances, Brian," I said as I stood to go. "At this point, pretty sure I'm just stealing any chances I find along the way."

TWELVE

CHASE

I'd never felt so weak.

I'd never been the best at anything, but I was a damn good surfer, and I could hold my own in the ring—even against Brandon, and that guy was a fucking beast. But walking for, shit, I didn't know . . . maybe an hour had tapped me out. Leaving me gripping my side and struggling to take deep enough breaths around the aches and pains and the guilt lashing out inside me.

I was sure Scarlet was going to give me hell because I doubted her version of *going for a walk* meant storming out of the shop and taking off for the beach. But I hadn't called anyone. I hadn't texted her.

And I'd ended up on a part of the beach I wasn't sure I'd ever been to, even though my feet had carried me there like I'd known the way. And as I stared out over the water, every violently clashing thought went back to her.

To the way she'd looked at me since I'd woken. To the way those eyes had shattered and dimmed and continued pulling back to me with so much hope and love, only to repeat the cycle.

And the worst was still to come.

Pulling my phone from my pocket, I unlocked the screen and slowly stretched my side as I brought up her number to call her.

"Are you okay?"

The question was immediate and filled with so much panic that I just froze for a second before straightening. "Are *you*?" I asked uneasily.

Her relief was palpable through the phone when she said, "You haven't—" She forced out a breath and whispered, "You just haven't called me since everything happened."

"Oh." I glanced around, my face creasing as I thought of what to say when Brian's words were saturating every thought. "Sorry, no . . . no, I'm good. I'm at the beach. You think you could meet me?"

"At the beach?" she asked, surprise and that damn hope wrapping around her words.

"Yeah. I, uh . . . I don't exactly know where I am. I just left the shop and ended up . . ." I glanced around again, looking for street signs, but Scarlet spoke before I could relay any identifying markers.

"I know where you are."

If I hadn't been so weighed down with the dread of what was coming, I might've laughed. As it was, my question came out sounding miserable. "You put a tracker on me, Scar?"

"I'm just pretty sure I know where you are," she said, the softness of her tone gripping at my heart and making it pump harder. "I'll be there soon."

"Scarlet," I said before she could end the call. When her

questioning hum came through, I just stood there. Letting the sound wash over me and embracing the way a *hum* could make me feel. "Drive safe."

I tapped the red button before she could respond.

Worried I'd start confessing everything right then. Worried I'd say all the wrong things when I still had no idea what I'd even done. Worried I'd ask if she'd *known*.

And at that thought, I lifted my phone again. Quickly searching for another number and kicking off my sandals as I headed out onto the sand.

"Hey, man," Brandon answered. "You ready to be picked up?"

"No, that isn't why I'm calling." Gratitude built and poured into my next words when I teased, "You can be off duty for the rest of the day."

"Finally," he muttered, but the amusement lingered. After whispering something away from the phone, he said, "All right, I'm in my office now. What's up?"

"Brian said some things, and I'm wondering why I didn't hear them from you," I said, getting right to it. "Said some other things that I wanted to go over with you so I can try to figure out what the hell happened."

A beat passed before he hesitantly said, "Okay?"

"Scarlet told me I was the last one to see her—" I swallowed the next word before it could slip free and glanced around the mostly empty beach. "Scarlet said I was the last one to see this guy . . . I'm guessing it was years ago. She said she didn't ask for details of what happened when I saw him, and I didn't tell her. Brian said *you* were with me when it went down."

"If she isn't telling you, she isn't ready for you to know," Brandon said, voice cold and lethal.

"Apparently, I already know."

"Yeah, but the guy who knew is a different person than the guy I'm talking to," he said unapologetically. "That guy, to her, was allowed to know things about her life."

I nodded for a while before pleading, "Just tell me what we did. You don't have to say why or the details surrounding it," I hurried to add. "Just tell me what we did."

Brandon was silent for so long that I was sure he wasn't going to respond. Just as I reached the shoreline, he muttered, "Beat the shit out of them."

"*Them*?"

"That's it, Chase."

A harsh breath left me as all those scenarios I'd been thinking of earlier came flooding back. "Brandon, unless you're in a ring, I can't imagine you voluntarily going to beat anyone up."

"You've been pushing for a front-row seat lately," he muttered wryly.

"I'm serious, man."

"And so was that situation," he said, tone letting me know he was done talking about it.

"Understood," I said, even though I wasn't anywhere close to understanding what could've happened. Releasing a slow breath, I asked, "Was I okay the morning of the accident?"

A stuttered breath sounded through the phone. "What?"

"Was I okay?" I repeated. "Did you notice anything different about me? Was I saying anything weird?"

Realization and dread weighed down his voice when he said, "Brian knew something."

"Need to know if I was okay," I said firmly.

"Chase, what'd you do?" he asked instead.

"For fuck's sake, Brandon."

"I don't know," he shouted over me. "I mean, yeah. You were you. We were here, working out like we always do. We'd gone surfing."

His tone didn't change. He didn't trail off.

But the way he'd gone from listing things off to not saying anything at all had that guilt exploding.

Because I could feel it. Creeping through the phone and crawling down my spine.

I might've been trying to keep it from my best friend, but he'd noticed it too.

"You weren't talking," he finally said, words slow. "You were going harder in the gym than usual, and you wouldn't talk to Konrad or me."

Fuck.

"We kept joking about it because you'd had a shitty run that morning on the waves. So, we thought you were just pissed about that." He cleared his throat, his voice dropping even lower when he said, "Now that I think about it, you'd been quiet at your parents' the night before. I forgot because of the accident, but Bree actually asked us if you were okay after you and Scarlet left that night."

I closed my eyes tightly, my head bobbing as something Brian said pushed to the front of my mind. "It was an accident . . . right?"

"What—your wreck?" he asked, the words exploding from him when he realized what I was asking. "Fuck, man, are you kidding?"

"You were there."

"Yes, it was an accident," he snapped. "No way you could've seen it coming or prevented it. Now, tell me what Brian said."

"Nothing definite, but enough to let me know I fucked up."

"Chase," he muttered, my name nothing less than a disappointed sigh.

"Said I came into work a few days before the wreck, raging and threw my chair. Was so anxious that he and Marissa thought I was on drugs. When Brian cornered me the next night, asking if things were okay with Scarlet, he said I snapped. Punched a wall. Was cussing between saying things like 'What am I gonna do?' and 'I didn't know.'"

"That doesn't mean anything," he said after a while. "That could've been about literally anything."

"Well, was Scarlet okay during those days?"

Silence filled the phone before he uncertainly said, "I think so. She might've been thrown off by you at dinner because you weren't talking, but I think we all were."

"So, she was fine, and I wasn't. And I remember waking up to someone in bed with me," I reminded him. "And everyone has been showing me how my memories are really just twisted versions of my life. Tell me again that those days and what I said could've been about anything."

"Shit," he hissed before repeating his warning, "If you cheated on her . . ."

"I fucking get it, man." I turned as if on instinct and felt my entire being react when I saw Scarlet making her way across the sand. Body buzzing and pulse kicking up this erratic beat in my veins, all while it felt like I was crumpling under something I didn't understand. "I gotta go. She just got here."

"You gonna tell her?"

"I have to."

Silence settled over the call before he said, "Don't hurt her more than you have to—just tell her what you know. Because you don't know what you did yet."

"You still think I didn't?"

"Knowing you?" he challenged. "Knowing what she means to you? I just can't believe you *could*."

I gripped the phone as the smallest glimmer of hope tried to break through the well of guilt in my stomach. "Gotta go." Slipping the phone into my pocket just as Scarlet reached me, I nodded to her in greeting but let myself take in her face for long moments before I ever spoke.

The mesmerizing shape of her eyes and the unadulterated excitement there.

The tempting slant of her lips and the way I wanted to get lost in them all over again.

"How'd you know where I was?"

That excitement grew as she fought a smile. "This is a special place."

I looked down the shoreline as my brow furrowed. "This isn't where we surf, is it?"

"No," she said on an amused breath. "Do you not remember anything about this place?" When I just slanted my head, she drew in a sharp breath and nodded. "Something in your memories is trying to come back. It has to. Because this place was special to *us*."

"Tell me."

"Chase—"

"Scarlet, please," I whispered at her obvious reluctance, reaching for her without meaning to and grasping her fingers.

A line of apprehension appeared between her eyebrows as

her gaze drifted from our loosely joined hands to my stare. After another beat of hesitation, she explained, "This is where we used to come before we were together. This is where you asked me to marry you."

"Right here," I said in confirmation.

"Not—well . . ."—she looked up the beach, a soft smile pulling at her mouth as she nodded in the direction we'd both come—"we weren't standing in the water."

"I see." A smile of my own had crossed my face to match hers but quickly fell when I remembered why I was there. Lifting our joined hands, I brushed the tips of my fingers along her jaw. "Remember what I told you earlier?"

Her eyebrows rose in forced amusement, but a deep dread had filled her eyes at my question. "You said a lot this morning."

"I won't stop you from leaving."

Her body caved on a heaving breath and her expression crumpled, but she forced herself to straighten when she assumed, "You know something."

"I have more questions than answers."

"But you know something," she ground out as her jaw trembled.

"Yeah," I confirmed and released her when she turned.

Hands moving quickly as if she didn't know what to do with them. Interlacing on top of her head and then drifting to her neck before sliding to her chest as she hung her head.

"Whatever it was happened a few days before the accident," I said when she just stood there, then repeated the stories Brian and Brandon had told me.

"But I was with you," she said once I was done, eyes glassy. "That weekend . . . the week before . . . I was home. I was with you other than when I was doing my classes or at brunch. And you were—" She'd started gesturing away from herself but let her arm fall limply. "Except for when you were at work or at the gym or breakfast with the guys, you were home. Unless you weren't actually at those places."

"Think they would've told me if I'd skipped out on one of those."

She blinked up at me. "Then we were home, and we were fine. Everything was fine. I mean, I remember what Brandon said . . . sort of. You were quiet, but I actually think I just chalked it up to you being exhausted because of how busy we were. We're always coming and going with work or our friends."

My head bobbed quickly before I repeated, "I won't stop you from leaving."

A strangled sound caught in her throat. "Stop saying that. You—we don't even know what happened. We don't know if anything happened."

"Something had to, Scarlet," I said undoubtedly. "I was keeping something from everyone closest to me. You, most of all."

"But you told Brian, 'I didn't know,'" she reminded me as if I hadn't been replaying his words for the past hour and a half. "That doesn't sound like something a person would say who cheated on their fiancée."

That dull spark of hope flared a little brighter, even as I shook my head. "I can feel it. This morning, when you said you can't sleep because of my need to convince Harper I hadn't cheated on her, I had this twisting in my gut like I was afraid *you* would find out."

Her body bowed and swayed toward me as her hand

pressed to my chest, pushing all that fear and grief into me and amplifying my own. "What are your memories?" she asked as her fingers curled against my shirt.

"Of what?"

"Of whatever happened?" She cleared her throat and looked up, holding me captive in that gaze. "What you were trying to tell Harper after you woke up. Why you were saying you hadn't cheated on her."

I drew in a slow breath as those days assaulted me, feeling just as real as Scarlet's hand did against my chest.

And yet, I could sense it now . . . the difference in my memories from growing up and what I remembered as the last year. Even in their vividness, they felt off. Like there was a hazy film layered over the latter.

Grabbing Scarlet's hand, I turned, leading us out of the calf-high water and up to sit on the sand as I spoke. "This girl I work with, Trish—"

"You don't work with a Trish," she said, making me nod in acknowledgment.

"Right," I mumbled, then corrected, "*Worked* with . . . thought I worked with. Anyway, none of it makes sense because she's—she *was* gay. I met her girlfriend a ton of times. But she showed up at my party for whatever reason. Next thing I know, I'm waking up to Bree screaming at me, and Trish is in bed with me, wearing only my shirt." I placed a hand to my chest and hurried to defend what hadn't—or possibly *could've*—happened, "I hadn't even been drinking. I don't even remember the party."

"Okay." The word left her on a breath as if just the coma-induced dream made Scarlet nauseous because of the possibilities. "You . . . you work with *Riss*," she added hesitantly, expression scrunching up in disbelief.

"Yeah, just found that out. And there's no fucking way."

"No," she agreed wholeheartedly. "But when you started talking about your *supposed* life with Harper, I easily fit it all together into what had been *real*. I still can't make sense of this."

Her head shook as she glanced back at the ocean, getting lost in her thoughts for a while. "I can't remember the last time either of us was at a party unless you count Brandon and Harper's wedding or your parents' New Year's Eve parties. But we've gone home *together* after those. And even before we moved into the house, it's been you and me, every night in the same bed."

Her lips pressed tightly together as she stared straight ahead, but nothing could've hidden the deep sadness that burst from her when she realized what she'd said.

When she was reminded of the changes in our relationship since she actually remembered it. Because we hadn't even been in the same room for weeks.

Clearing her throat, she forced a smile when she added, "As for the last part, I mean, the only thing, I guess . . . there's a woman you're convinced is in love with me."

A breath of a laugh worked from me. "Yeah?"

"At the coffee shop. Her name's Erin, she actually owns the shop, but she's our favorite. Anyway, she always compliments me, and whenever she's there, there will be a heart on my cup —but only my cup." She batted her lashes playfully before a soft laugh danced across her lips.

"Is she trying to steal you from me?" The tease left me

before I realized I was thinking it, and I knew it came out exactly how it was supposed to.

Is. Not *was*.

Because even though Scarlet wasn't mine in the way that mattered, this chaotic mess of emotions she ignited sure as hell felt like possession.

A humming sound left her that was all amusement. "Again . . . you think so." She gave me a wry grin. "Too bad I'm hopelessly straight."

My next laugh was louder and had a whisper of pain pulling at my side. "So, that's all that kept you with me."

Her smile slowly faded and her head listed. "Among a few other things," she said before adding, "Chase, what if you didn't?"

"I did *something*," I said unquestionably. "Saying, 'What the hell am I gonna do,' and acting how they described doesn't exactly sound like someone who's innocent."

She looked like she'd give anything to deny it, but she eventually gave a slight dip of her chin. "How do we figure it out without your memories? What do we do until we know?"

I didn't know how to figure anything out other than asking the people closest to me the way I'd already done.

So, I just kept my tone gentle and even when I asked, "You leaving tonight?" Refusing to ask if she was leaving *period* because I didn't want to know, and I didn't want to put that pressure on her.

I'd already told her she could go, and I'd meant it. If she chose to leave at any point, I would understand. And I didn't want her to feel trapped by an answer she gave me years, months, or days before.

"Depends on your definition of leaving," she said carefully.

"Because I fully intend on leaving this beach and going home with you."

I fought a smile as I stood, reaching to help her up as I did. "PT and Chinese food?"

A laugh broke from her as she smacked at my hand and stood on her own, beautiful and free and touching every part of my soul with the purity of it.

Making me feel lighter than I had since I'd woken in the hospital. Making it feel like I could breathe easier.

I was pretty sure I'd been waiting my entire life to hear that sound.

Jesus Christ, what was this girl doing to me?

"You're ridiculous," she said as her laugh trailed off, her smile bright and making my heart beat impossibly fast when she looked up at me. "You can't keep using that. We aren't even fighting."

"I'll use the Chinese food thing forever if it'll keep you laughing like that. If it'll make you look at me like that." And then I was moving. Curling my arm around her waist and pulling her close as if my body had a mind of its own. Unable to go another second apart from her, even though I'd just been thinking I would let her go.

Like that was a possibility.

I watched as her eyes widened with surprise and need and hope when I pressed her body against mine and gripped her tight, claiming her with that simple motion.

"You want to leave, then I'm going to let you because you don't deserve the shit I've put you through," I said before shaking my head. "But understand that I'm only giving you a ten-minute head start before I'm chasing after you and begging you to give me any fucking chance that's left."

"I'm not going anywhere."

I lowered my head to hers but kept my lips a breath away when I pled, "Don't say that yet."

"I'm here," she whispered, the words their own plea. "I'm here; I'm not going anywhere. Chase, I love you."

I broke.

Crushing my mouth against hers and swallowing the remnants of her words. A claim that felt all new and like a welcome home. Prickling at the top of my spine and begging me to hear the familiarity in it all while the overwhelming urge to put my own claim on this girl tried to drown out the voice beating on some invisible barrier I was just beginning to sense.

I lifted my hand, curling it around her jaw and tilting her head back to deepen the kiss. Falling deeper into her and getting lost in the way her lips moved against mine.

Soft and sure. Desperate and playful. Driving me out of my goddamn mind when she smiled before attacking the kiss with a renewed fierceness.

All intoxicating whimpers and teases of her tongue that about had me falling to my knees.

And I needed more.

I needed *her*.

As impossible as it was, I had a feeling I needed all of her forever.

"Chase—no," Scarlet had choked over her tears, then curled her hands around my neck and pressed her forehead to mine. "No, no, no, don't do this."

"One of us has to," I'd said, my own voice weighed down

with exhaustion and emotion. "We can't keep doing this. I can't keep doing this."

"Don't," she'd begged. "Don't say things like that."

"Fuck, you think I want to?" I'd gripped her hands, intending to move her away, and had ended up holding her tighter. "But I'm the idiot still waiting around for you to choose him when you won't."

"No, no, no, that isn't it," she'd said over me. "You know that isn't it! I've chosen you. *I want a life with* you. *Only you."*

"Then tell me why we're here," I'd demanded through clenched teeth. "Tell me why we're still each other's goddamn secrets." When a choked sob had been her only reply, I'd said, "Anything less than everything isn't enough anymore, Scar. I need all of you forever or nothing at all."

"Forever," she'd cried out. "All of me. You have me, I swear it."

"Chase. *Chase*," Scarlet snapped, panic coating her voice as if she'd been trying to get my attention for a while.

I blinked quickly and found myself looking at the same dark, hypnotic eyes I'd just been staring into.

Only these were different.

Everything about the scene was different, even though it was the same.

There was still sand beneath my feet and waves were crashing close by, but the world was lit up from the late afternoon sun rather than drenched in deep blues and purples from the night sky.

And while Scarlet was clinging to me, it was in an entirely different way, and I only had a hold of her with one arm because the other was still in a sling. And the look on her face . . .

That love was there in an undeniable sort of way—the same love I'd been refusing to acknowledge over the last weeks. But the pain and grief and fear I'd just been staring at were now a mixture of worry and the heated remnants of our kiss.

"Are you okay?" Scarlet asked as her hand slid over my arm and then up to rest on my chest.

"What?" I asked, slow to catch up with reality when it felt like I'd never left it.

"What just happened?" she pressed anxiously. "You suddenly went still—like *completely* still."

My head moved in a slow shake as I tried to make sense of everything. Because I was sure I'd just had a memory—a real one—but it had bled so fluidly into the present that I would've never known what'd happened if it hadn't been for the mind trip of switching from day to night and back again in just a handful of seconds.

"I, uh . . ." I shook my head harder and pulled away from her, feeling so damn unsteady when I'd finally felt stable for the first time in weeks.

It wasn't until I eventually turned to look at the water that had been a constant throughout it all that I realized Scarlet was watching me, looking completely lost.

I cleared my throat and nodded toward the rocks that led up to the street. "Ready to go home?"

"Yeah, okay," she whispered, then slowly started toward me.

Eyes trained on me. Worry lining every part of that beautiful face. And I had no idea what to say to her.

It should've been a good thing—something to be celebrated. I was sure the first thing I should've done was tell Scarlet that I'd gotten one of the memories I'd lost.

But I was scared . . .

I'd just started falling for my fiancée, and in the span of a few seconds, I'd realized the consuming need I currently felt for her was *nothing* compared to the actual love and unending devotion I'd felt for her in that memory. In a few seconds, I'd realized the pain from my so-called 'memory' of losing Harper couldn't come close to touching the incapacitating grief of just trying to walk from Scarlet—of not having her fully.

And I'd fucking *done* something I shouldn't have. Something I knew down to my soul had the power to hurt her and ruin us.

So, yeah, I was scared.

I was absolutely terrified of what I'd remember next.

THIRTEEN

SCARLET

A whispered curse fell from my lips when my towel slipped off the rod I was trying to hang it on. Snatching it up before it could hit the ground, I had to try another two more times before I finally got it to stay.

It was still early in the morning, but it was clear this was how my day was destined to be . . .

Unable to find my keys that were right in front of me. Missing perfect waves because my thoughts were somewhere else. Forgetting how to shower because I was just *that distracted*.

But that was what Chase had always done to me.

And after a week and a half of this? Of mind-blowing kisses and having him stop me from wherever I was going so he could just look at me in this indescribable paradox of a way —like his soul knew mine in an irrevocable way but was still learning mine for the first time. Of falling harder for the man I knew while falling for this new Chase all between dinners and physical therapy that was horribly, sexually charged and left me wanting and aching . . .

But we never went there.

Chase never went there.

My head was permanently in the clouds and on him. My lips were permanently swollen from our kisses and tipped up in a smile.

But whenever we started getting carried away, he'd stop us. He never said anything—not anymore. Just gripped me tighter like he was trying to remind himself why we needed to stop, all while staring at me in that way.

But I heard his unspoken words each time. Loud and clear.

"Did you . . . did you want to sleep in our bed tonight?" I'd asked hours after we'd gotten home from the beach a week and a half ago.

"You leaving?" he'd asked instead.

"Chase, what? I already told you I'm not going anywhere."

His head had moved in a mess of subtle nods and shakes. "It's going to hurt when we find out—I know it is. Not going to hurt you any worse by letting myself have you when we know what's coming."

"We don't know—"

"Until we do," he'd said over me, words soft but unyielding. Gripping my side, he'd pulled me close and pressed his forehead to mine. "You consume me."

So, he'd continued sleeping in the guestroom. And we'd never gone any further than the kisses that had slowly gotten a little longer, a little heavier, and were sure to be my ruin judging by the start of my morning.

"Jesus," I hissed and then laughed in irritation when I smacked into the door as I turned to leave the bathroom. Rubbing my hands over my face, I groaned into them before letting them fall. "Gah, this morning!"

Grabbing the partially closed door, I slid it the rest of the way open. My gaze pulling to the canvas of Chase and me until a nagging sensation had me looking at the door just as my hand fell from it. Because I hadn't closed it—even partially—when I'd gone into the bathroom to take a shower. We rarely closed that door.

A chill raced down my spine and icy fingers gripped my lungs as my stare snapped back to the bed.

Above it.

To the canvas there.

The photo of us that had been missing ever since Chase came home from the hospital was back. And—

"Oh my God," I breathed before staggering toward the bedroom door. But my feet felt heavy and my body felt limp as the last remaining air in my lungs ripped from my throat in a cry for Chase.

Frozen.

I was utterly and completely frozen as the fear gripping my chest consumed me.

Because someone had been in the house—in the *room*—and I didn't know if they were there still. I was afraid to move. Afraid to look. I just stood there, staring at the hallway as tremors racked my body and a hollow ringing filled my ears and dulled the sound of thundering steps until he was there.

Crashing into me and pulling me into his arms. Hands quickly searching my body and cupping my face, forcing me to look at him as he shot questions too fast for me to comprehend.

But then it was pouring out of me.

Just as quickly as he'd been demanding answers and without sense as I choked over words and gestured wildly behind me.

"It's here—someone's—the door. They closed—I ran into the door after the shower, and then I saw the picture. It wasn't here. It wasn't here, remember? They left the picture," I hissed, voice dropping to a whisper as if that could save us now. "They were here when I was in the shower. We need to leave! They burned my face!"

"Wait, what?" he snapped, holding me tighter to him and taking a step into the brightly lit bedroom. Stare sweeping my face before scanning the bedroom and widening with dread when he saw the canvas above the bed frame.

"What the fuck?" he breathed before glancing around the bedroom again. "What the actual—where's your phone? Get your phone." Before I had a chance to move, he was charging into the room with me still tucked securely against him to swipe my phone from the nightstand.

In seconds, he was calling nine-one-one as he turned, looking everywhere while he kept one of his hands on my head, preventing me from seeing the canvas again.

I don't remember much after Chase told the dispatcher someone had broken in and left a threatening message. I remembered being moved to lock ourselves into the bedroom while we waited for police to show and search the outside of the house before Chase had quickly led us to the front to let them in . . . but that was it.

I don't remember even worrying over the possibility that the person might still be in the house as we'd rushed to the front door. I barely remember moving—only that we made it there and were suddenly outside, talking with officers.

I wasn't sure if it was the shock or disbelief of it all, or if it was because my mind was so weighed down with the worry of *who* had done it.

"Yes, the door to the bathroom was partially closed," I told the officer again, glancing at the canvas that was being carried away for evidence.

"And how certain are you that you hadn't closed it?" the officer asked, and I tried to hold back an irritated sigh.

"I can't remember the last time I actually touched that door before this morning," I finally responded, tearing my stare from the ruined picture of Chase and me. "We don't close it, and it doesn't slide without force."

He nodded at the answers I'd already given him multiple times before asking, "And is there anyone you've been able to think of who might want to scare you or send this kind of message to you?"

My gaze flitted to where Chase was talking with another officer. My stomach dipped with worry and that doubt that fueled my sleepless nights. "No one," I muttered as I met the officer's gaze again. "It's obviously personal, but—" My stare snapped back to Chase as a thought slammed into me. "My fiancé used to have sketchbooks all over the house. At least half a dozen. I'm not sure when they went missing, but we haven't seen them in a few weeks, so probably around the time the canvas did. I'm not positive, but it's possible whoever did this also took his books. They would have to know what those meant to him."

"Have you noticed anything else missing?" the officer asked as he quickly wrote in his notebook.

"No. Not that I'm aware of," I added as an afterthought.

"And who would know about the sketchbooks?"

My lips opened and shut a few times before a defeated laugh tumbled past them. "So many people," I admitted. "Anyone who knows him knows he has one near him at all times. But, again, they were scattered all over the house, not just in one place. It's weird for them all to be missing except for one we found hidden away in a closet."

The officer made some sort of grunting sound before leveling me with a look like he was about to ask something I wasn't going to enjoy. "You said you don't keep a hideaway key outside, and the door was locked when we arrived. Is there any way your fiancé's the one behind this?"

"No," I said adamantly, then repeated, "No," when he continued watching me, waiting for me to doubt myself.

"It isn't uncommon for the partner to be the one behind these sort of occurrences," he said simply, then blew out an unsteady breath. "Just as often, it's someone they're having an affair with who's feeling scorned."

I kept my eyes on the officer even as the drop in my stomach made me feel lightheaded and weak. Made that doubt he'd been looking for come rushing to the surface.

"Best scenario, it's a friend playing a joke. But it looks like someone is trying to get your attention, Miss. Whether the threat is real or not, keep a watchful eye out. Keep yourself safe. And if I were you, I'd change the locks on your doors today."

I nodded and mumbled my thanks as he turned to leave, then glanced over to find Chase watching me.

Jaw locked tight. Brow drawn close in worry and fear and a deep rage as he listened to the officer he was talking to. With a quick dip of his head, he shook the officer's hand and then hurried over to me. Pulling me against his body and cradling my cheek as his forehead fell to mine.

"You okay?" he asked, voice tight.

"You aren't wearing your sling."

"Fuck the sling, Scar. Need to know if you're all right."

I hesitated for long moments before confessing, "The officer said it's often someone the partner's having an affair with."

Chase just held me before nodding. "Yeah," he breathed. "Yeah, I got asked about four times if I was or had been seeing someone else."

I didn't ask what Chase had told them. I already knew he was constantly beating himself up with the *what-ifs*.

"My face was burned," I muttered as I placed one of my hands over the harsh pounding of Chase's heart, just in time to feel it falter.

He gripped me tighter in response, clinging to me like he could keep me there, and I could practically hear the words he was thinking.

I did something.

I did something.

I did something.

"We'll figure it out," I whispered, trying to assure us both.

"If this is any indication," he began, only to finish with a harsh sigh.

"I'm not going anywhere." I grasped his shirt and slanted my head to press my mouth to his. The kiss brief and soft, nothing more than a brush of our lips, but it had me feeling lighter than I had all morning. "Except for now. I want to leave this spot."

His lips curled into a brief smile before he stole another kiss. "Where do you want to go?"

"Inside."

He leaned back enough to meet my stare. "You want to stay here?"

"As long as we change the locks."

"I'm already on it," he assured me. "But if you're not comfortable with being here, we can go anywhere."

I lifted a brow, voice bordering on a tease despite the heaviness surrounding us and the multiple police vehicles still just feet away. "*Anywhere*, anywhere?"

"Within reason."

"And what's reasonable?"

"Anywhere I can keep you close." His answer had been immediate and sure and had my heart taking flight.

I fought the smile threatening at the edge of my lips even though his light eyes were locked on me, catching every reaction. Every hitched breath. Every dip of my head to hide the blush rising to my cheeks. Every way he stole another piece of me.

"That sounds like everywhere," I murmured.

"Then name the place."

"Inside," I said without hesitation. "I'd like to be in our home."

His head slanted in acknowledgment as his gaze bored into mine. "I won't let anything happen to you."

"I know," I said, even as a whisper of doubt twisted through my veins.

Not that I thought something would happen to me or that Chase would allow it to happen. I just had this gut feeling something like this morning would happen again, and Chase wouldn't be able to stop it.

But the fear I'd been paralyzed by had receded after my conversation with the officer because, the more I thought of it, the more sure I was that this was simply someone trying to get my attention. But *only* my attention.

They wanted to send a message to *Chase*.

They'd taken the picture of us and returned it with my face severely burned, but they'd taken his sketchbooks—where all his dreams and thoughts and secrets were.

It was almost as if they wanted to remind Chase I wasn't supposed to be the girl in his picture. As if they wanted Chase to worry about what they knew or could reveal—except he didn't remember anything at all.

But that fear of what Chase could've possibly done? That was more real than ever.

FOURTEEN

CHASE

"I don't know, man," Brandon said a few hours later after I'd finished telling them about the fucked-up morning, then glanced to Konrad in question.

Konrad held out a hand before letting it smack down on the kitchen island—because I refused to be farther from Scarlet than I was right then. Where I could hear her laughing and coaching her friends through their workout session. Where I could get to her if she screamed.

"Fuck if I know," Konrad said. "I'm just surprised Scarlet wanted to come back into the house."

"Honestly," Brandon agreed. "They were in the fucking room with her when she was showering."

I worked my jaw at the reminder, then shook my head to rid my mind of the dark path I kept traveling down. Because it could've been anyone in the house with her. Anything could've happened to her.

And I hadn't been there.

"But I don't know how many sets of keys you gave out—

we all have keys," Brandon went on, circling back to what I'd originally been asking them, then corrected, "*Had.*"

"Right," Konrad murmured. "Us, your parents . . . we all have access to each other's houses. Does Brian have a key?"

"No," I said immediately before backtracking. "Well, I don't know. He could, for all I know."

Brandon grunted in understanding, then leaned closer to the island from his spot on the barstools next to Konrad and lowered his voice. "Do any of Scarlet's friends?"

I lifted my hands in a show that I didn't know. "Didn't exactly think it'd be a good idea to go putting it in Scarlet's head that one of her friends could've been the one who came in."

"Why the hell not?" Brandon demanded. "You asked if *we* had keys."

"I asked to get an idea of who had keys and if you still had them—like if you'd lost them or let anyone borrow them," I ground out. "But the cops seem to think the person who was in here is someone I'm currently—or was—sleeping with. So, if it's one of Scarlet's friends . . ."

"Shit," Brandon whispered as he sat back. "Really?"

My eyebrows rose. "Apparently."

"You really cheated on Scarlet?"

"I don't know, Brandon," I snapped, every defense rising in response to the deep disappointment in his voice and the guilt that was a constant reminder in my gut. "I don't know what I did. I know what I remember, that apparently never happened. I know that picture of us disappeared after I got home and just showed back up this morning with a clear-as-fuck message on it. So, all I know is I did something bad."

"Why didn't you tell us the picture had gone missing?"

Konrad asked as he reached forward for the box of pastries that was sitting on the island, even though we'd just finished eating. Snatching one of the large muffins out before pushing the pink box over to Brandon.

"Honestly, I forgot," I said as I stepped forward from my spot against the other counter to catch the box when Brandon slid it toward me. "It disappeared the day after I got back from the hospital. Scarlet got pissed—thought I'd taken it because I was mad about what was and wasn't real. I was sure it fell. We didn't talk about it again until today—she probably thought I was hiding it somewhere until it appeared this morning."

Brandon started responding just as Konrad groaned, "God damnit. Are these Litany's?"

I looked from the muffin he was holding to the box in my hand. "What?"

"Shit," Brandon said through a muffled laugh as he took a massive bite. "Eat it fast."

"Why are they so fucking good?" Konrad asked, tossing the question out like an accusation as he tore into the muffin.

"Every time," Brandon said around the next mouthful. "She's probably drugging us, and we don't even know."

"Wouldn't care," Konrad said with a wry grin, then gestured to me. "Why aren't you eating?"

"These are for Litany?" I asked as I glanced toward the garage where the girl in question was working out.

"She made them," they said at the same time.

"But she's a handful," Brandon said with a harsh shake of his head.

"That's polite," Konrad murmured as Brandon added, "So, we eat fast."

I looked at the remaining muffins before hesitantly pulling

one out and sliding the box back to the center of the island. But that constant twisting in my gut was impossible to ignore as my stare slowly drifted from the box to the large pastry in my hand.

Sparing another glimpse toward the garage, I asked, "What do you mean she's a handful?"

Konrad muttered something I couldn't understand, but it was laced with irritation and had Brandon huffing out a laugh.

"Have you met her yet?" Brandon asked, then hurried to add, "You know her. But in the last few weeks, have you seen her? Met her again?"

I nodded subtly as I remembered the day just a week before, my lips pressed into a tight line to keep from saying anything.

Because Scarlet's friends had patiently let Scarlet introduce them to me, even though they'd clearly already known me. And when I'd turned to the last of her friends, I'd known her name—her nickname—before anyone had said a thing.

Even worse, I'd almost said it out loud before Scarlet had the chance.

I'd been stunned into silence for a second too long before I'd managed to say, *"All right. Good to meet you,"* to the smiling blonde. Because, once again, I'd been worried about what I'd remember next.

Not to mention, there'd been a clear warning in my bones to step away from LT. And I'd been fucking horrified by the possibilities of why I'd remembered her even over Scarlet.

"Yeah, I met her last week," I mumbled as I started tugging the muffin wrapper off.

"Then you probably already got a good dose of it," Brandon began. "She's—" He glanced over his shoulder when the door to the garage opened and mumbled a curse as he dropped the mostly-eaten muffin onto the island.

"One, two, three, lucky me," LT said as she came skipping into the kitchen, shoulders quickly bunching up and down in an attempt to continue bouncing her breasts once she'd reached the end of the island we were gathered around.

"Litany," Brandon said impatiently.

"Aww, look at you guys," she murmured in a too-sweet voice. "If I would've known you wanted to eat my muffin, I would've been in here earlier, offering it up."

"Jesus," Konrad hissed before letting the last bit of his fall. "Still taken."

"Still married," Brandon said, their tones suggesting this was a normal conversation.

I glanced between them before realizing that I'd apparently had a part in it too and gestured in the direction Litany had come from. "You were just with my fiancée."

"You guys are always so silly," she said as she began tugging on her boobs, trying to fix her cleavage, then sighed heavily. "Well, I know a lost cause when I see one, and I don't see one. So, I'll be back."

I snatched my arm away when she trailed her fingers over it and watched Brandon twist from her touch when she reached for him as she headed for the hallway that led to the guestroom.

My jaw clenched tight and my stomach in knots as thoughts and worries nearly choked me.

"Handful," Brandon ground out.

"Delusional," Konrad corrected. "Why is she such a good baker?"

"She always like that?" I finally managed to ask, the question sounding like broken glass over gravel.

"Always," they said at the same time.

My head moved in slow wide shakes. "She wasn't last week. But we were in front of Scarlet then."

Konrad scoffed. "Well, we wouldn't know about that. We try to avoid your house if she's gonna be here."

I scrubbed my hand over my face and finally managed to tear my stare from the hallway she'd disappeared down. "I wouldn't have . . ." I gave a hard shake of my head, struggling to voice the question. "I wouldn't have—"

"With Litany?" Brandon asked over me before bursting into laughter.

"Hell no," Konrad said without a doubt.

"Absolutely not," Brandon agreed. "You can't stand her. And one of the things you said to Brian was, 'I didn't know.' I promise you, you're aware that Litany's borderline insane and can't keep it in her pants."

I managed something close to a nod, but that fear was only growing stronger, gripping at me and making it hard to breathe. "Scarlet know she's like that?"

Brandon lifted his hands before setting them on the counter, pushing the muffin away as he did. "Figure she does."

"Bree and Harper do," Konrad added. "And those girls talk."

Brandon nodded at him. "He's right. Scarlet has to."

I stiffly stepped backward until I was resting against the counter again when a hallway door opened but didn't say anything else as Litany came bouncing in again.

Talking in blatant innuendo and asking what we thought of different parts of her body—like if we thought her ass was getting tighter—as she moved around the kitchen, making coffee like she'd done it a thousand times.

"Well, unless one of you is going to give me a reason to stay, I need to get going," she said with a dramatic sigh as she finished fitting the lid onto her travel mug.

Konrad huffed a laugh as Brandon waved toward the front of the house.

When she looked at me expectantly, my knees nearly gave out as that fear exploded inside me. Because I didn't miss for a goddamn second the way the heat in her eyes changed when her attention shifted to me. The way her hope flared and her longing deepened into something desperate and familiar.

Shit.

Shit, shit, no . . .

Forcing myself to move, I nodded toward the entrance of the kitchen and gritted out, "Goodbye, Litany."

"Every time," Brandon said when the front door shut.

"She ruined the muffins," Konrad muttered, forcing an amused huff from Brandon.

"I'd say I'll never be able to eat one of hers again, but . . ."

"So fucking good," Konrad agreed on a groan before biting out a laugh. "God damn her."

I swallowed the guilt choking me and asked, "Thought you said you avoid my house if she's here."

"We do," Konrad said, then hurried to amend, "We try. We never have breakfast here on Tuesdays or Fridays because those are the mornings the girls are working out here."

"But you seem to know her well," I said, letting the unspoken question linger as I looked between them.

"She's always showing up at random," Brandon explained, gesturing to the pink pastry box. "Dropping off pastries and shit. I don't think Scarlet even likes her all that much, but she's Samantha's cousin, so she's always around."

"Do you know who Samantha is?" Konrad asked hesitantly.

I lowered my chin. "Scarlet's best friend."

"Right, well, she's the one we can thank for all the sexually-charged confrontations."

"Got it," I murmured as my thoughts drifted and that fear twisted deeper.

I wanted to believe I wouldn't cheat on anyone ever.

More than that, I wanted to believe I wouldn't have hurt Scarlet—the girl I'd been so undeniably in love with.

But with each day and each new situation I was presented with, I couldn't see how this would end without us learning anything less.

FIFTEEN

CHASE

"So, have we just given up on the sling completely?" Scarlet asked as she walked into the living room late that night, disapproval lacing her amusement.

I glanced up from the book I'd been sketching in—one of the handful she'd picked up for me the week before—and froze when I saw her there, leaning against the entrance of the hallway as she finished tying a silk scarf over her hair.

Shorts clinging to her skin and barely covering her ass that was becoming one of my favorite distractions during our therapy sessions. Breasts pushing at the torn collar of an old, baggy shirt that was clinging precariously to one shoulder and teasing me with all those tattoos and soft skin hidden underneath.

Then again, she could've been wearing anything, and I would've had the same reaction.

Heart kicking up to a frantic, desperate pace. Fingers twitching and hands aching to be filled with her curves. Body begging to claim what already felt like mine.

"You're beautiful." The words slipped free unbidden and seemed to catch her off guard.

Shoulders straightening against the wall and eyes widening as she studied me before a soft huff tumbled past her full lips. "You can't charm your way out of having to answer."

My head shook as I glanced at the image I'd been repeatedly sketching before slowly closing the book. "It's right beside me. I took it off when I started drawing. Doesn't change that you're beautiful."

A hum left her as she pushed from her spot and started toward me, fighting a smile as she did. "You're saying ready-for-sleep Scarlet is what does it for you?"

The corner of my mouth twitched into a smirk as she slid onto the couch beside me, tucking her legs underneath her and pressing close to my uninjured side. "You say that like it surprises you. Did it not before?"

"Didn't say that," she said, voice soft and filled with amused wonder. "But the workout clothes are what used to get you. I could barely make it out to the garage without you pulling me back in."

"They still do," I said immediately and watched as her cheeks filled with heat at the roughness of the words. "But you, at any time, is what gets me."

"Ditto," she whispered as that smile she'd been fighting broke free, sending my body into pure chaos for the few seconds before I was slammed with the reminder of everything that'd happened that day.

The canvas.

Litany.

What I'd been sketching . . .

"What—" she began, only to hesitate. "Chase, what's going

on?" Shifting so she could look at me easier, she said, "There have been so many times today when you've gotten this same expression. Like you're devastated and worried and . . . I don't know."

"With everything that happened this morning, you're not?" I asked as my stare fell to the book again. My hand curled around the cover as if I could contain what was on the pages.

Scarlet took a steeling breath before saying, "I wouldn't have wanted to stay here if I were worried."

"You're not even worried about what it could mean?" I challenged gently and nodded when she didn't respond. "*That*."

"We don't know anything yet," she reminded me, but I just gave her a look that said we knew enough, then forced myself to ask the same question I did every night.

"You leaving?"

"I'm right here," she whispered as she slid her hand over my leg.

I slanted my head because I knew that answer would change. One day. And even though I was afraid of revealing anything that would push us closer to that day, I felt like I was drowning under the things I was keeping from her.

"Scarlet, I'm starting to remember things," I confessed and let a dark huff bleed from my lips when her expression shifted to dread. "And there it is."

"What are you remembering?" she asked, her voice barely a whisper.

"Not even a hint of excitement because you know as well as I do that I did something," I said without answering.

"I never said you did anything," she argued. "And I want you back, Chase. I want your memories back. But I'm allowed to be worried. I'm allowed to let that worry free when you start it off in a tone as somber as that. If there would've been no reason to worry, you would look happier right now."

"Fair," I said and then cleared my throat. "I still don't know what happened. But I remember us on the beach, arguing. I was going to walk away because you weren't leaving your ex, and I —" I pressed my hand to my chest, my head shaking because I could feel all of it as if it'd just happened.

"All of me forever," she said under her breath in realization. "I left him that night."

"I know," I muttered. "The memory ended before that, but I somehow knew that a few hours later."

"What else?" she asked, more encouraged than before, but I just shook my head, afraid to give her this.

"Litany," I finally said after nearly a minute had passed. "I knew who she was. I knew her name—knew her as *LT*." I met Scarlet's eyes when she went still beside me. "And I knew I shouldn't be near her."

"LT," she said numbly. "You . . . you remember *her*."

The hurt-fueled words weren't phrased as a question, but I still said, "Yeah. Just her name and that feeling. She came into the house today when Brandon and Konrad were here, and I felt like I was choking on the guilt I've been living with whenever she looked at me."

Scarlet sat back with a pained huff. Eyes wide and stare faraway before she gave a quick shake of her head and looked at me. "But you—you can't stand her."

"That's what the guys said."

"No. No, you *hate* her," Scarlet informed me as if she couldn't wrap her head around it, even as emotion shook her words. "I'm always asking you to be nice to her, and you tell me she doesn't deserve anyone's kindness."

I lifted my hand and then let it fall to hers. "I felt like you needed to know."

"Okay, but it still doesn't mean anything," she said, the words almost a plea. "It could've been because a part of you remembered you don't like her. It could've been—" She floundered as she tried to explain the rest. "It could've been so many things."

"Right," I murmured as uncertainty built and built between us. "Does she have a key?"

"To our house?" When I grunted in response, she gave a quick shake of her head. "No. Well—I don't . . . I don't know. Maybe. Anna and Samantha do. I might've given one to her too." From the way Scarlet's expression abruptly fell, I had a feeling that she'd just remembered she *had*.

That she'd just started wondering if one of her closest friends could've been behind this morning on top of whatever else had the potential to tear us apart.

"You leaving?" The words pushed from my lungs on a hesitant breath and had her sagging against the back of the couch.

"Chase," she said just as softly as her pained stare met mine.

For what felt like an eternity, we just sat there. Watching each other as the weight of the question and her answer pressed against us.

"It's like you said to me that night all those years ago," she finally began, voice steady and words careful. "Anything less than everything isn't enough. I need all of you forever or nothing at all."

My body stilled to the point of pain and my heart twisted as I sat there, silently begging her not to do this, all while I knew I would let her. After today, I would make it easy for her to go, knowing she deserved so much better.

And I'd tear my fucking heart out as I watched her walk away.

"When we met, I gave you my heart without thought," she went on. "But I was too afraid of consequences and hurting people to give you the rest of me the way you deserved and the way I wanted to. And I almost lost you because of that mistake. But right now, we're just assuming. So, until the day I find out with one hundred percent certainty that you *chose* to stop giving me all of you, I'm not going anywhere."

A strangled breath left me as I reached for her. Grasping her chin to press my mouth to hers. The kiss nothing more than feather-soft brushes and teasing claims.

"Don't deserve you," I whispered against her lips as I pulled her closer.

"That isn't true." Weaving her fingers through my hair, she pressed her forehead to mine as she effortlessly slid one of her legs over mine so she was straddling me. "Until we know, stop thinking that way. Stop saying those things." I started to argue, so she hurried to add, "You're getting pieces of things that can be explained away as anything else. Don't let those incomplete pieces make you believe you did something."

I nipped at her full bottom lip and muttered, "No promises."

Her eyes rolled as she leaned back. "What else?" When I lifted my chin in question, she asked, "What else have you remembered?"

I drew in a slow breath as my gaze drifted to where my sketchbook rested between us and then snapped back to her. To her chest that was barely covered by that old shirt and the design I could see peeking out between her breasts.

"That," I said a little uncertainly because I could only see the top of it.

"You remember my boobs," she said dully, eyes dancing with amusement when I met them.

"No, the tattoo." I started reaching for the shirt, only to stop. "Can I?"

Understanding and need mixed with her amusement. "It's weird to have my fiancé ask if he can see one of my tattoos. Especially considering he did it."

"I did your sternum?" I asked as I kept my hand hovering just over the torn collar.

"You've done a lot of them," she said as she tugged the material so it fell off her shoulder.

Before it could fall all the way, she caught the shirt against her breasts. Watching me. Seeming to wait for my reaction. But I had already forgotten what we were doing. All I knew was I needed to stop this.

Stop us.

As much as I wanted Scarlet, I couldn't let myself have her when I didn't know how—or *if*—I'd betrayed her.

And yet, I just sat there. Blood pounding and roaring with need as I stared into those dark, hypnotic eyes. And then the material of her shirt fell. Pooling around her waist as her hands covered her breasts.

When she spoke, her voice was barely above a whisper. "It's even weirder to feel like this is the first time I'm undressing in front of you."

"It is, Scarlet." I lifted my hand to trail the tips of my fingers up her arm and across her shoulder. "To me, it is."

Heat bloomed in her cheeks as her gaze searched mine. After a few moments, she cleared her throat and hurried to ask, "So, do you remember my tattoo?"

"Can I look?"

The corners of her mouth twitched before a small smile broke free. "I've already taken my shirt off, Mr. Grayson. Do you ask all your clients if you can look at the place where you're about to tattoo them?"

"I'm not tattooing you," I informed her. "And I don't need my memories to know you've never been a client."

Her eyebrows scrunched together in a way that was all adorable confusion. "I just told you that you've done most of—"

"You've never been a client, Scar."

In an instant, her confusion was replaced with need and that unmistakable, unending love. "Right," she breathed. "You can look."

My heart felt like it was going to tear out of my chest as I let my stare drift over her face and down the elegant slope of her neck. Lingering on the flawless skin of her chest and swell of her breasts, barely hidden beneath her hands, until I was trailing the design I'd been drawing.

Black lines and dots decorated her brown skin and surrounded a small quarter-moon and flower in an elegant pattern.

"I drew this," I muttered as I studied each part of the tattoo.

"That's right."

I met her elated stare before dropping mine to the tattoo again, head slanting as I explained, "This past week. In some of the sketchbooks you just grabbed for me—a few times."

Excitement and hope practically burst from her when she asked, "Really?"

"Scarlet, I—" I dropped my hand and shook my head as I reached for the sketchbook. "There's something else. Something I've been drawing repeatedly. But it . . . it isn't from a real memory. Well, with everything else you've figured out, it could be," I hurried to add when I felt the force of her excitement being stripped away. "I don't know anymore."

"Tell me," she pleaded softly as she sat back on my thighs and shrugged into her shirt.

And I hated it.

Not just that she was covering herself, but the way she was doing it. Pressing the collar of her shirt close to her chest. Looking like she suddenly felt vulnerable when she'd been a breathtaking and contradicting display of strength and shy innocence just seconds before.

"There's this—" I cleared my throat and tried to orient my thoughts. "In what I *thought* had happened when I first woke, there was this symbol Harper used to draw all the time. I found a ring of it and gave it to her for Christmas, which I'm guessing never happened."

"Not that I know of," Scarlet whispered as she looked at where I was thumbing through the pages of the sketchbook.

Not that I needed to go looking for it. I'd drawn it on almost every page so far, unable to stop thinking about it.

Opening to one of the pages, I made sure the symbol was on there and then turned the sketchbook around to show Scarlet. "Does this mean anything to you or us?"

SIXTEEN

CHASE

S carlet looked from the symbol on the page to me a few times before she bent. Pressing her head to my chest as a breath rushed from her lungs that was at once amused and grateful and relieved.

"Does that mean *yes*?" I asked, reaching for her chin so I could study her expression.

"Harper drew this?" she asked. "In your not-real memories?"

"All the time."

"And you gave her a ring of this symbol?"

"The metal was twisted into it," I confirmed as I watched her eyes dance and warm with all that love. "Did I give it to you?"

"No," she said as a slow smile spread across her face. "But do you know what that is?"

"The trinity symbol," I said without hesitation.

But Scarlet just watched me expectantly as if waiting for a different answer, her smile widening. When I didn't offer anything else, she said, "Chase, Trinity is my last name."

"You're serious?"

A soft laugh left her as she leaned forward to press her mouth to mine. "You know me," she said against the kiss, her revelation filled with relief and joy. Lifting her hand to brush against my chest, she whispered, "All of your memories of us can be wiped away, but your heart still knows me. Your soul still recognizes mine."

Always.

I would always know her.

My mind could try to steal every moment of Scarlet from me. I could think I was in another life and in love with someone else. But there was no denying this. There was no denying her.

There was no denying that I loved Scarlet in a fierce, irreversible sort of way.

Curling my arm around her, I pulled her closer until she was pressed firmly to my lap. Her whimper climbing up her throat and getting lost in the kiss when she rocked against my hardening length.

And then again.

I knew I needed to stop this. Needed to stop us before we got to a point where I'd be so blinded by her and my need for her that I wouldn't want to.

But then a shiver rolled through her the next time she moved against me, and my name left her lips on a breath like a plea, and all reason left me.

"Fuck," I growled as I banded one arm around the small of her back and curled my other hand around her jaw. Pressing her harder against me as I claimed her mouth.

Taking more of the kiss and more of her that she readily

gave until she was trembling. Chest pitching with ragged breaths and body vibrating with barely concealed need.

"I want you to see me," she said as she reached for the bottom of her shirt, a sound of uncertainty and protest getting caught in her throat when I grabbed her hands before the material could pass over her breasts.

Slowing the kiss until we were nothing more than clashing chests and frenzied breaths, I met her pleading stare and gently removed her fingers from the shirt. "This is my job."

The change in her features was instant. Heat filling her cheeks as an indescribable look filled her eyes. All open trust and sensual need. Familiarity mixed with the thrill of something new.

And fuck if I didn't feel that down to my bones.

Because as I lifted her shirt over her head and let it fall to the floor, everything inside me shifted into absolute chaos at the sight of this girl. Sitting above me with all that trust, bared to me for the first time.

But there was that feeling again—like someone was beating against an invisible barrier in the back of my mind—shouting that I knew this. That I'd spent my time studying her and worshiping her and learning her body.

"Fucking beautiful," I whispered as my hands slowly moved up her waist and over the sides of her breasts before I was filling my hands with them. Teasing her nipples and leaning forward to flick one of the hardened peaks with my tongue before pulling it into my mouth.

And the whimper that fell from her lips? God damn. I wasn't sure I'd ever get that sound out of my head.

I slowly released her, relishing in the gasp that tore from her as my teeth scraped across her nipple, then softly blew on the same spot. A smirk tugging at my mouth when she shivered against me as chills skated across her skin in response.

But just as I was moving to her other breast, she curled her fingers around my jaw and tipped my head up. Crushing her mouth to mine in a fierce claim as she rolled her hips. Rocking against me until I was grasping for the control I'd lost somewhere along the way.

My hands moved back to her hips, guiding her, even as I told myself to stop her movements. I parted her lips and swept my tongue into her mouth, tasting her and swallowing her needy sigh, even as I fought to pull back. And when she began lifting my shirt off my body, I took it off the rest of the way for her instead of putting an end to everything.

This would hurt her worse in the end. I knew that.

But this girl was in my head and in my veins. She'd buried herself under my skin and embedded herself in my soul.

I needed her body, heart, and soul in a way I'd never needed anything.

Gripping both of her hands in mine when she grasped the band of my athletic shorts, I tugged on her full bottom lip and met her heated stare. "First time I fuck you isn't gonna be on a couch."

"First time." The words were barely a breath leaving her as amusement played at the edge of her mouth. "If you only knew how many times you've done exactly that," she said before kissing me again. This time softer, slower, as she fought against my weakening hold to dip her hand inside my shorts.

My eyes rolled back and a groan raked up my throat when she sat up enough to grip me through my boxer briefs.

"Fucked me. Right here," she whispered as she slid her hand along the outline of my hard length.

Moving my hands to her thighs, I met her stare again as I curled my fingers tight against her. "Bed," I said in warning as I prepared to stand.

Just as my muscles tensed, Scarlet slammed one of her hands against the wall over my head and gripped me tighter with the other, forcing a hissed curse from me as I relaxed into the couch.

"Scarlet," I said through clenched teeth, her name all carnal wants and reproachful demands. And then another groan was building in my chest at the wicked little smirk she gave me when she resumed her teasing touches before slowly moving off the couch.

"I know how you fuck me, Chase Grayson," she said once she was on her feet again and bent close, lips just out of reach. "It's slow and sensual. It's hard and savage. And it's always perfect."

I reached for her waist and curled my hand into a fist when she stopped my attempt with a gentle touch to my forearm, never once taking her eyes from mine.

"And the way you hold me . . ." she continued as she reached for the band of my shorts and boxer briefs, pulling them down until I stopped her just before they freed me. "It's tender and possessive and powerful, and as your physical therapist, I'm telling you that you can't do those things."

"Wanna bet?"

Her smirk briefly widened into a bright, stunning smile as she leaned forward to place a soft kiss to my lips. "Let me take care of you."

"It's my job to take care of you," I countered easily, the words slipping from me as if I'd said them dozens of times.

"Chase," she whispered. *Begged.* My name tearing at me

because her plea went so much deeper than not wanting me to injure myself further.

She needed this.

I captured her mouth again in response. Easily parting her lips and deepening the kiss as I released my hold and lifted my hips to help her remove the rest of my clothes.

And then she was moving. Leaving a searing trail down my chest and stomach until she was on her knees in front of me and taking me in her hands.

Jesus Christ.

I bit back a groan as she stroked me. Slow and teasing. Grip just firm enough to make me feel like I was going to go out of my goddamn mind before this could really begin.

Those hypnotic eyes shifted from what she was doing to mine, keeping me locked there until one of her hands left my cock and drifted up. Trailing to the ridges of my abdomen as she sat forward to take me in her mouth.

"*Shit.*" My head fell to the back of the couch at the feel of her surrounding me. Pumping me slowly as she moved her head up and down. Taking me in again and again until I hit the back of her throat and swirling her tongue around the tip like she was about to release me, only to do it all over again.

I met her dark stare again, getting fully enraptured in the way she was watching me as she brought me closer and closer to an end I wasn't ready for.

As if she'd been waiting for this. Craving this. Needing this, exactly as I'd thought.

And I needed her.

I let my fingers trail over where she was gripping my stomach before reaching for her. Brushing my thumb over her cheek and gently demanding, "Come here."

Suddenly, that desperate voice in the back of my mind was there. Screaming at me. Begging me to remember.

And in a way, I did.

I knew this. I knew *her* . . .

The way she continued sucking my cock before slowly releasing me because she refused to stop until she was ready. The way her body moved as she pushed to her feet and rid herself of the little shorts she was still wearing, all sensual swaying that was purely Scarlet and not at all for show.

Reach for me.

Just as the thought entered my mind, one of her hands stretched toward me as the other slid across her belly. The action somehow sensual and timid and so damn sexy.

"I know you," I said as I pulled her onto my lap, bringing her back to where we'd begun.

Where she belonged.

With me. Pressed close to me.

Wonder and hope wove through the heat and desire in her eyes, and her eyebrows lifted when she asked, "Yeah? Tell me."

"There's nothing; I can't explain it." My head faintly shook. "I just know you."

A ghost of a smile pulled at her mouth. "I see it when you look at me," she whispered in understanding. "I feel it when you touch me."

"Touch you how?" I asked as I dipped my free hand between her thighs, teasing where Scarlet was bare and slick and pulling a shuddering whimper from her.

"Oh God," she breathed as she rocked against me. Her eyelids fluttering shut when I slid a finger inside her before moving back to her clit. "Oh God, like that."

Pressing our joined hands to my chest, I laid her palm flat against the thunderous pounding there so she could feel exactly what this was doing to me as I spent my time touching and teasing her. Tracing just past where she was aching for my touch before finally focusing on her clit. Alternating between light, barely-there touches and giving her exactly what she needed until she was trembling.

Watching the way her lips parted and her chest's movements deepened. Listening to the hitches in her breath and the hushed whimpers that pulled from her. Memorizing everything about her because I never wanted to forget any part of this.

When her body tightened above mine, I pressed two fingers inside her and crushed my mouth to hers. Swallowing her moan when I curled my fingers and hit that spot, sending her into an orgasm that had those tremors rolling through her body and her fingers digging into me in a simple but powerful claim.

"I need you," she breathed through the kiss.

"Bed," I agreed, repeating my earlier demand as I slowly removed my fingers and trailed them over her sensitive clit.

Her head shook as those tremors continued rocking her, and then she was kissing me. Deep and passionate as she situated herself over my length and began lowering onto me.

My eyes rolled back at the feel of her—

"Shit." Tearing my mouth from hers, I hurried to still her hips and met her confused but satisfied gaze. "Bedroom," I said through clenched teeth because it was taking everything to keep from moving. To keep from driving up into her and fucking her when she felt *that damn good*. "At least to get a condom."

Amusement bled from her on a breath as she leaned in to kiss me again. This time soft, almost teasing, as she shifted.

Sinking a little lower on my cock and forcing a groan to rake up my throat.

My fingers flexed against her hips and her name left me on a warning as memories I could no longer trust ripped through my mind.

Because I had always been careful to a fault, not leaving anything to chance . . . except for one time. One weekend. And my entire life had changed because of it.

At least, from what I could remember. And as we'd been finding out, every one of my coma-induced memories was laced with truth from my life. It didn't matter that I'd already planned on spending the rest of forever with the girl in my arms; I couldn't take that chance with her.

Or maybe . . . maybe it was that, with something as impactful as this, I was afraid to trust my mind and the possibilities.

"I don't know what you remember," she began, her fingers skating up and weaving into my hair as she playfully bit at my lip, "but that isn't us. You won't find anything in our room because we've never used anything."

My fingers curled tighter against her at the understanding and honesty in her voice and my eyes shut for a second as I fought against the urge to continue. To claim her when I already had her right there. Where she clearly belonged.

"And what happens when you get pregnant?" I asked before meeting her wide stare. "What happens when I go through it all again—the absolute fucking joy of finding out I'm going to be a dad and the appointments—only to wake up in a hospital to find out none of it was real?"

Her chest shook with the impact of her next exhale. "Chase . . ." Sorrow etched across her face as her forehead fell to mine, and then her hands were curling against my jaw and slanting my head just enough to kiss me.

Soft.

Slow.

Full of so much love and pain and passion that my heart ached as my own love for her clashed with the fears I'd been keeping at bay and the guilt that had been slowly destroying me.

"You know me," she reminded me. "You know me because we're *real*. Let me show you that. Let me give you the pieces of us you've forgotten."

I held her there for a moment longer . . . lips brushing with each breath. Bodies connected and begging for the movements I was keeping us from.

"Just be there when I wake up," I softly begged before forcing her down until she was fully seated.

"Oh God," she whimpered as another tremor rolled up her spine.

Nothing . . . nothing had ever felt like her. I could've stayed in that moment forever, with her in my arms as she stretched around me, gripping me so damn tight. Her heated stare locked on mine and her full lips parted. Begging me to kiss her. To taste her.

To claim her in every way.

And then she began moving.

Hips rolling in a way that had a groan building in my chest and my grip on her tightening. Urging her to continue.

"*Fuck*," the word scraped up my throat when she shifted until only the head of my cock was still inside her before sliding back down. Taking me in again and again before she resumed her rocking, quicker than before. Driving me out of my goddamn mind because everything about this girl screamed that she was made for me.

The sensual rocking of her hips. Her unexpected, teasing movements that had my eyes rolling back. The way she clung to me and breathed my name when I captured her mouth.

Mine.

I wrapped one of my arms around her hips, keeping her close as my other hand trailed up her back and curled over her shoulder. Holding her. Claiming her with my touch alone. Forcing her down harder and harder as she rode me and pulled me closer to that ledge.

A whimper bled from her and got lost in the kiss when her movements changed. Became almost desperate as she clenched around me, nearing her own release.

Unlocking my arm from around her waist, I slipped my hand between us as I deepened the kiss. Demanding more even as she struggled to catch her breath, and goddamn if she didn't give me exactly that.

More of her addictive mouth, attacking the kiss as if she needed me to breathe.

More of her mesmerizing body, moving with me like she was afraid she'd never be able to have this again when I began teasing her clit.

More of her as she let go, pulling me off that ledge with her as she shattered above me. Her body vibrating and chest heaving as I poured my release into her. Whispering, "I love you," against my lips before pressing a soft, lingering kiss there.

I love you. I love you.

The words tore through my mind on repeat as we slowly

came down together, but I held them back. Because at the end of all this, I needed to protect her more than I already was.

Trailing my mouth to her jaw and then her neck, I gave a teasing bite to the soft skin there and said, "You consume me."

Words that were just as true but weren't nearly enough.

Wrapping my arms around her, I held her close and pressed my forehead to her shoulder just as her soft voice met my ear.

"I'll always be there when you wake up."

My eyelids shut and a shuddering breath left me at the depth of her words, and I gripped her tighter. In gratitude. In adoration.

In a plea to make her words *true*.

Pressing a kiss to her shoulder, I sat back to look into her eyes and said, "This changes nothing." When confusion and rejection touched her face, I hurried to clarify, "If one day you decide you need to leave, I'll let you go. If you want me to continue staying in the guestroom, then I'll say goodnight right now and go in there."

"If I *want* you in there?" Scarlet choked out on a stunned laugh. "I want you with me. That's all I ever want."

"Then I'm taking you to bed tonight and every night that you'll let me," I informed her. My voice dropping when I added, "And I'm about to show you how wrong you are."

I stood from the couch with her in my arms and began stalking to the main bedroom as a shocked gasp tore from her.

"Chase!" she cried out as she hurried to wrap her legs around me even as she scolded, "You need to put me down. You can't—"

I stopped her with a firm kiss and felt my blood begin to pound all over again at the frustrated sound that got caught in her throat and turned into a pleading whimper. "I'm taking that bet now."

"You're going to make your injuries worse," she reprimanded, but a laugh still bubbled free when I dropped her onto the bed.

Climbing onto the bed after her, I situated myself between her legs and held myself just above her. Watching as all that light and excitement in her eyes began mixing with an endless need when I ground my hardening length against her.

"Ask me if I give a fuck," I muttered as I dipped down to capture her lips, my mouth twitching into a smirk. "After I'm done with you."

SEVENTEEN

SCARLET

"I have to pee!" Litany called out as soon as our workout session ended a few days later.

"Oh my God, what a surprise," Anna said dryly, eyes rolling as she moved her head exaggeratedly to watch LT escape into my house.

"You're always so annoyed with her," I said to Anna as I began gathering weights to clean and put away.

"Because I always have to deal with her before coffee," Anna said irritably, then gave Samantha an apologetic look. "No offense."

Samantha lifted her hands. "I know how she can be. But she's really great too—she's always been there for me."

"She's great because she feeds us," Anna countered, then laughed. "On second thought, maybe not. Bitch is keeping me from dropping a pant size."

"You love her," I chided gently, and Anna rolled her eyes.

"Obviously," she conceded as she dramatically flipped open her sunglasses before putting them on. "I'm not outwardly mean to just anyone. They have to be one of my people and be able to handle it."

"How sweet," I muttered, a laugh bursting from me when Anna swung at me with her purse.

"Hey, are we getting new keys to your place?" she asked as she began walking out of the garage. "And what do I do with the old one?"

"Throw it away?" I said, making it sound like a question, then turned to continue my after-session routine as I went on. "And, yeah, we plan on having copies made for everyone. We just haven't yet."

I held my breath, waiting for either of them to call me out on the lie, but Anna just shrugged and said, "No rush. Obviously. But I have to run; love you both."

We called out our goodbyes, and I waited until she was far enough away before saying, "Hey, Sam, can you hang back until after LT leaves too?"

Her eyebrows lifted as she fixed her blonde hair into another messy bun. "Of course. Everything okay?" When all I could offer her was an unconvincing hum, she nodded in understanding and asked, "Can I help you while we wait for her to pretend she isn't making coffee?"

A laugh danced across my lips, but I just shook my head. "No, I've got it."

Besides, I needed the distraction of this. Of the repetitive back and forth throughout the garage and mindless cleaning. Of letting my mind drift as I thought of what to say to my best friend.

Because Chase and I'd had copies made when we'd gotten the locks changed on our doors last week. But after everything Chase had revealed that night, what memories he'd had, I hadn't been able to give my friends their copies when I'd seen them at brunch the next day. Not when I'd spent the entire meal picking apart every word that had left LT's mouth.

I'd told myself at least a dozen times over the weekend that I was being ridiculous. That it so obviously couldn't have been one of my friends who'd come in, stealing and replacing a picture of us, and who was the potential missing piece in Chase's memories.

But then the girls came over this morning, and I'd found myself watching LT all over again. Overanalyzing what she was saying and feeling this deep pit of anger growing inside me whenever she so much as hinted at Chase.

Ridiculous because, as I kept telling Chase, we didn't know.

Still . . .

"Bye!" Litany called out from the street as she hurried to get into her car.

I didn't even bother waving that time.

"She knows that you know she steals your espresso, right?" Samantha asked with an affectionate laugh.

"Oh, I'm sure," I muttered, head bobbing quickly as I forced myself to calm my racing heart and clear my thoughts. "It's just a game we play where we pretend she doesn't do it."

"Such a brat," Samantha said in that same gentle affection, then blew out a quick, determined breath. "Okay, so what—"

"Do you think LT could be the one who broke into my house?" I asked before she could finish speaking, then looked over to see her eyes widen in shock.

"What?" she finally asked, choking over the word. "LT. My cousin, Litany. That's who we're talking about right now?"

My shoulders sagged with a heaving breath as I turned to face her fully. "I didn't want to say anything, really, but—"

"Wait, wait," she hurried over me, voice still somehow managing to keep that endless calm she encompassed. "You've *been* thinking this?"

"Please don't be mad," I begged as I stepped toward her. "I didn't at first—she never even crossed my mind. No one did. But then Chase said something . . ." I gave her a helpless look and walked over to one of the large exercise balls.

With a sigh, I roughly fell to it and told her what the police had said about the likelihood of it being someone Chase was seeing and how Chase had remembered Litany. His guilt when he'd seen her and that *sense* he'd described about needing to stay away from her.

"And now," I went on, lifting a hand to gesture to where Litany always parked, "I can't stop dissecting everything she says. She asked about him three different times today. If he'd remembered anything new. If he was home. If we'd learned anything new about the break-in and what Chase thought about it . . ." I trailed off meaningfully and lifted an eyebrow.

"So, I don't know," I muttered. "Before all this, I would've never believed Chase would cheat on me, and I still don't. And I don't *want* to think LT would do anything, but I realized I'd given her a key at some point. And I just . . . well, I wanted to see what you thought."

Throughout it all, Samantha had stood there. Listening as mixtures of shock, concern, and sadness flitted across her face.

"If I thought Chase might have cheated on you, or if I think he could've cheated on you with LT?" she asked softly, then hurried to add, "Or if I think she's the one behind what happened last week?"

I thought for a while before shrugging. "I guess all of it."

Samantha's head moved in slow shakes before she reasoned, "LT has her moments, but she isn't crazy. She isn't going to come into someone's house and steal things or leave *burned pictures*."

A shamed breath left me as I dropped my face into my hands. "You're right."

"And Chase . . . Chase has mentioned in front of me that he can't stand her."

"He has," I acknowledged with chagrin, then looked at her again. "But what about him remembering her and all that?"

"I don't know," she said after a moment, shrugging as she did. "It could've meant so many different things."

"That's what I told Chase." I straightened on the exercise ball and asked, "Do you hate me for even considering it?"

"Of course not," she said with a scoffing laugh. "I think you've been going through something really difficult, even before someone left a super scary message in your bedroom. I'd be suspicious of everyone."

"Even me?" I asked, twisting the question into a playful tease.

"Especially you," she tossed back with a wink.

Grabbing one of the rubber bands near my feet, I flung it at her. "Brat," left me on a huff just as a familiar Jeep pulled onto the driveway.

"And there he is," Samantha murmured. "Guess that's my cue to leave."

"You don't have to," I assured her as I tore my stare from where Chase was saying something to Brandon as he climbed out of the idling Jeep.

"Except I do," she said with a sigh. But just as she began

stepping away, she turned toward me again. "I don't know him well, but from all the things you've told me about Brandon, he's this loyal, trustworthy, incredible guy."

"Brandon?" I asked on a laugh, my stare darting to the Jeep again for only a moment before snapping back to her. "You know he's married, right?"

But Samantha just waved a hand through the air, dismissing my question. "If this conversation had been about someone like him, I'm sure there would be no doubts. From you, from him, from any of us. But it's Chase, Scarlet. You *want* to believe him, but have you ever really been able to trust him?"

My eyebrows knitted together as I stood. "What?"

"I just . . . I don't know. I don't know what I'm saying," she forced out on an apologetic rush as if she was sorry for having said anything at all. "I'm being ridiculous. This whole situation just has me looking for things that aren't there because you're my best friend, and I'm worried about you."

"Samantha—"

"But it'll be fine. I know it," she offered. Her gentle encouragement somehow not managing to encourage me as she started backing away. "Let me know if you figure anything out —either of you."

"Yeah, of course," I murmured as I tried clearing my head of the doubt she'd unintentionally placed there. "See you Friday."

"Love you," she called over her shoulder as she grabbed her bag and hurried down the driveway, saying something to Chase as they passed that I couldn't hear from where I stood.

But it had Chase pausing.

Brow furrowing as he glanced back at her, and then again as he continued toward me.

"What is it?" I asked as he pulled me into his arms and pressed a soft, teasing kiss to my lips. "What'd Samantha say?"

He grunted as he shifted to look at where she was pulling away from the curb. "I know her? I mean, I know I do. You've said she's your best friend. Right?"

"Right," I said warily, my stomach dipping as I waited for what he would reveal next.

His head bounced quickly. "She didn't say anything weird, just 'Hi, Chase.' But it gave me this—I don't know. Didn't feel like a memory, but like the distinct feeling I'd heard those words in that tone at the shop. Have I tattooed her?"

"A few times," I said as I glanced at the place she'd just been. "I think the first time was when she and I got our sternum pieces together."

His brow furrowed tighter like he was trying so damn hard to remember. "Matching?"

"No, hers is different. We just got them done at the same time."

"Yeah, I don't know," he mumbled after a while, then pulled me closer. "How'd your session go?"

My head moved slowly as I tried to force away the completely unfounded and insane thought that something could've happened between Chase and Samantha before I managed to say, "Good. Good, it was fine."

"You sure?" he asked cautiously, eyes taking me in like he was looking for anything that would say otherwise.

"No, it was great," I assured him, then forced a teasing smirk. "I think I'm just tired because someone wouldn't let me sleep last night. Or the night before. Or the—" A gasp tore from my lungs and ended on a giggle when Chase lifted me into his arms and started walking toward the door.

"When's your next session?" he asked before stealing a quick, hard kiss.

"A little over an hour." Another laugh bubbled free as I vainly reached for the equipment. "But I have to clean—I have to prepare! And you have a meeting in less than that."

Setting me down just inside the house, he kept one hand on the open door and trailed the other down my spine and over the curve of my butt. A smirk shaping his lips at my next inhale when he continued the path until he was teasing just between my thighs. "If you want me to let you go . . ."

Taking his hand off the door, I let it slam shut and then reached for the bottom of his shirt as he grabbed the band of my workout pants. "It can wait."

———

"So, we come here a lot?" Chase asked late that afternoon, expression the same as it often was lately as he took in our favorite coffee shop.

Like he was trying to remember. Like he *wanted* to.

And couldn't.

Tomorrow would make a month since his accident. And even though things between us were so much better than they'd been when he'd first woken from the short coma, our lives were still incredibly different than they used to be.

Mornings weren't the same without him in the water with us. There were dozens of inside jokes that would go by without a reaction from him. He was getting more and more restless to get back to the shop and doing what he loved. And even though his truck would be replaced soon enough, according to the meeting he'd had today, Chase wouldn't be able to drive—or surf—for another few weeks, at least.

Something he'd voiced his displeasure about at the doctor's office about an hour ago.

But as the doctor had reminded him, even though his bones were healing extremely well, head injuries needed to be treated carefully.

Something the rest of us understood far too well, considering *we* remembered all the years Chase had lost and still wasn't getting back.

The doctor had said to be patient. To continue giving it time and that we were doing all we could. But it was everything else he'd quickly tossed out as possible explanations that had made me pause. Had worried me.

"It's Chase's mind that needs to repair itself," the doctor had said. "It's up to him to get his memories back. We don't know what will trigger them, if anything. It could be something as simple as a smell or a sound. It could be that, along with protecting his body from the physical trauma of the accident, his mind is protecting itself from the emotional trauma. Maybe he just doesn't want to remember. We just can't know."

Emotionally traumatic . . . the accident had been exactly that. Brandon and Konrad had described witnessing it in detail. I'd seen the aftermath. I'd been shown videos and early photos from before I'd gotten to the scene.

It'd been horrific—no one should've been able to survive that.

So, I understood the idea of Chase's mind protecting itself. But if he'd already been so torn up over something he'd *done* . . . was it possible his mind was blocking out not only the accident, but also these past years, to protect *us*?

"We come here all the time," I finally answered and then cleared my throat as I gave him an encouraging smile. "It actually opened up not long after we met, so it became one of our places."

He nodded as a humming sound rose in his throat.

But still, that look.

Not one bit of recognition lit his blue eyes, and I could see it aggravated him.

Grabbing my hand in his, he started leading me across the small parking lot and toward the building. "Then let's see how it is," he murmured as if a part of him didn't already know. Pressing his mouth to my temple, he asked, "Chinese food tonight?"

A stunned laugh burst from me at the unexpected comment. "What? No! Where did that even come from? We aren't fighting."

"You were still yelling at me about the sling on the way to the doctor. When he said I could be done with it, you rolled your eyes and said, 'Don't say a word,' so I'm not. I'm feeding you."

My chest shook with amusement. "Because you're thinking 'I told you so,' aren't you?"

"But I've already got the apology lined up," he said as a grin tugged at his mouth.

"You're awful," I tossed back as I let him lead me into the coffee shop.

"That isn't a *no*."

I slanted my head and gave him a look like I planned on saying exactly that, only to mutter, "Well, I'm never going to turn down Chinese food."

"Now, about surfing—"

"No," I said unquestionably as I brought us to a stop halfway to the counter. "Absolutely not. You heard the doctor."

One side of his face scrunched up adorably, but the words that left him and the tone of his voice were pure sin. "You also told me I couldn't fuck you, and I—"

"Chase," I hissed, pressing my hand against his stomach and looking wildly around, making sure no one was close enough to hear him.

When I met his stare again, his eyes were all wicked amusement and carnal promises.

"I've proven you wrong," he continued. "Repeatedly. I'm also fine."

My head shook as I fought the smile threatening on my lips. "You definitely owe me Chinese food now," I said under my breath as I turned toward the counter again, then added, "No surfing. Period."

A contemplative hum sounded in his chest as he caught up with me. "We'll see—what the fuck are you doing here?"

My head snapped up at his harsh demand to see him staring straight ahead, looking horrified and furious and like he was about to be sick.

A question lodged in my throat as I followed his line of sight to where Erin, the owner, was standing next to the barista who was waiting to take our order. Her stunned stare shifting quickly between us before landing on me.

"Did I miss something?" she asked, then jerked back when Chase charged the counter.

"Do you have any idea what you've done?" he ground out. "What the *fuck*?"

"Chase!" I shouted over him. Grabbing his arm and trying to pull him back, only to stagger a few feet away when he shoved from the counter and raked his hands through his hair as he seethed.

"The hell did I ever do to you?"

"Chase, *stop*," I demanded as I reached for him again. Gripping his arm tightly and putting myself in his line of sight. "What is wrong with you?"

His wild stare snapped from me to Erin repeatedly before something like understanding and dread seemed to fall over his expression.

Blinking quickly, he studied me longer and longer before focusing fully on Erin and demanding, "Who are you?" Before she had the chance to respond, he met my stare again as he pointed at her, voice dropping to a rough whisper. "That's Trish."

"Who—*oh God*," I breathed as the story Chase had told me —the *memory* that had never really happened—rushed through my mind and made my heart ache for him. "No. No, no, no."

"Yes," he said through clenched teeth.

"She isn't—" I roughly shook my head and looked at Erin and the other baristas, who were watching us with varied expressions of shock and alarm. "Erin, I'm sorry. He thinks— he thinks you're someone else."

She nodded as she glanced between us, having already heard about the entire thing when I'd broken down during one of my visits when Chase was still in the hospital and furiously angry that I was claiming to be his fiancée.

"From the coma," she said slowly, a little uncertainly, then gave a soft laugh as she looked at Chase. "Not sure what to think if you hate me, but I guess it's something to have been in those memories."

"Yeah." The word broke from me on a huff, but my brow furrowed as I wondered why she had.

This shop had opened after Chase and I met, and he didn't remember it. And yet, Erin had played such a crucial role in Chase's memories when I hadn't been in them at all.

At least, not physically.

Chase's body vibrated beneath my hand, all pent-up anger he was trying to suppress as he studied the woman on the opposite side of the counter. Clearly seeing things that weren't happening. That had *never* happened.

"I don't know you?" he finally asked, voice like gravel.

Erin's eyes met mine as a smile pulled at her painted lips. "I mean, you do . . ." she began, drawing out the last word and trailing off for a moment. "Sometimes I take your order. Sometimes I make your coffee. Sometimes I just say *hey* as I walk around, checking on things. But I see you a few times a week."

Icy blue eyes flashed my way, hard and shamed and so, so confused, before they drifted away again. "I don't work with you?" he asked her, trying to cover every base as if he was struggling to trust anything.

Anything he knew. Anything he saw. Anything he was told.

"Do you want to work here?" Erin's smile turned mischievous as she glanced at me again. "Been trying to get Scarlet to come work for me for years now."

"No." The response came hard and fast and dripped with the loathing he still felt for the person he *thought* she was.

"Got it," she murmured, then leaned closer, expression

scrunching up in mock hesitation. "Do I want to know what I supposedly did?"

"No," I said quickly, pleading with my touch alone for Chase to let this go. "No, can we just—can we just order, please?"

"Of course," she said, popping back up and nodding to the awaiting barista as she reached for a marker. "I got this one."

Erin continued trying to make small talk while we ordered and waited on the drinks as if nothing had happened. As if it could wash away Chase's tension or the heaviness that had filled the shop.

I wasn't sure what all I offered to the conversation, if anything. I was too focused on the man beside me.

The way he was holding himself as if he was afraid to move. The rigid set of his jaw. The way his hardened stare stayed locked on some obscure spot and the way his thoughts seemed to be somewhere else entirely.

When we left, there was a heart on my cup.

Something we didn't joke about, the way we always had before. Something I'd been sure we still would've in this new, uncertain life, considering I'd explained about Erin and the hearts.

But Chase still wasn't speaking or looking at me, even after we got home. He just grabbed one of his sketchbooks and headed to the back patio without a word, staying out there long after I finally went to sleep that night.

No physical therapy. No Chinese food.

No nothing.

EIGHTEEN

SCARLET

I'd just finished slipping into a pair of loose sweats the next morning when I heard the guys jogging up the beach behind me. My head moving in small shakes and my chest pitching as I tried to pull myself together. Without looking back at them, I tugged off my rash guard and then hurried into a tank top before working off the top of my bikini beneath it. My movements rushed and jerky, bordering on frantic.

"You good?" Konrad asked, looking confused as he gestured to an ocean full of some of the cleanest waves we'd had in weeks.

"What's wrong?" Brandon asked, grip tight on his board and brow furrowed as he studied me. "Something was up when you got here too."

I paused for only a moment from where I'd been shoving my wet clothes and towel into my bag. "Chase texted when I was riding that last one in," I said, voice strained as I unnecessarily held up my wrist to show my watch that I'd received the text on. "He's on his way to see her. Right now. He got a car, and he's going to see her."

Dropping the bag to the sand, I dragged my hands over my face before meeting their edgy stares.

As if, in that vague response, I'd told them enough to begin putting pieces together. Pieces they were afraid of.

"Something happened yesterday afternoon—after the doctor appointment. We went to get coffee, and Chase lost it. Started yelling at the owner and asking what she was doing there. If she had any idea what she'd done to him." At their shift to utter confusion, I explained, "He thinks she's the reason he lost Harper . . . in his *other* memories. He thinks she's this person who worked with him and ended up in his bed somehow."

"Shit," Konrad muttered as he lowered his board to the sand. "Did you explain it to her?"

"Yes—sort of. I don't know," I stammered. "She already knew about the coma and the life he thought he had because of it, but I didn't tell her who Chase thought she was. That isn't what matters," I said quickly, sharply. "It's that after that happened, Chase wouldn't talk to me or look at me. When we got home, he went outside and stayed there all night. When I woke up this morning, he was—" A pained breath left me, shaking my chest with the force of it. "He was asleep in the guestroom."

Brandon flashed a worried look Konrad's way before hesitantly asking, "So, he's going to see this person?"

"No," I muttered, my heart wrenching as I snatched my bag. "He's going to see Harper."

"Fucking hell," Brandon hissed as he followed suit. Grabbing his towel and other clothes, but not bothering with changing as he began stalking up the beach.

"Are we following him?" Konrad asked as he hung back

with me, taking his time to gather his own things.

"What do you mean?" I asked as I picked up my board, mind miles away and weighed down with worries that were so far past this beach and Brandon.

"Just wanted to know if we were following Brandon to his house or if I needed to be following you." He held a hand up as he bent to reach for his board again. "I know what Brandon's going to do, but someone needs to be with you right now, and I can't magically transport Bree here."

A breath burst from me that edged on amused as I began walking up the path we'd been taking for years. "I have every intention of beating Brandon to his house."

Konrad just shrugged and began following me as if he had all the time in the world. "Not if I beat both of you there."

———

We all got there within a few seconds of each other. Not that it mattered because Chase wasn't there.

Neither was Harper or her car.

When Brandon called her, she simply said, "I'll talk to you soon," before ending the call.

And just like Chase had the day before, Brandon exploded. All harsh reactions and pleading, terrified demands as he threw his phone against the wall.

"What is he trying to do?" he shouted as he turned to Konrad and me. "I understand he's confused—I fucking do. I can't imagine waking up and having an entirely new life implanted in my mind. But he was getting it. He's *been* getting it. You can see that he knows *that* wasn't his real life."

"I know," I murmured as I sank into one of their kitchen

chairs, not bothering to try to calm him when that same fear of the unknown was gripping at my own chest.

"He loves you," he went on, a harsh laugh leaving him. "Jesus, he's in love with you *now*. As this person who's struggling with his memories and didn't even know you a month ago. So, *why*?" Brandon demanded. "Why is he letting this take him back to a place where he thinks he's in love with someone who never belonged to him? Why is he letting this drive the two of you apart when you're all he can talk about?"

"I don't know," I whispered and then released a weighted sigh. "At least you can be comforted knowing your wife only loves you. My fiancé has memories of someone else and has told me multiple times what he remembers of their *being* together and how much he loves her."

Konrad slowly looked at me, his wide stare matching Brandon's. As if I was missing something so completely obvious.

"Tell me," Brandon began, voice like grating steel, "before the accident, would it have bothered you if someone continuously told Chase she was in love with him? Not playfully—but *I love you*, and *you love me* with absolute certainty. If she told Chase, right in front of you, the two of them had been having an affair. If she tried *convincing* him of it, even if you knew it wasn't true."

My heart twisted and slowly sank as I looked at the situation from Brandon's perspective for the first time. And I hated that I'd been so consumed in my own pain that I hadn't once thought of how all of this had been for him.

"Because then that thought isn't just in your head; it's in Chase's head too, right?" he went on, voice hardening as he stepped up to his kitchen island and planted his palms firmly on it. "It doesn't matter how secure I am in my marriage. I never want my wife to have someone trying to convince her she's supposed to be with him. I never want my wife to be pulled into an enclosed room with another man so they can talk alone —especially about their *relationship*."

"Brandon, I'm sorry," I said, head shaking and my tongue darting out to wet my lips as I struggled with my shame. "I didn't—I should've realized what this was doing to you, and I'm sorry that I didn't take the time to stop and see."

"You have enough going on without trying to look out for everyone else," he said, shoulders slightly lifting. "But don't think that I don't hate this. For you. For me. I know what Harper would and wouldn't do, but when someone comes in, trying to change that, it doesn't make that fear any less real."

"I'm sorry," I repeated in understanding, then pushed to my feet when the front door opened. Hurrying after Brandon when he went stalking in that direction and releasing a sound of frustration when Konrad wrapped an arm around my waist to stop me.

"If it's just Harper, then we need to give them a minute," he mumbled. "If it's both of them . . ." He hesitated before releasing me, a look crossing his face as if to say Chase deserved whatever was coming to him. "Better not to be there when Brandon reacts."

But before I had the chance to respond to Konrad or worry over how Brandon might *possibly* react to Chase if he were there, Harper's mildly impatient sigh filtered into the kitchen seconds before she came walking in with Brandon directly behind her.

"I hung up because we were saying goodbye, and it wasn't really a good time to answer," she said, eyes rolling before she offered me a worried smile.

"Wasn't a good time to answer your husband," Brandon said dryly. "Who wouldn't have known you were even going somewhere with Chase if it hadn't been for Scarlet."

A soft laugh left Harper as she turned on him, looking down at him even though he towered over her. "Chase told me that he'd texted Scarlet. Considering you were out surfing with her, I figured she would've let you know. I also figured I would've been home before you." Her brow was lifted when she turned for the fridge and her tone fell into something uncomfortably sarcastic. "I can't imagine why you cut surfing short today of all days."

"You honestly think I'm just gonna—"

"I expect you to trust me."

"I don't trust him," Brandon snapped, the sharp claim reverberating in the kitchen and filling the open space with a pressure that each of us seemed to feel.

Konrad muttered a curse just before I staggered back to fall into the same chair I'd been occupying, and Harper's expression when she faced Brandon again was all shock and disappointment, twisted up with that same worry when she glanced my way.

"Fuck, I didn't mean that," Brandon said, voice soft but still rough. "You know he's like my family; you all do." He met each of our gazes, holding mine for a little longer before focusing on Harper again. "But this Chase who doesn't fully trust *us*? Who can't even trust his own mind? It's hard to trust *that guy*."

"I understand," I whispered when no one else responded, head bobbing subtly. "He's Chase, but he isn't. You trust him, but you don't know how. Everything about him is the same and so completely different. He's unpredictable."

"Right," Brandon murmured before dragging a hand over his head.

"He doesn't think he's in love with me," Harper said after nearly a minute of uneasy silence. "At least, I don't think he does. He never once mentioned anything like that."

"Then why did he want to see you?" Brandon asked when she went back to looking through the fridge.

"Well . . ." A huff left her as she turned back around, waving a leftover slice of pizza at us. "I'm not actually sure it was me he wanted to see. But he called and said he needed to see me. Asked if I could meet him, and said he was already headed to the coffee shop. When I started hesitating, he said it was important."

"So, you just went," Brandon said, still clearly not okay with the entire thing. I wasn't exactly thrilled either.

"Yeah," Harper said with a shrug. "It was the way he sounded. Like he was breaking. There was this strain in his voice that I've never heard from him before. And like you said, he's family. But when I got there, he wasn't alone. He was sitting at one of the tables with, um . . ."—she waved the slice around again—"I always forget her name. Long, dark hair. Tons of tattoos. Super pretty."

"Fantastic," I breathed as she continued.

"I'm not sure if she owns the coffee shop or just works there."

"Erin?" I asked, her name snapping from me as I straightened in the chair.

"Yes," Harper said as she took a large bite of the cold pizza.

"Chase was with *her*?" I asked, tone disbelieving and a little apprehensive as the encounter from the afternoon before burst through my mind.

Harper hummed in acknowledgment, head bobbing as she leaned against the counter. Looking like she was getting ready to launch into the story. "At first, I thought maybe she was just checking in, trying to see how he was doing after everything. But as soon as I sat down, he pointed at Erin and asked me, 'Do you know her?'"

"Oh no," I said under my breath, worried about what she would reveal next.

"I told him that we all go to that shop all the time, so I see her often enough," she went on. "But that I didn't know Erin outside the shop or anything like that, and he just kind of grunted. Like he wasn't sure if he was happy with my answer or not, and then he asked Erin if he'd done any of her tattoos."

"Has he?" I asked when she took another large bite.

She hurried to swallow, head shaking as she did. "Erin said she has a guy she's been going to for a super long time. I'm not completely sure if Chase believed her, but he didn't say anything. He just stared at us. Like, this *intense* staring as if he was waiting for something from us, and the longer he waited, the more discouraged he got. Then, out of nowhere, he shoved from the table and started storming out of the shop.

"Erin seemed really surprised and confused by the entire thing, but I followed Chase," Harper said, then gave Brandon a meaningful look. "Which wasn't long before you started calling. I asked what was going on, and he said, 'I thought this would be it. The two of you—that's what made everything fall apart. At least, in the memories that aren't real, that's what made everything fall apart. You hated that she was always at my station whenever you stopped by and that she only wanted *me* to do her tattoos. You didn't trust her at all, and I never listened to you. She's what ruined us *right* before the accident.'"

"So, was he just trying to see how you would respond to each other or—"

"He was trying to get his memories back," I said over Brandon, and Harper pointed at me with her free hand. "That's why he was watching them. He was waiting for it to jumpstart something."

"He thought it would be *the* memory that would unravel all the rest," Harper added.

"Okay, well, why didn't it work?" Konrad asked as he gripped the back of the chair beside mine.

"Who knows?" I said as I thought over the possibilities in my head. "It could be because he has the wrong people. The few memories he's gotten back have been when they're caused *by* that person. And he put Harper in my place, and Erin in—" I pressed my lips tightly together, stare falling as the words on the tip of my tongue taunted me with their truth.

He'd put Erin in someone else's place . . .

Chase was right. If he hadn't cheated on me, *something* had happened with *someone* that he'd been too afraid for me to find out. Something that had the ability to ruin us, if his memories were any indication.

"Chase is sure Erin worked with him," Konrad began.

"As Trish," I added.

"What?" he asked, and I could practically feel the question being echoed by the others.

"He thought Erin's name was Trish," I explained. "Which is just one more thing to make this that much harder to figure out because he's remembered everyone else's name. And we don't know anyone with that name or a variation of that name."

"Okay," Konrad went on, drawing the word out. "But he's sure he worked with her, and one of the things he said was that Harper hadn't liked that Trish-Erin wanted only Chase to do all her tattoos. If what he's trying to do is see someone or something that could potentially get back that one crucial memory, then I think he needs to be looking at work."

Harper, Brandon, and I looked at each other before facing Konrad.

"You think it's *Marissa*?" Brandon asked in a disbelieving tone.

"No," Konrad said quickly, firmly. "I just mean, *at work*. He's tattooed a lot of people. Who knows what he'll find out or remember if he sits there long enough."

"Oh my God." The words left me on a horrifying breath as things began falling into place.

I hadn't wanted to believe it, and yet, the clues were right there in front of me.

"Scarlet, *what*?" Brandon asked, sounding as if he'd been trying to get my attention. When I looked their way, Harper's expression twisted with worry.

"Do you know who it is?" she asked gently.

"No," I lied as I shakily stood, my head moving as denial twisted through me. "I mean, I don't know. There's never been anyone that I've complained about the way Chase said Harper complained about 'Trish.' But . . ."

I pressed a hand to my stomach as I thought back to the dozens of conversations Chase and I'd had about one person in particular. Always the same. Always ending with me rolling my eyes because I'd thought he was being ridiculous.

.   .   .

"I just don't see why you think it's weird," I'd said during one of the many conversations about her. "Why wouldn't she want you to be the one who tattoos her? You're incredible."

"Because I'd prefer it if she went to anyone else," he'd said as he opened the door to our favorite coffee shop, letting me slip inside before he'd followed. "Anywhere else."

I'd turned to face him, a patient laugh leaving me. "Why do you hate her so much?"

"Scar . . ." he'd murmured, his eyebrows lifting in a way that said he didn't know how I didn't see it. "I don't understand why you like having her around."

"Because she's one of my closest friends," I'd said, all reprimand, and gently smacked my hand against his stomach. "You need to be nice."

"She needs to stop making appointments with me," he'd said, refusing to back down. "Every few weeks, she's in my chair, saying shit she really has no business saying. And it's driving me to a breaking point."

I'd paused at that because it'd been the first time he'd ever hinted at a true reason for not liking her. "Saying what?"

Chase had studied me for a while, jaw working before he'd wrapped an arm around my waist. Leading us toward the short line as he'd finally admitted, "She doesn't know how to keep her mind or her mouth out of her pants, doesn't matter who her target is."

A laugh had burst free. "LT's like that with literally everyone. But she's harmless."

"She's fucking trash."

"Chase!"

"I'm sorry," he'd said quickly as he'd lifted his free hand in a placating gesture. "I'm sorry. But, Scar, she makes more

appointments than anyone I've ever tattooed. She's at our house at least twice a week. I can't escape her, and I want to."

I'd rolled my eyes and turned in his hold to face the counters, waving at Erin as I did. "Okay, Chase. Next time I find you eating one of LT's pastries, I'll be sure to remind you of this conversation."

Chase had called her trash . . . *trash.*

Oh God.

"I need to talk to Chase," I said through thin breaths as I turned, only to come to a stop when Harper spoke.

"I don't know where he went."

"What do you mean?" I asked as I looked back at her.

"He said he was going for a walk. That he needed time to think." She lifted a shoulder and glanced at Brandon before focusing on me. "He seemed to be struggling a lot more this morning than he had been during the last couple of family nights. He also said something about embarrassing you . . ."

My eyebrows drew close in confusion as her words hung in the air.

"Something about losing it," she said before lifting her hands. "That he'd lost it and embarrassed you, and wondered if you realized 'how it was going to end yet' because it was only going to get worse. That's when he said he needed time to think."

I nodded when I couldn't seem to speak around the knot in my throat, then offered everyone a weak wave as I continued out of the kitchen and house. Moving in a daze as I thought through everything I'd learned and realized.

Fitting pieces together and coming to roadblocks the way

we had this entire time. Feeling only the slightest bit of relief that Chase hadn't been pushing me away last night. He'd put that barrier between us again for *me*—a barrier I still didn't want. And struggling to wrap my head around the fact that the person we'd been looking for was one of my closest friends . . .

Trash had become *Trish*. His frustrations with LT always hitting on him—and every other man she saw—and wanting him to do all her tattoos had twisted into Harper being upset with those very things. She hadn't worked with him, but she was there often enough. Always at his station, as he'd liked to complain about.

She was everywhere.

But Chase's words had been "I didn't know" and "what the hell am I going to do," according to Brian. And I couldn't figure out how that came into play. I still couldn't see something happening between them because I *knew* Chase would've never laid a finger on LT.

And if we were going with the theory that the person in Chase's memories was the same person who'd taken the canvas and sketchbooks, I still found it laughable to picture LT even attempting something like that.

She probably would've stopped halfway through hanging the canvas back up to run into the bathroom, yelling, *I have to pee!*

So much made sense, and somehow, nothing did.

But I knew one thing, at least. Konrad was right. Chase needed to go and just sit at his station.

Grabbing my phone once I was in my car, I pulled up Brian's number and tapped on it. Already preparing an apology for waking him that involved tons of greasy food as I started toward the one place I knew Chase would always go.

NINETEEN

CHASE

J *ust sit. Please.*

That's what Scarlet had asked me to do when she'd dropped me off at the tattoo parlor about forty-five minutes before.

When she'd found me nearing the beach not long before that, she hadn't asked for an explanation or details on my conversation with Harper. She hadn't said anything as she'd driven us here. Just continuously stole glances my way until we were pulling up to the shop.

And then it'd been those three words.

Pleading. Worried. Full of so much damn meaning as if she'd already known what I'd been attempting to do.

Trying anything to get those memories to come rushing back, all while I was terrified they *would*.

"I can't believe you didn't say anything," Brian called out again from where he was messing around at his own station, getting things ready for when the shop would open in a few hours. All between giving me shit and eating the breakfast he'd shown up with, tossing one of the bags at me with a *compliments of your future wifey.*

"Bri," I said on an irritated groan and dragged a hand over my face.

"I'm just saying."

"There was nothing to say," I told him for probably the fifth time, then hurried to amend, "Nothing that would help our situation."

"There's everything to say," he countered. Standing and turning to look at me as if I'd offended him. "You tell her you're a motherfucking idiot for sleeping in a different bed last night. You tell her you love her."

"Brian—"

"You tell her you still want to marry her."

I ground my jaw, my head shaking as I thought over yesterday and last night and then this morning . . . where I'd let Scarlet drive away without ever saying so much as *hi* to her.

"I knew," I began firmly. "I *knew* after talking to you that there was something I'd done that was going to hurt her. I tried keeping some sort of distance between us because of it. Because the closer we get, the more it's going to hurt when I remember what it is. But she . . . Jesus."

"You love her," he said, enunciating each word and talking to me like I was an asshole for not having said it to Scarlet before then.

"I know that," I ground out. "It feels insane to be this in love with someone my mind thinks I barely know. But I can also *feel* that I've loved her for so damn long. But, Brian, it's going to ruin her. I fucking feel that too. Every time I get another hint of something, this dread and guilt inside me tears at me, screaming I'm going to destroy her. And I'm trying to soften the blow the only way I can."

"By ignoring her," he said with a shrug. "Smart."

I hissed a curse. "Fuck off, Brian."

"I mean, what do I know?" he asked, gesturing to himself. "Been married to my lady love a damn long time. Done a lot of things wrong and done a lot of things right. And, my dude, this is a *wrong*."

"I already did a wrong," I snapped, arms spread wide as if he'd somehow missed that.

His head moved in slow shakes as he turned, rooting around in one of his drawers for a hair tie to pull back his long mass of curly hair. "You don't know that, Chach," he began sadly, words eerily similar to Scarlet's. "What you said and that feeling you're having . . . it could mean anything. You could've done something, sure. Except, none of us believe you *would*. But maybe you just *knew* something, have you thought of that? You kept telling me, 'I didn't know,' so why is it so crazy to think that you just had information that was going to hurt her?"

I thought over the possibility for a while before the memories I *did* have—even if they weren't real—had me shaking my head again. "Because that isn't what this feels like. It feels like I got caught. Or like I was going to."

His brows lifted as he considered that. After a minute, he said, "But I'm telling you, you're making a mistake by keeping that damn ocean you love so much between you and your girl. You keep expecting her to leave . . . one day she just might because you're not giving her a reason to stay."

My body went tight as the impact of his words slammed into me.

As I realized that, in trying to protect Scarlet from whatever was coming, I was ruining whatever future we could possibly have once my mind finally righted itself, and our lives went back to normal.

"Right," I managed to say.

"Damn right, I'm right," he said with a huff, then turned back to his desk, bending over an outline there. Murmuring as he continued. "Always so surprised when I come out with all my awesome wisdom-ness."

I didn't respond or react. Just sat there. Thinking over the disaster in the coffee shop the day before and how there'd been nothing when I'd been in front of Trish—*Erin* and Harper this morning.

No stirrings. No beating on that invisible barrier in the back of my mind. No whisper of what I might be missing.

All while thoughts of Scarlet slipped through. Invading everything, the way she always did—even when I'd still been in the hospital. Only now, it was flashes of her. Of us.

Her smile. The way she fit perfectly against me when we slept. The way she leaned toward me when she laughed. Those fucking mesmerizing eyes.

Her soul.

Because it was *her* that I was drawn to again and again. And I was hurting her . . .

In trying to save her more pain later on, I was hurting her now.

Fuck.

I turned toward my desk, my trembling hands hovering just over the wood there as I took slow, measured breaths. Trying to calm and control the battles raging and building inside me.

My want to keep Scarlet at arm's length and my need to

hold her close. My fear of what I'd done and my rage over the inability to access my own memories.

All of them creating this chaotic, destructive storm until it felt like I was going to explode.

Grabbing one of my drawers, I yanked it open. Reaching in and looking over in surprise when I didn't find what I was looking for. Rolling my chair closer, I ground my teeth and continued trying to control my breaths as I studied the neat rows of different inks when I'd expected to find my catch-all drawer.

Slamming the drawer shut, I quickly opened and shut other drawers. Finding everything all out of order and getting more and more frustrated.

"Someone rearrange my desk?" I asked just as I opened the drawer I was looking for.

"Code," Brian said as if that should've been obvious. "We don't touch each other's shit."

Except nothing—

As soon as the thought started entering my mind, I realized it was entirely possible I'd rearranged my own desk years before, and I just didn't know.

Pushing aside the pens and gum, I grabbed one of the pencils and my earbuds. Tossing them both on the desk before reaching back in instinctively, only to remember my sketch-book wasn't in there because I hadn't brought one with me.

Just as a mumbled curse began slipping free, my fingers touched something at the back of the drawer that had a sickening chill spreading across my body. Quick and sudden.

And there it was.

That *thing* I'd been waiting for—had been *hoping* would appear this morning in the coffee shop. That pleading pounding at the back of my mind, begging me to understand. To remember.

I curled my fingers around the small, spiky ball and pulled it out of the drawer. Eyebrows furrowing as I looked at the inoffensive, crumpled-up paper in my hand. My heart pounding out this unforgiving beat because the twisting in my gut told me this was what I'd been looking for. And somehow, I knew there were more.

Dropping the paper onto my desk, I yanked my drawer open even farther and bent to look inside as I reached for the very back. That twisting becoming nearly incapacitating when I grasped at what felt like a half dozen more of the same.

Once I was sure I had them all out of the drawer and on my desk, I sat back. Staring at them as if they had the power to destroy everything.

Heart still racing and my throat feeling like it was filled with broken glass.

"Some kind of weird origami?" Brian asked as he appeared beside me, making me tense because I hadn't even heard him come near me.

"I don't know," I said as I reached for one of the papers. Curling my fingers around it, I held my fist up and looked at him. "But I have this feeling—"

"You're fucked up, you know that?" I'd asked Brian as I'd stepped back into the shop, a laugh slipping free as I'd held the balled-up paper between my fingers.

He'd straightened from where he was tattooing a guy's calf. "My dude," he'd said, one hand out to the side. "This isn't news."

An amused hum had built in my throat as I'd hurried back to my desk and tossed the weird-as-shit note that had clearly been a prank into my catch-all drawer. "Keeping this forever now. And just for that," I'd gone on before Brian could comment, "I'm going to consider not getting food for you."

Brian had slammed his hand against his chest as Jeff, one of the other artists, had loudly laughed. "Betrayal," Brian had yelled. "Absolute betrayal."

"I said consider,*" I'd called over my shoulder before heading back outside and to my truck. Another laugh had scraped up my throat as I'd glanced at my windshield where the note had been. "What an idiot."*

"I thought it was you," I told Brian, who was waving at my face as if he'd been trying to get my attention. I smacked his hand away. "I thought these were from you."

"I can't origami, my guy," he said as if I should've known.

"No, Brian," I began, then raked a hand through my hair as I shifted the paper so it was between the tips of my fingers and directly in front of his face. "I thought you were pranking me. Leaving weird notes on the windshield of my truck. Here. At the shop."

Understanding lit in his eyes half a second after confusion and denial began filtering in. "You remember something?"

"Yes. These. I remember these. And I don't know how, but I know I found out it wasn't you."

"Well, what are they?" he asked hurriedly. "You can't say *weird notes* and not open that shit up." Before I had the chance to do anything at all, he pointed at me. "You told me, 'I didn't know.' This is *it*, my guy. This is it. I know it."

My jaw worked and my head slanted because, even though I knew these notes were a major piece of whatever I was missing, I knew it wasn't everything. I knew it wasn't *it*, as Brian was saying.

Holding the note for a second longer, I finally began working it open as Brian reached for one of the others to do the same. My heart feeling like it was in my goddamn throat as I worried over what I would find on the pages.

By the time we had them all open and facing up on my desk, that dread in my stomach felt like it was devouring me.

"Fuck me, Chach," Brian muttered, voice dripping with worry and uncertainty. "Does this mean . . . no. Right?"

I tore my eyes from the papers and focused on him, unable to say the words.

Unable to make sense of anything anymore.

TWENTY

SCARLET

I didn't know what to do.

Was I supposed to call the police, or was this not one of those situations? Was I just overthinking this?

I glanced around for probably the third time since I'd walked up to our porch, unable to make myself get closer to our front door than where I stood, a good six feet away.

But it was just another morning on our street. The usual cars in the driveways and on the street. The same moms with their strollers out for a morning walk.

And one of Chase's old sketchbooks propped up against our front door.

I glanced at my phone, unsure of what to do when all I wanted was to call Chase. Beg him to get home in any way possible, but I'd just left him at the shop not even fifteen minutes before.

He needed to be there. He needed to see what memories might resurface from that place.

I couldn't pull him away from that just because I was afraid of a book.

Besides, for all I knew, one of his friends or someone in his family could've found it and dropped it off while we were gone. I stared at the leather cover as I slowly stepped closer, sure from the color and wear of it that it was one of his old ones.

With a shaky breath, I dropped to a crouch and reached out. Hand trembling as I fingered the cover, carefully working the sketchbook open and realizing when my lungs began screaming that I was holding my breath.

But with each page that only revealed more of Chase's clear style, I felt my body relaxing. The vice on my chest easing.

Grabbing the entire book in my hands, I fanned through the pages, my blood running cold when I saw the bold words and lines marking up so many of the pages I hadn't made it to.

Starting back at the beginning, I quickly moved through each page until I found the first that had been ruined by a permanent marker.

"She burned," I whispered the words out loud, my brow furrowing as I read them again and again before looking at the sketch that had been crossed out.

It was my lilies.

Something Chase sketched often—making small changes and additions each time, depending on his mood that day.

Burned. Oh my God.

The canvas. The canvas . . . they'd burned my face.

"What the fuck?" I breathed as I moved through another few pages of sketches and came to a stop at the next bold words. My gaze bouncing between the words SOMEONE ELSE and the beautiful, elaborate design Chase had made up—my name hidden within.

The next was a furiously crossed out, partially completed sketch of my face beside the words TO BE WITH YOU.

On and on it went until I'd reached the end of the book.

By the time I did, I was shaking. With fear or rage or shock, I wasn't sure. But I was trembling as I stared at the back cover of the sketchbook.

Just as I was pushing to stand, a thought hit me, and I fell to the porch instead. Sitting as I flipped back to the beginning and began the slow process of going through the entire book.

Studying each page. Each crossed-out sketch. Taking pictures when needed and typing the broken message into a note on my phone so I had it all laid out.

Waiting until I was done before calling the police and absolutely refusing to go into the house until after they'd arrived.

"I touched it," I told one of the officers as I handed him the sketchbook. "I mean, every page. I looked through it."

He just dipped his head as he took it from me with gloved hands and turned for where the cars were parked.

"Where's your boyfriend?" the officer I'd been speaking with asked, the same one Chase had spoken to the morning the canvas had been returned.

"Fiancé," I corrected, head shaking a little as I explained the entire messy situation we were in. From the wreck and coma to the amnesia and his need to be where he currently was.

"He doesn't even know I found one of his sketchbooks yet," I ended with a heaving breath. When one of the officer's brows ticked up, I hurried to add, "He will. I'll tell him. But what he's doing is important."

"For his memories," the officer said with a nod. "He mentioned something about that when we were here last time. Wasn't sure what to think *then*, considering he only said, 'I don't know if I've cheated on her or done anything that would cause someone to do this,' when I'd asked about the burned photo."

"Right," I said shakily. "Right, it's complicated."

"I see that now," he said with a sympathetic smile. "Well," he went on, folding his notebook and putting it in one of his pockets, "we'll routinely patrol around here. Make sure we don't see anyone who shouldn't be here. If you could give us a list of cars that are normally here, that would help."

I hesitated as I gestured to mine. "I teach classes out of the garage. There are always people coming and going."

"Well, we'll still keep an eye out," he said with a shrug. "Also, we know they had a key and went through a door last time since the house was locked up tight. Now, I don't know if you've changed the locks since we were last out—"

"We did."

He nodded for a while before saying, "If you gave out spare keys to the exact same people, then that doesn't help us. But if you didn't, the people without keys should be considered as possible suspects since it doesn't seem like they went into the house today, and the book was left on the porch."

"I understand," I said as my thoughts drifted to Litany. That horrible mixture of denial and sadness and fury filling my veins

"Not saying it is one of them," he added as if he hated putting the thought in my head that it could be someone close to us. As if it hadn't already *been* in my head. "Again, just something to consider." With a wave, he started backing away to the cars. "Call us if something else happens. And maybe look into getting one of those doorbell cameras."

"Right, thank you," I called out, even though I had a feeling it wouldn't be necessary.

I was positive I knew who was behind all this.

Well, *mostly*.

If I'd been one hundred percent positive, without a doubt, I wouldn't have called the police to come get the sketchbook.

But for every sign that pointed to Litany, there were bigger ones that pointed away from her and to no one at all.

———

I finished pulling my shirt over my head and hurried out of the bedroom about half an hour later when Bree yelled, "I have coffee!" just before the front door slammed shut. "Tell me *everything*."

"I adore you," I said as I ran my hand through my still wet hair from the shower, an amused huff tumbling from my lips when I actually *saw* Bree. Purse and computer bag falling off her arm as she juggled a drink carrier and phone in one hand and her keys in the other.

Absolutely chaotic.

"Wait, did you have class?"

"Um, don't even start with me, friend. Family always comes first. So does drama," she said matter-of-factly, scrunching her nose at me.

"Bree," I began hesitantly as I took the drink carrier from her, worry touching my voice, "you didn't have to skip class for this."

"Hush," she said with a wave of her hand. "Tell me all the things. What's happened since family night?"

An unsteady breath left me. "What's happened just this morning," I muttered and then gave her a look. "You might want to sit down because it's a lot."

She took a long drink of her coffee before saying, "Nope, I'm ready. Hit me."

———

Bree and I were sitting at the kitchen table by the time I'd finished telling her everything from Chase flipping out on Erin and ignoring me yesterday to meeting with Harper and Erin this morning to everything with the sketchbook.

"What a psycho," she said as she slid my phone to me after looking through the pictures of the sketchbook pages. "I mean, sorry if it *is* your friend, but come on. Who even does that?"

"I don't know," I muttered as I spun my phone around and around.

"And what did all the words end up saying?" she asked, stare drifting as she thought. "I was too focused on the crossed-out things to put them all together."

"'*She burned someone else to be with you. She'll do the same to you*,'" I said from memory. "And they only crossed out sketches that had to do with me. They left the others untouched."

Bree's eyes widened as she finished taking another sip. When she did, she whispered, "What the hell?"

"Right," I murmured, then pressed my hand on top of my phone before reminding her, "Only a small group of people knew that I was dating someone else when I met Chase. And only a handful of *those* people know where we live."

Bree was nodding as I spoke, but her head suddenly jerked back. "I'm not the psycho," she said quickly, eyes wide as if she hadn't realized until just then that I might've thought that.

A soft laugh broke from me at the absurd thought. "Hadn't even crossed my mind."

"Okay, okay." She gestured at me with her drink, her tone musing when she continued. "So, the cops think this person is someone who Chase had an encounter with, and *you* think this person could be whoever Chase thought Erin was as 'Trish.'"

I nodded before asking, "Why'd you call it an 'encounter?'" When she just looked at me in confusion, I explained, "You said it was someone Chase had an encounter with, but the cops keep hinting it's someone he had an affair with."

Bree snorted. The sound wholly amused and adorable and utterly her. "Because there is absolutely no way in hell my brother cheated on you. He's too in love with you. Like, obsessive and possessive over you in ways that are nauseating to hear about. So . . . he definitely, only, *encountered* this crazy person."

"He doesn't think so," I told her, voice soft, even though that was nothing new to Bree.

"Well, he also thought he was in love with Harper . . ." She drew out the last words, letting them linger as she fought a smile at the absurdity of it all. Lips pressed tightly together before a soft laugh left me. "Exactly. He can be wrong."

"I think that's the first time I've laughed over the whole Harper thing," I admitted.

"Oh, well, then it wasn't nearly good enough," she said with a wry smile. "Let it out, friend."

"Yeah, one day, I'll probably find it a lot more amusing. But I still needed that," I told her and gave her a grateful smile. "So, thank you."

"That's what I'm here for," she said with a nonchalant

shrug. "To drink coffee. Devour gossip. Knock my brother upside the head when he gets out of line. Fight off crazy people who leave creepy messages for you . . ."

My next laugh was louder, freer. "I don't know what we'd do without you."

"Um, nothing. Because your lives would be incredibly dull." She leaned against the table, expression set in determination. "Now, let's go down the list of things we know and put them against all the women that are regularly in your and Chase's life." She looked around, hands up. "Paper . . . I need paper and a pen. This is going to get confusing."

Confusing. Heartbreaking. Infuriating.

With all the signs pointing at my friend, I fully understood Chase's fear of getting his memories back. Because as much as I wanted to know, I wasn't ready for how badly this was going to hurt.

TWENTY-ONE

CHASE

I tore my stare from the passing neighborhood when Brandon said, "Read the notes to me," that afternoon.

A sigh bled free as I grabbed the smoothed-out papers from my pocket, my mind feeling weighed down as I unnecessarily shuffled them around since I had no idea if there was any sort of order to them.

"Is it going to make a difference?" I asked before I began.

"Can't hurt." He glanced over at me, a helpless kind of smirk slanting his mouth when he said, "Brian sort of yelled a general version of what they said in about ten seconds. So, read them. Slower."

I nodded, slapping the papers against my palm a few times before I began, jaw clenched tight and knee bouncing rapidly. "'*Have you thought about us? Does she know? Do you touch her the way you touch me? I still think about your hands on me. In my dreams, it's only you and me. I'm dying to be touched by you again.*'"

"Jesus," Brandon murmured, looking at me with a mixture

of shock and disappointment when he pulled up to a stop sign. "The hell?"

"Yeah."

"What if Brian's right?" he began, and I shook my head, already knowing what he was about to say. "What if it's just someone who's obsessed with you? Maybe we should really be focused on that whole 'I didn't know' thing."

"But that isn't what it feels like," I said irritably, getting tired of explaining this. "I see these, and that fucking pit in my stomach swallows me whole. I see these, and that part of me that *knew*—that *knows*—what they mean tries to warn me that these notes are what lead to me hurting Scarlet."

"I don't know, man," he said as he continued toward my house. "I know I've had my say on if you *did* do something to hurt Scarlet, but this doesn't feel right—not that any of it did before. But keeping proof of it right there for anyone to find?"

"I know."

"You even told Brian you thought it was him playing a prank on you."

"Brandon, I know," I muttered and dragged my free hand through my hair. As soon as he pulled onto the driveway next to Bree's car, I turned in the seat to face him. "Look, last thing I want to believe is that I did something. Swear to God, it fucking tears me up even considering it. But for as much of this can be explained one way or another, I feel it. Here." I gripped at my stomach. "It hurts her. No question."

He nodded after a while. "Yeah, all right."

"Come on," I said on a sigh as I grabbed the door handle. "Help me get my sister out of the house so I can talk to Scar."

Brandon sucked in a breath through his teeth, feigning hesitation as he got out of the Jeep and headed around the front. "I don't know. Your sister can be terrifying sometimes. If she's on bodyguard duty?"

Despite everything over the past twenty-four hours, a sharp laugh left me. "If she is, we're both screwed."

"Fuck you. You'll be on your own, and I'll be back in my Jeep so fast."

Another laugh worked from my chest. "You know Konrad would be the first one out."

"Absolutely," Brandon said, smile widening. "He'd see that look she gives and would be gone before she could turn it on him."

"Asshole," I muttered as we stepped into the house to loud music and Bree's animated voice.

When we entered the kitchen, I stopped. Head listing slightly as I took in all the papers scattered on the island and table.

"Maybe they're building a time machine," Brandon whispered as he gestured to where Scarlet stood, arms folded and paper hanging from her fingertips as she studied the paper Bree was quickly writing on.

"Idiot," I said on a breath before stepping deeper into the kitchen. "We interrupting?"

"Hey," Scarlet said as she turned to us. Stare quickly falling over me before narrowing on my face. Trying to figure out what was going on with me when I couldn't even do that. "How'd it go?"

I nodded and spared a glance at my sister before focusing on the girl who could bring me to my knees with that vulnerable, pleading stare. "Can we talk?"

"Yeah, Bree, time to go," Brandon said unapologetically.

"No, we're busy," Bree said as she waved a paper at us. "We're being detectives, *hello*. You can't just stop that."

"Is that what this is?" I asked in dry amusement.

Brandon hummed like he was trying not to laugh. "We need to let them talk, so we're going."

At that, Bree's eyes narrowed on me. "If you're about to say something that upsets Scarlet, then I'm definitely not leaving. So, you can keep whatever conversation you think you're going to have to yourself, jerk."

"There's the beginning of that look," Brandon mumbled.

"I found something at the shop," I said before he could do something, like leave.

"A sketchbook?" Bree asked on a gasp as Scarlet nodded.

Her soft words were lined with an undercurrent of fear and anger when she said, "I found something too."

I ignored my sister as I erased the last of the distance between Scarlet and me, unable to stay away from her any longer. Sliding my hand around her waist like it was the most natural thing to do, I drew her closer and asked, "What'd you find?"

"One of your old sketchbooks," she said, then gestured around as if to say Bree and the chaos in the kitchen should've explained that.

"Where?"

"The front door. It was propped up against it when I got home this morning."

My grip on Scarlet tightened. "You didn't call me?" I asked, jaw clenched tight as I thought about every possible thing that could've happened to her. "You're just in the house alone with Bree?"

"The police came," Scarlet said, trying to placate me. "They checked the house and took the book."

"And you didn't call me."

"You needed to be where you were," Scarlet said without remorse. "Clearly, if you found something."

"No, something like the picture or this morning happens, I need to be here. I need to be with you." Lifting my other hand, I cradled her neck and tilted her head back so I could study her face. All that strength and vulnerability and beauty. "Understand?"

She nodded. Her eyes searching mine as wonder and so many questions filled them.

"We're going to talk," I promised softly. "About yesterday, about today—all of it. But first, I need you to tell me if—"

"I'm not leaving," she said over me, voice trembling with emotion and exasperation.

My head shook as I brushed my thumb over her jaw. "Need you to tell me if we can work through this—whatever happened." Dropping my voice even lower, I assured her, "Never asking again if you're leaving because *that's* something I don't survive."

"Chase." My name was a strained breath as she absorbed the weight of my statement. With a shaky nod, she said, "Anything. We can work through anything, I promise."

I pressed my forehead to hers. Trying to swallow back the words that were gathered in my throat because this wasn't the time or place to say them.

But when I slanted my head, they bled free. Falling from my lips just before my mouth brushed across hers. "I love you."

One of her hands had been flat against my stomach. But at

the claim, her fingers grasped at my shirt, pulling me closer as her body seemed to sway. Falling into me and the kiss as she whispered, "I love *you*." Her voice twisting with joy and gratitude.

"I told you," Bree muttered, slowly drawing my attention to her. My eyes narrowing in a way that warned her she should be anywhere else right then. But she just lifted the paper she'd been writing on and said, "Detectives. You're the one who interrupted. Now, what'd you find?"

Scarlet just sighed as she rested her head against my shoulder, the sound all contentment and amusement and not matching her tone when she said, "Couldn't have been worse than the sketchbook."

"Wait, what was wrong with the sketchbook?" I asked, pulling away from her to look between her and Bree.

Scarlet's conflicted gaze drifted to the island. "It's all over there. I printed out the pictures I took of it before I called the cops."

I turned, looking at where Brandon had clearly been studying them. When he met my stare, he lifted a hand toward the island. "No way it isn't the same person as your notes."

"What notes?" Scarlet and Bree asked at the same time.

"Found them in my drawer at work," I said, words coming out slow and unsure as I headed over to stand beside Brandon so I could look at the printed-out pictures. "Almost as soon as I did, I remembered getting them. Or one of them, at least."

Digging the notes from my pocket again, I held my hand out to Scarlet but kept my grip on them when she began taking them. Meeting her confused and worried stare, I explained, "I kept finding them on my windshield when I was at work. I always thought they were a prank Brian was playing on me.

But I'm positive I found out before the accident that it wasn't Brian."

"Well, who was it?" Bree asked as she looked over Scarlet's shoulder once I released my hold on them.

"I don't know," I said as I returned to the photos. "I knew before the accident. Not sure how I know that, but I do."

"You can't keep saying it wasn't someone obsessed with you," Brandon muttered. "On top of all the shit they were saying, it looks like they were—and still are—doing everything to put doubt in your mind for your relationship."

"Freaking *psycho*," Bree hissed as she tossed some of the notes onto the kitchen table. "Who is this Litany chick anyway?"

"Litany?" Brandon asked in surprise, considering I hadn't mentioned we thought it might be her.

But I just slowly looked to where Scarlet was carefully watching me, knowing from the weight pressing down on her that she knew something I didn't. Had figured out something else.

With a dip of my head, I glanced at Brandon and murmured, "Had a feeling last week when she came into the kitchen. Like all that shit I've been worrying about has been because of her."

"No," Brandon said with a laugh. "There's no—"

"Even if I hadn't, you and Brian are sure it's someone obsessed with me. You know what she's like. Every word and every look is overly suggestive. And, shit, Bree just called her a psycho. Weren't you the one who said she was insane and couldn't keep it in her pants?" I gestured around us to the printed-out pictures and notes. "What about all of this doesn't scream Litany?"

"Then it's *her*," he said firmly, shifting to look at Scarlet too. "It's *only* her. Not her and Chase."

I gave him a look because I was so fucking tired of people dismissing the truth I could feel in my veins just because I didn't have full access to my memories. "Brandon . . ." I gave a rough shake of my head and then stepped back to lean against the counter.

"You called her *trash*," Scarlet said, forcing my attention back to her. When my brow furrowed, she shrugged. Her face pinching in a heartbreaking show of defeat. "I told you LT was harmless, and you said, 'she's trash.'"

I continued watching her, trying so damn hard to understand what she was telling me. "I don't . . ." My head shook. "I don't understand."

"After realizing *Erin* was the *Trish* in your memories, I couldn't figure out why your mind had changed her name. Or, at least, the person who it must have really happened with. This morning, Harper said something that reminded me of one of the times you were complaining about how LT was always around. You hated that she was always in your chair—making appointments with you every few weeks—and wanted her to get tattooed anywhere else. By anyone else. That's when you called her *trash*. I'm positive we were at the coffee shop during that conversation and that Erin was there."

"Shit," Brandon murmured just as the weight on Scarlet seemed to settle on me.

Pressing heavier and heavier as if I weren't already under water. Drowning in a sea of unknowns and so much fucking guilt.

"Wait . . . *Harper*?" I asked, head slanting. "You talked to Harper?"

"We thought you'd gone to my house to meet her," Brandon said, then gestured to Scarlet when I looked at him. "We headed straight there from the beach."

"Got it," I murmured before meeting Scarlet's stare again. "So, you already know everything that happened there?"

"From when she got there," she answered with a small nod.

"And I was caught up on your epic meltdown yesterday," Bree said cheerfully, ignoring when Scarlet hissed her name to roll her eyes at me. "Kind of mad I missed it. But I'll allow this one."

A hum rose in my throat as I let my stare fall to the floor. Thoughts racing as all the bullshit, information, and new memories from the last day fought for my attention.

"What happened yesterday shouldn't have. I apologized to Erin, and I'm so damn sorry I did that to you," I began, head bobbing quickly before I lifted my eyes to look at Scarlet again. "Think it just threw me right back to the morning—"

I gave a hard shake of my head and cleared my throat as I once again had to rearrange what was and wasn't real in my mind. "To what I *remember* as the morning I got in the wreck because it was the first time I've seen her since. But after we got home yesterday and I calmed down, I could see everything for what it was.

"Her blatant shock yesterday," I said, lifting my eyebrows because it'd been so damn obvious. I just hadn't been able to see it in the moment. "The way she'd been looking at us *then* and the way she looked at me this morning. It was all different from what I remember." A hesitant laugh crept up my throat. "Really put things into perspective when she asked about Scarlet probably five times before Harper even showed." The corner of my mouth tipped up in amusement when Scarlet rolled her eyes. "Apparently, Erin really is trying to take Scarlet from me."

One second, I was hearing the beginnings of Bree's *Duh,* and Scarlet's laugh.

The next, I was standing a couple feet away from where I'd been as everyone repeatedly said my name.

Scarlet's hands were curled around my cheeks, trying to get me to look at her, all while I held myself in place. One hand pressed firmly to the fridge. The other gripping the island so tight that my entire body was shaking.

Or maybe that was the crippling pain and sorrow. The rage. The need for revenge—to make him *hurt.*

All of it rising up and rushing through my veins.

My eyes finally locked on Scarlet's as the last of the memory faded, but the feelings stayed just under the surface. Stronger than any of the guilt or worry I'd been drowning under.

"Get out." The demand was all grit and steel as I continued staring at the girl in front of me, searching her eyes. Looking past her worry to the strength and love there. Finally tearing my gaze from her, I glanced from Bree to Brandon and repeated, "Get out."

"Rude," Bree said with a scoff.

"*Bree.*"

"Fine, fine." She lifted her hands in surrender, but just as she began collecting her bags, she asked, "Wait, what are we going to do about Litany?"

Scarlet looked toward Bree on a delay before focusing on me again. Her brow furrowed and her words coming out slow and uneven. "I don't know. I'll probably mention the sketchbook when she's here on Friday and see how she reacts."

"Wait, wait, wait," Bree said, looking at all of us like we'd missed something crucial. "Knowing she could be a total psycho, you're still going to let her come back to your home?"

"Yes," Scarlet said as she seamlessly drifted her hands across my shoulders and down my trembling arms until she was pulling my hands away from the places I'd been holding onto.

Keeping myself grounded.

Once she had her fingers laced through mine, she said, "It's the easiest way to find out since we don't know for sure. Because if I'm wrong . . ."

"You aren't wrong," I said through clenched teeth.

Her eyes snapped to mine and widened. "Is that what just happened?" she asked, voice a whisper. "Did you remember something about her?"

My head moved just enough to let her know it hadn't had anything to do with Litany. "But they need to leave."

"We are," Brandon said quickly, clapping my shoulder as he headed around the island. "Konrad and I will be here when Litany comes over," he added when Bree continued staring at all of us in shock. "Happy?"

"Fine." Bree grabbed the last of her things and blew kisses our way as she hurried through the kitchen. "Love you both the most!"

"If Litany doesn't bake something to make up for the fact that we have to deal with her . . ." Brandon gave an irritated grunt as he turned, still backing up out of the kitchen when he asked, "You gonna be good?"

I just nodded and repeated, "Out."

Once he rounded the corner into the entryway, I looked at Scarlet. My heart hammering as we waited until we were alone.

Her eyebrows twisted up in worry as she pressed herself closer to me and tightened her hold on my hands. Because, even though she didn't know, she seemed to sense that what I'd just remembered was something big.

As soon as the front door shut behind them, Scarlet asked, "What happened?"

But I simply held her there.

Studying her for a moment longer before I pulled her close. Wrapping one set of our joined hands around her back and keeping her against me as I lifted our other hands to her chin. Tipping her head back to brush my mouth across hers in a ghost of an apology.

"I love you," I whispered before pressing another soft kiss to her lips.

Her entire spirit seemed to tremble at my words.

"Chase." Worry fueled my name and lingered between us. "Chase, you're scaring me. What do you remember?"

"Because this is real," I said, grief weighing down the words as if everything was happening *right then* and not years before. "Finding out I'm gonna be a dad and having it ripped away."

I knew the second she realized I was talking about *us* and not the fake life my mind had created. Felt it in the way a little jolt went through her body before it locked up completely. Saw it in the old pain that lined her eyes.

"We'd just found out you were pregnant before it happened," I said, my head moving in the faintest nod as understanding washed through me. "It's why you don't know what happened the last time I saw your ex."

"I have an idea," she said, voice soft and filled with a heavy sadness.

I continued nodding as I stole one last kiss before pressing my forehead to hers. Letting everything I'd just seen, everything I could remember with vivid clarity, replay again and again.

The unexpected shock of finding out Scarlet was pregnant just a month after she'd first moved in with me. Something neither of us had questioned because, even though her mind had kept her from choosing between us for too damn long, I'd known exactly who her heart and body had belonged to. Whose bed she'd been in, even before she'd finally left her ex.

Our unrestrained excitement that had quickly overwhelmed every other thought and emotion.

And a few nights later, the way she'd looked when she'd come home from working at the physical therapy clinic she loved so much. Trembling. Sobbing. Unable to speak or even look at me as she'd gone straight for the bathroom, holding her ripped shirt close to her chest.

It'd taken hours before she'd broken. Crying from where she'd been curled into a ball in our bed and confessing everything as if *she'd* done something wrong. As if her ex and his cousin keeping her tied to one of the therapy tables and raping her had been *her fault*.

She'd started bleeding the next morning.

The doctor hadn't been sure if it was the stress of what'd happened or if it was something already set into motion. Whatever the reason, we'd only had five days before that unrestrained excitement was torn away. Twisted into a devastation so whole and absolute.

That night, I'd waited until Scarlet was asleep before calling Brandon. He hadn't hesitated, not that I'd expected him to.

"She made her choice, and he—fuck." I'd snapped as I'd raced through the darkened streets to the house Scarlet had shared with her ex. *"After tonight, I want him to be afraid to go near her. Talk to her. Fucking think about her. I'm done with Aaron trying to take Scarlet from me,"* I'd ground. *"Taking fucking everything from me."*

His cousin had been there too.

A few of them had. But it'd been clear really damn quick which one had helped Aaron, so Brandon and I had only focused on the two of them. Only leaving once they were unable to get up on their own.

Once I'd gotten home and had been cleaning up in the bathroom, I'd felt Scarlet's grief and confusion slam into me. Wrapping around me and making my knees shake as my throat had tightened with my own anguish.

"It's my job to take care of you," was all I'd said in explanation when I'd finally met her stare in the reflection of the mirror.

Red, swollen eyes had drifted to my busted knuckles before lifting to mine again. And I'd known in the way she was looking at me that she'd known exactly what I'd done. Where I'd gone when she'd been sleeping.

But there hadn't been any judgment there. Just the smallest whisper of gratitude before she'd turned for the bedroom again.

Giving me those minutes to be alone in my grief before I'd slipped into bed behind her. Holding her close and trying to take on her pain.

"His name's Aaron," I muttered, eyes rolling when Scarlet just continued watching me. "I'd forgotten. But that night, I told Brandon, 'I'm done with Aaron trying to take Scarlet from me.'" Brushing the tips of my fingers over her cheek, I dropped my voice even lower. "I think I just said something kind of similar about Coffee Shop Erin."

"I see," she said just as softly as if speaking any louder would destroy something about this moment we were in.

This incredibly unsettling moment because I felt ripped open. Heart exposed in the cruelest way, all while I knew— deep down—everything I was feeling and remembering happened years ago.

And somehow, beyond that and the guilt that lingered below it all, I knew I had never loved Scarlet more than right then.

In that moment.

"I love you," I said again because I needed her to hear it. To know.

Her head moved in quick, faint nods as tears gathered in her eyes. "And I love you."

"We need to talk about everything," I said as I began backing her out of the kitchen. "What happened yesterday and this morning. The notes and the sketchbook. LT . . . we need to talk."

"I know," she murmured, her fingers gripping mine tighter when I pressed her body even closer to mine to steal a brief kiss.

"First, I want to take you to bed," I said as I loosened my hold on her only slightly. "I want to show you what you mean to me and what you do to me just by looking at me. I want to hold you as you come down from the highs I'm going to push you to."

Scarlet's glassy eyes flared with need and her full lips parted on a stuttered exhale.

Turning her down the hall that led to our room, I lowered my hand to the hem of her shirt. "I want to take care of you."

"You do," she said, stopping us just as we entered the bedroom. "You've always taken care of me."

The way her voice dipped and twisted, I knew her words went so much deeper than sexual.

She meant when we'd lost the baby. She meant Aaron.

She meant in life.

My head lowered in acknowledgment. "Need to take care of you," I murmured, hoping she understood that, right then, I needed her on an emotional level just as desperately as I needed her on a physical one. "More than I've ever needed anything."

"Then take me to bed." Her words edged somewhere between a plea and a tease as she lifted up on her toes to press her mouth to mine.

Taking the bottom of her shirt from my hands, she slipped the material over her body. Revealing her bare breasts and all that flawless skin as she moved away from me, toward the bed. Holding my stare with those fucking captivating eyes as she slowly continued undressing. Body moving in these subtle sways that had my hands aching to be filled with her.

Grabbing the back of my own shirt, I pulled it over my head and let it fall to the floor as I took a step toward her. And then another as I reached for the button of my jeans.

And then she smiled.

Just the smallest twitch of her lips, but that damn look gripped my heart and had me moving. Erasing the last of the space between us and pulling her into my arms as I slanted my mouth over hers.

Tasting that smile and drinking down the hushed laugh that

moved through her and bled into the kiss. Invading my senses because that voice in the back of my head said I knew that laugh—that soft, husky sound that always made the corner of my mouth twitch with amusement. That made my heart beat a little faster because it meant *this*.

It meant her in my arms.

Body pressed to mine.

Lips moving in perfect sync with my own and making me want to stay in the moment forever.

It meant *Scarlet*.

TWENTY-TWO

SCARLET

A plea tumbled from my lips when Chase lowered me to the bed. Strong hands gripping and shouting their claim as they worked down to my thighs. Mouth moving in a slow, tantalizing trail down my stomach and over my hip until he was there.

On his knees. Broad shoulders between my legs. Fingers curling possessively into my skin. Teeth grazing the sensitive part of my thigh.

"*Chase.*" His name tore from me on a gasp that encompassed my shock and desire and absolute *need* for this man.

But he took his time.

Exploring me. Learning my body all over again as he loosened his hold to make lazy patterns along my skin while he kissed and nipped a path down my thigh and back up.

Bringing him closer and closer to where I was aching for him until my chest was pitching. Until the heat swirling in my belly begged for the promised bliss. Until every inch of my body felt alive and ultrasensitive and so attuned to his.

The way he moved. The way his mouth shifted into a

smirk against my skin when another whispered plea left me. The simple warning he offered when his hands curled tighter again.

Holding me there.

Keeping me suspended in that moment until I was nearly writhing in anticipation and need.

"Oh God," I breathed when he finally tasted me, licking me from entrance to clit in a move so slow and so sensual that it rocked me.

My body. My spirit.

My eyelids fluttered shut as I quickly reached out to hold on to anything to keep me grounded. One hand gripping his hair as the other fisted the comforter just as he did it again before setting his mouth on me.

Pulling my clit into his mouth and using the edge of his teeth to give the slightest sting of pain. Forcing a whimper from me because everything had already felt like too much before he'd even begun.

The heat in my belly.

The buzzing of my body.

And now he was there. Drawing me closer and closer as one of his hands slid from my thigh. Tormenting me with the telling, feather-soft trail he made until he was dipping a finger inside me.

Gentle.

Teasing.

So at odds as he began devouring me, but I wanted them both.

Wanted the way he tortured my clit with his tongue before pulling it into his mouth again. Wanted the way he slowly brought his finger out to tease my entrance as if he had all the time in the world to touch and explore me before he pressed two inside me again.

Each pump of his fingers was a slow devotion. Each flick of his tongue was a wicked promise.

All Chase.

All the man I'd fallen in love with and was still getting to know.

And then he curled his fingers, hitting that spot deep inside me just as he focused on my clit, and I shattered.

Body arching as all that heat raced through my veins. Burning hotter still as he continued working me, drawing out my orgasm until I was a trembling mess as I reached for him.

"I need you," I said through my thin breaths. A whimper scraping up my throat when he pressed a slow, open-mouthed kiss to my sensitive clit before moving away.

Blue eyes all fire and need as he dipped down to press another kiss to my stomach before pushing off the bed. Stare never drifting from mine as he removed his jeans and boxer briefs until he was standing there before me.

By some miracle, *whole*. Muscles rippling beneath all those colorful tattoos as he drew his hand up and down his long length. Movements still slow and measured when he knelt on the bed again and pulled me into his strong hold.

One arm rested against the comforter while the other brought my hips off the bed as he settled between my thighs. His thick cock sliding against me and promising me with what was still to come.

"God, please," I whispered when he pressed against my entrance, his body trembling with the restraint it clearly took to stay there.

Right there.

At the precipice of ecstasy.

Keeping both of us from what our bodies were craving as he moved his lips over my jaw and to my own. Pressing a slow, teasing kiss there as he gave just the slightest bit. A knowing smirk tugging at the corner of his mouth at the whimper that left me.

"That sound, Scar," he muttered as he began inching in. Taking his time. Drawing out this torturous pleasure until he was seated to the hilt. "I need you always."

I swallowed the moan that built in my throat when he pulled out, only to push back in. Again and again. Driving me out of my mind as he increased his speed until one of his hands dropped to my hip. Gripping tight and telling me exactly what he was about to do.

But just when I expected him to slam into me, hard and fast, he stilled.

I focused on his icy-blue eyes, but the question on my tongue faded to nothing at all the intensity I found there.

The love.

The certainty.

The need.

"My mind's a chaotic war of blank spaces and false memories and a life I desperately want to know," he began, voice a rough confession. "But in everything, there's you. It'll always be you."

I pressed my hand to his chest instinctively as my own heart began wildly slamming against my ribs and felt the same erratic beating against my palm. "Chase—"

"Marry me," he pled. "Marry who I was. Marry who I am. Just so long as I'll get the chance to do this with you forever."

A stunned breath fled from me. "Are you serious—of

course I'll marry you," I said, stumbling over the words before I crushed my mouth to his. "Like that was ever in question?"

"Scar . . ." He slanted his head before claiming my mouth for another kiss. This one all soft lips and slow, teasing tongues before he said, "With the shit I've put you through the last month alone? Yeah, it was in question."

"Not for me," I said resolutely.

He drew the side of his nose along mine until they were barely touching. Until he was looking down at me in a way I knew I would never forget. Because it was old and it was new, but the love there was so profound, it had chills rising on my skin.

"You consume me," he muttered before claiming *me*.

Hard.

Fast.

Drawing a cry of surprise and pleasure from me that faded into a hushed moan when he did it again. And it was all I could do to match him thrust for thrust as he drove into me with carnal abandon. To hold on when he forced me into another orgasm so sudden and unexpected. To make sure he felt my absolute love and need for him as he loved me. Fucked me. Made me his in this all-new way.

Hard and savage. Slow and sensual.

Perfect.

I gripped him tighter when he stilled above me, his body tensing and muscles trembling as he poured his release inside me and stole the remaining pieces of my soul.

Because this wasn't just us coming together emotionally and physically and falling in love. This wasn't just Chase asking me to marry him.

This was having everything—a life and a future—only to

have it ripped from us. This was somehow finding our way back to this exact place despite it all.

The pain of what we'd gone through only made it more profound.

More beautiful.

A shudder worked through my body and seemed to pass to his when he pulled out. His chest heaving and lips hovering just over my own for those long moments before he stole a soft, slow kiss. Lips barely brushing against my own. Tongue nothing more than an affectionate tease.

And then his hands were moving. Wrapping around me as he shifted us so we were on our sides and facing each other. Laying in silence as we continued coming down from the intensity of the moment.

It wasn't until both our bodies had stilled from the subtle aftershocks that he said, "I can feel it."

My eyebrows lifted in question, but I just wove one of my hands through his and waited for him to explain.

"You know when you can't think of a word, and it feels like it's right there, on the tip of your tongue?" When I hummed in acknowledgment, he said, "That's what it feels like. Like I know what happened. Like I know my life, my *real life*, but I can't fully grasp it yet. It's just sitting there. On the edge of my mind. Waiting to be freed by that one push that'll send everything rushing to the surface."

"Is that a new feeling?" I asked, an appreciative sound rising in my throat when his fingers began trailing over my spine.

"Started noticing it in the kitchen after I remembered what happened to you," he confirmed as his hand drifted over my hip and between our bodies to brush along my stomach. "Is that why we don't use condoms?"

"You don't remember that," I said in understanding, my head bobbing softly as I tried to clear my throat—the emotion that built there swiftly and unbidden. "At first, it was because we were careless. Got swept up too fast in the moments and didn't stop to think until it was too late. Then because we couldn't imagine anything else. But after losing—"

I swallowed again and again, eyes unfocused for long moments as flashes of those days tore through my thoughts before I could block them. The pain and humiliation. The agony and sorrow. All of it stealing the small joy we'd had.

"We decided we'd let whatever happened happen," I finally said, lifting one of my shoulders.

His eyes searched mine, and I could see the question lingering within that well of worry and pain. Wondering if anything had happened *since*.

"It's just been us," I answered when nearly a minute passed in tense silence, the tremor in my voice betraying me when I added, "Funny how life works, huh?"

His eyebrows slanted low just before his forehead fell to mine. Head moving subtly as he roughed out, "Nothing about that's funny."

He captured my lips before I could respond and easily parted them the way he'd always done. Silently asking. Softly demanding. And then he was kissing me . . .

Slowly. Deeply. Sliding his tongue against my own in a gentle, adoring dance as he continued that soft brush against my stomach.

"One day," he breathed against my lips.

"I know." I wasn't sure if there was any strength behind the words or if I'd only mouthed them, but it didn't matter. Chase heard them all the same. *Felt* them.

One day, we would have what we'd lost.

One day, we would have the wedding we'd been planning.

One day, our lives would be the way they used to.

First, we needed to make it the rest of the way over this hurdle that was doing everything to break us.

TWENTY-THREE

CHASE

"Are we just going to keep staring at the box?" Konrad asked a couple days later, stretching his arms across the island and nearly touching the pink box that sat in the middle, practically begging to be opened.

"Go ahead," Brandon said with a smirk. "Open it and see what happens."

Konrad pushed back to cross his arms over his chest. Eyes rolling irritably. "Asshole," he murmured.

Brandon and Konrad had shown up with breakfast long before Scarlet's friends had arrived for their Friday morning workout, as promised. None of us had said a word to each other or Litany when she'd come running in to toss the box of pastries on the island and use the bathroom.

She also hadn't done or said anything other than giving us a flirty wink with a *"Boys"* as she'd hurried for the garage.

I hadn't known what to think. Both Konrad and Brandon had sworn up and down that she'd never been that tame, and none of us knew what it could mean.

But we were waiting.

We'd *been* waiting.

Because, as Scarlet had told me, Litany came into the house after every session, without fail. Scarlet was also planning on mentioning the sketchbook and notes to the girls to see how LT reacted.

If she gave herself away then, we'd clearly know. If she tried to skip coming into the house, we'd know.

Any way it could possibly go, we'd know. I felt the certainty of it down to my soul.

"They should be done," I muttered as I glanced at the clock for what felt like the hundredth time since Litany had first come running through. My body practically buzzing with all the restless energy built up inside me.

"Haven't heard any yelling yet," Brandon said, eyebrows lifted knowingly.

"You think she's going to keep pretending," I said, already understanding the look without needing him to explain.

"I just don't think anyone would give it up that easily after what they've been doing," he said, one hand raised placatingly. "But being Litany? She's crazy enough without all this other shit on top of it. There's no way she's going to be like, 'Yeah, you know what, I did all that.'"

My head moved in tight, fast jerks. "She's going to fess to it," I said undoubtedly. "I know she is."

That feeling I'd gotten the other day, as if my memories were on the tipping point of being freed, had only grown. Now every little thing felt like it might break that invisible barrier. Like the softest sound or the slightest movement had that dam weakening. Had my memories crying out. Grasping. Begging for me to just reach out and *take* them.

"But if she doesn't—"

"I'm anxious as fuck," I snapped, cutting Brandon off. "It feels like I'm crawling out of my skin. It's coming to a head. I know it is."

"Chase," he began, voice gentle but no less firm. "I'm on your side. I want this to end for you."

"Then trust me."

"All right," Brandon said, lowering his head. "All right, man." Reaching forward, he snatched the box and dragged it toward him.

"Finally," Konrad said on a near groan, only to let his head fall back with a heaving sigh when the door to the garage opened. "Damn it."

"Just in time!" Litany said with a giddy smile as she practically danced our way. Touching Brandon's shoulder, she trailed her fingers toward the other side, looking from the box to the three of us. "I put a little something *special* in there this time. Let me know what you think."

With a much more understated wink than before directed at me, she turned and left for the hall.

And it took every ounce of agitated energy I had to just watch her leave. Not to demand answers from her.

"Every time," Konrad muttered as Brandon pushed the box, sending it across the island to where I was standing. Bouncing. On the verge of pacing.

"Aside from her ruining food," Brandon began as he leaned across the counter, voice a whisper, "she didn't look like someone who's about to get caught."

"She looks like she thinks she's getting away with it," I said under my breath. "Remember the way she winked at us before they began working out?"

"I like to forget what she does," Konrad murmured as

Brandon lifted his chin in confirmation.

"She just winked at me. It wasn't anything like that. It wasn't anything like the way she looks at us when she's being overly flirty or sexual." Before I could tell them how she'd looked at me the week before, as if she'd known me in a way I really hoped she didn't, my phone vibrated from where it rested on the counter.

"It's Scar," I murmured as I snatched up the phone and opened the message just as another one came through. The smallest whisper of doubt pushing into my veins when I read the words there.

Scarlet: *She asked questions the way she does about everything. Not too interested. Not interested enough. She didn't seem suspicious in any way.*

    Scarlet: *Sam's coming to keep an eye on LT when she's around you.*

"She didn't pick up on anything," I murmured, answering their unspoken question as Konrad and Brandon eagerly waited.

"I don't think Litany's going to admit to it," Brandon began, his low voice dropping to a nearly imperceptible whisper when the door to the garage opened. "But I can't see how it's anyone else."

"It can't be," I murmured, then lifted my chin at Samantha when she came in. Steps hesitant and eyes wide as she looked around for her cousin. "Bathroom."

"Of course," she said with an affectionate eye roll as she came to a stop near me and opened the pastry box. "I just always figured she went straight to making her coffee that she pretends Scarlet doesn't know about."

I grunted in understanding and pointed at the scone she'd pulled out just as Konrad said, "I wouldn't eat that."

Samantha's hand stilled with the scone in the air as she looked around at us. "Why?"

"She said she put something *special* in them," Brandon informed her as I went back to eyeing the hall.

Samantha laughed, soft and gentle, as she broke a piece off the scone to eat it. And something about that sound had my head slanting. Had that dam weakening a little more. Had my gaze darting to her for a second. Then two, before I went back to waiting for her cousin to reappear.

"She puts something *special* in everything she makes," she told the guys. "Like cinnamon or cayenne pepper where you wouldn't expect it. She isn't poisoning you."

"Wait until she leaves?" Konrad asked Brandon, and Brandon murmured his agreement, forcing another laugh from Samantha.

"You're all so weird," she said as she turned toward me, her voice dropping to a whisper. "So, how are you doing with everything? Scarlet seems pretty freaked out."

"We're fine," I said through clenched teeth. But that anxiousness, that feeling like I was going to crawl out of my goddamn skin, was overwhelming now.

"Chase," Samantha breathed as her hand fell to my trembling arm.

My gaze snapped back to her. Body already shifting instinctively away from her when it happened.

That break.

That flood.

And it about took my knees out with the strength of it.

"If you wanted me wet, you could've just asked me to come stare at you instead of making me work out for the last hour," LT had said as she'd come walking through the kitchen one Friday morning, eyebrow raised suggestively as if I might've missed exactly what she'd said.

"Jesus Christ, LT," I'd whispered, head shaking as I'd gone back to making coffee. Voice all an irritated mumble when I'd reminded her, *"Still engaged. You were just out there with my fiancée. You're one of her closest friends. Don't know why."* The last I'd added under my breath, too soft for LT to have heard.

"Details, details," she'd said in a singsong voice as she'd walked toward the hall that led to our guest bathroom. *"Don't miss me too much. I'll be back for you soon."*

My head had swung toward the sound of the door opening once again, but my disappointment at not seeing Scarlet there had quickly shifted to irritation when Samantha had appeared instead. "Get control of your cousin."

"What'd she do now?" she'd asked, eyes rolling playfully.

"What she always does. And she made an appointment with me for tonight—another appointment," I'd ground out as I'd turned to face her, setting my mug on the counter as I had.

One of Samantha's eyebrows had lifted. "Are you saying you don't like having clients?"

I'd given her a dry look because she'd known damn well that hadn't been what I'd meant. "I'm saying I don't like having to tattoo someone who's constantly telling me what they want to do to me."

"And what about me?" she'd asked as she stepped close. Too close. Just as I'd begun taking a step back, she'd asked, "What if it was me who made the appointment? What if it was my body your hands were on?"

My feet had become one with the hardwood so abruptly that I'd had to reach out and grab the counter to steady myself. My head had slowly slanted before shaking as if I might've somehow heard her wrong.

Taken Samantha's soft, gentle tenor and twisted it with her cousin's words.

But before I could ask her to repeat what she'd said, Samantha had stepped even closer, her voice dropping softer still when she'd asked, "Do you think about me when you're with Scarlet?"

What the fuck?

"Samantha, what the hell are you talking about?" I'd asked as confusion and doubt slammed into my veins.

Because, for just a second, I'd been sure it was a joke. That she was fucking with me.

But then those notes I'd been finding on my truck had rushed to the forefront of every thought, and I'd gotten a horrible, sinking feeling they weren't a prank Brian had been pulling on me.

"Do you know what it's like to watch you with her when I know what it's like to be touched by you? When I know you want me too?"

"Touched?" I'd ground out as she'd spoken, nearly choking over the word. "What the fuck, Samantha? Stop." The harsh word had snapped through the kitchen and reverberated back to us as I'd grabbed her wrist and shoved it away when she'd reached for me.

The tips of her fingers having just barely grazed the bottom of my shirt as if she'd done that move so many times when I'd only ever hugged her before then.

"The hell is wrong with you?"

"Oh?"

My head had shot up at the unexpected voice to find LT standing just inside the kitchen, eyes wide with surprise and a hint of amusement as she'd looked between the two of us. Samantha's wrist still in my grasp. Our bodies only inches apart because Samantha had somehow gotten closer.

"Not what—"

"Didn't realize there were so many of us vying for your attention," LT had said over me, all while I'd roughly shaken my head and forcibly moved Samantha farther from me.

"Not what it looks like," I'd finally said through clenched teeth, words hard and sure.

LT had just shrugged. "Guess we'll see about that." She'd gestured from me to Samantha and back again as she'd continued through the kitchen, toward the entryway. "I think I'll skip my coffee today . . . leave you two alone."

"You don't need to leave," I'd said quickly, ready to fucking beg Litany to stay anywhere near me for the first time since I'd met her.

"Oh no, you two clearly need privacy. Maybe a bedroom?" she'd offered with a wicked laugh, then had hurried to brush off the fear and rage I could feel bursting from me. "Don't worry, I won't say anything to a certain fiancée you like to keep reminding me you have. Think of ways to bribe me with keeping quiet, handsome. I'll see you tonight."

"Stop her," I'd begged as I'd turned back to Samantha. "Tell her there's nothing happening between us."

Samantha had just given me a wounded look, but her voice had remained assertive. "I'll be your secret, but I'm not going to lie to her."

"My secret?" The words had come out on a heaving breath and twisted laugh. "What secret? We're nothing. You are nothing to me other than Scarlet's best friend." Gesturing toward the garage, I'd stepped closer to Samantha. My anger leaking into every strained word. "You're her best fucking friend. What the hell are you trying to do right now?"

"I'm not nothing to you; I've felt the way you touch me," she'd said with a confidence that would've been laughable if it were any other situation. Before I'd been able to remind her that I'd never touched her in the way she was implying, she'd continued. "And you and I both know she'll just do to you what she did to Aaron."

My head had jerked back. "The hell did you say?"

"She burned him to be with you. She'll do the same to you."

"No, see, that was something that destroyed her," I'd said through clenched teeth. "That wasn't something she did to him —something she went through—for the hell of it. And that isn't something that'll happen again."

"Maybe it already is," she'd said as if she'd known something I hadn't.

But I hadn't believed her for a goddamn second.

"I know you don't want to be the one to leave her, but I know you want to be with me. So, it's nothing to help us get what we both want." An icy trail of dread had worked down my spine when Samantha had looked at me like she was about to offer me the damn world. "A mention that you might not be what she really wants. That she'd be happier with someone

else. A whisper about someone else's perfect qualities. Someone close to her. Someone she sees every day. Someone like Brandon . . ."

I'd entered some Twilight Zone. I'd been sure of it.

"The hell?" I'd breathed, my head shaking as I'd struggled to wrap my head around everything—literally everything— Samantha had been doing to us. "That's my relationship you're fucking with. Brandon's my best friend. He's married.*"*

"I want to stop hiding," she'd said as she'd once again moved closer to me. "And I know you do too."

"There's no hiding," I'd said furiously. My voice low but firm as I'd waved my hand in front of her. "There's nothing happening between us. And I've never fucking touched you."

In a move that had been nearly too quick to prevent, Samantha had grabbed my hand and tried pressing it to her breasts.

"Enough," I'd snapped as I'd ripped my hand from hers. "You need to—" The words had died on my tongue as soon as it had clicked into place.

The move she'd just tried to make. Where she'd tried to place my hand.

The tattoo I'd given her—that she'd specifically asked for.

"Samantha . . ." I'd begun, my tone low and filled with warning. "Samantha, that was a tattoo session."

Her head had quickly shaken. "It wasn't just that. Not with the way you touched me."

"Yes, it—" I'd sucked a breath in through my teeth when the words had come out too sharp and too loud. Waiting until I'd had a little more control, I'd informed her, "I literally have no choice but to put my hands on people when I'm tattooing them, and you wanted your sternum tattoo to go between and

directly beneath your breasts. My hands had to be on you when I was tattooing you. You and I both needed to move your breasts when I was at certain angles. That was it. Nothing more."

"Chase . . . no. No," she'd said adamantly, her voice twisting with a plea. "No, you're saying that because you're scared to leave—"

"Sam?" Scarlet's voice had filtered into the house at the exact moment the door to the garage had opened.

And I'd frozen. A chill had burst through my veins as if I were about to be caught doing something I shouldn't have.

Only I hadn't done anything except gotten trapped in the weirdest conversation of my life.

"Oh, hey," Scarlet had continued, a bemused look crossing her face when she'd noticed us standing there. "Saw your car was still here. Wanted to make sure you were okay." She'd glanced between us, and her voice had dipped with worry when she'd hesitantly asked, "Is everything okay?"

Samantha had laughed the way she always had. Soft. Gentle. Without a damn hint as to what had been happening in the kitchen. "You know Chase . . . he's just complaining about LT being LT."

"Chase," Scarlet had whispered, a pleading look crossing her face because she hated whenever I let my irritation with LT spill onto her other friends.

But this was so far past that.

I hadn't been able to stop myself from quickly looking between Scarlet and Samantha as that rage and confusion and aggravation had slowly built in me again.

I'd wanted to tell Scarlet that her best friend, the seemingly sweet, caring one of them all, had been leaving me fucked up notes and had twisted a tattoo session that Scarlet had been present for into some sort of foreplay. Had made it all up in her head that we were having some kind of affair because of it.

But I'd just stood there. Unable to speak because I was still too stunned by it all. More than that, I was terrified Scarlet would believe them.

Samantha was her *best friend. The person Scarlet went to for everything.*

How the hell was I supposed to tell the woman I loved that her best friend had been waiting and hoping for us to end for at least a year? That she was trying to ensure it would happen? That she was unable to be convinced that we weren't having an affair? How was I supposed to convince my fiancée that I hadn't done a thing when two of her closest friends had 'proof?'

My lips had parted as a dozen explanations had built and caught in my throat when I'd focused on Scarlet again.

Because I didn't know how to put that doubt in her mind.

I didn't know how to potentially destroy us that way.

I had no fucking clue what I was going to do.

TWENTY-FOUR

CHASE

I staggered to the side before I was able to steady myself, my hand shooting out to grip the kitchen counter as the force of everything slammed into me and nearly dropped me to my knees.

Random pieces of my life.

The memory.

The shock of what'd happened . . . *again*.

Holy shit, holy shit, holy shit.

Looking up, I managed to focus on Konrad and Brandon's concerned expressions before I realized someone was touching my arm. Gripping it.

Just as I began glancing toward the person standing at my side, I ripped my arm away from the slightly possessive hold when I remembered Samantha had been there—laughing at us and eating the scone. Remembered her laugh and the way she'd said my name and *her fucking touch* that had been what set everything off.

"What the fuck?" I yelled as I turned on her, already backing away to put the necessary space between us and not missing for a second the hurt that tore across her face before she looked between the three of us, feigning confusion.

"What happened?" she asked as Brandon and Konrad stood from the barstools, calling my name as I quickly shook my head. "Chase—"

"Stop," I ground out, trembling hand shaking as I held it in front of me, warning her not to come toward me. "Stop saying my name. Stop acting like you don't have a goddamn clue what's going on."

"Oh?"

My head snapped to the side at LT's voice, giving me the wickedest sense of déjà vu when I found her standing just inside the kitchen with a satisfied smirk.

Folding her arms over her chest, she slanted her head and asked, "Now, doesn't this look familiar?"

"Nothing," I seethed. "Not a goddamn thing has ever happened between us, and you know that."

"*What*?" Brandon demanded as Konrad sucked in a stunned breath.

"Do I?" LT asked mockingly, her expression showing just how much she was enjoying this.

"I know what you tried to do," I shouted. "I fucking know."

"What is going on?"

And there it was.

That ice that splintered in my veins and gripped at my lungs at the sound of Scarlet's voice, making it difficult to breathe. That guilt that had been a living, breathing thing inside me for weeks, even if I'd been misinterpreting it.

It'd been warning me of this moment when I would have to tell Scarlet what happened—to hurt her the way this was clearly going to. To cause that doubt I'd been agonizing over all those weeks ago and potentially lose the woman I loved because this was my word against two of Scarlet's best friends.

One who would do anything to bring me down and another who was wholly convinced we were in love with each other.

And that person? Scarlet trusted her with her life.

"Chase," Scarlet said, *begged*, when the edgy silence in the kitchen only lingered and grew heavier.

Turning fully to face Scarlet, I drew in a slow, steeling breath as my fear of the outcome of this conversation threatened to cripple me right there.

This was my fucking nightmare.

This was the end of my twisted memories—my false life. Right here.

"What we thought, what *I* was worried I did, never happened," I muttered as I gestured weakly to her. But the relief we should've felt over that revelation wasn't there, even for Scarlet, because she knew from the tension building and my tone that I wasn't finished. "But I didn't know how to tell you what was going on."

She shifted. Straightened. Seeming to draw herself up as if putting on armor as she glanced around at the five of us before focusing on me. With a slight lift of her chin, she asked, "Right before your accident?" When I nodded, she asked, "What was going on?"

I stood there for what felt like an hour. Trying to figure out the best way to tell her and coming up empty, just as I'd done in the days before my wreck.

Because there was no *easy* way to tell her everything.

Samantha had been the only one of Scarlet's friends that she'd confided in when Aaron and his cousin had abused her. She'd been the only one Scarlet had let come over when we were grieving the loss of our baby—the only one I'd trusted to stay with Scarlet when Brandon and I had left that night, seeking vengeance. She had been the first person Scarlet called when we'd gotten engaged and was supposed to be her maid of honor because she was *everything* to my fiancée.

How was I supposed to convince Scarlet that she was lying?

I slowly looked at Samantha to find her watching me with the same expression she'd given me a month ago. As if she'd done all of this for me— for *us*.

What the actual hell?

"It wasn't LT," I finally said, voice gruff and full of apology. "The notes I used to get on my truck, and I'm assuming the canvas and my sketchbooks too, were all Samantha."

Scarlet's chest shook with the force of her amused exhale, relief filling her features as she drew in another large breath. "Funny."

My head listed as apology after apology after explanation gathered on my tongue, trying to figure out how to fall.

And when nothing came out, when no one laughed with her or offered anything else, Scarlet's expression fell. Disbelief and surprise and hurt clashing on her beautiful face as she took a step back. "What? No. No, because—*no*."

"Scar—"

"No," she said firmly, a shockwave of that pain I'd been anticipating bursting from her and slamming into me, gripping at my already straining lungs.

"Chase wants to be with me," Samantha said confidently as I quickly shook my head, slashing my hand through the air as if I could physically stop her from speaking.

"You need to stop with that shit." Keeping my hand out, I

pointed at Samantha as I focused on Scarlet's horrified face. "I tattooed you and Samantha on the same day—the sternum tattoos. Right? Hers was different. Bigger. More elaborate and went beneath her breasts. Because of that day and the fact that I had to *touch* her to complete the tattoo, she got it in her head that I wanted her. But you were right there the entire time; you saw what I was doing. I never actually fucking touched her the way she's insisting I did."

Scarlet just looked from me to Samantha, blinking slowly as if she was in a daze.

"I thought Brian was leaving the notes for me. I thought it was a joke until, a few days before my accident, Sam started saying all this shit that made me realize they'd been from her. *Informed* me she was my secret, even though all of that was news to me right then. Said she knew I wanted to be with her and knew you would leave me—cheat on me the way you'd cheated on Aaron. So, she was trying to make sure it happened."

"What?" Scarlet asked, the word barely audible as she pressed a hand to her stomach. Her stunned yet condemning stare shifting to Samantha as I went on.

"She'd been telling you things to question being with me and to get it in your head that you might want to be with someone else—Brandon specifically."

"Wait, what?" Brandon asked as a shocked breath ripped from Scarlet.

And I could see on Scarlet's horrified expression and in her devastated eyes that Samantha had been doing exactly that. Maybe not in a way that Scarlet had ever realized until just then, but she'd been planting those seeds.

"All of it was to get you to leave me so she and I could be

together because she'd created this entire damn thing in her head. And in the middle of that," I ground out, my eyes narrowing on where LT was standing, still looking pleased with herself. "LT came out of the bathroom when I'd been stopping Samantha from touching me and took it as something it wasn't. She'd already had an appointment set up with me that night and came in, wanting me to *do something for her*—preferably *with her*—to keep her silent. When I told her she could fuck right off and that I hadn't actually done anything with Samantha, she said you wouldn't believe that, considering she'd seen it with her own eyes." I let my stare drag back to Scarlet when I added, "You know LT. She had a really active imagination about what *could've* been happening when she'd found Samantha in the kitchen with me.

"I didn't *want* to think you'd believe either of them," I went on, shoulders jerking up agitatedly. "But I couldn't be sure when one friend was saying she saw it and your best friend had imagined an entire affair and couldn't be convinced it wasn't happening." I gestured from LT to Scarlet, remorse dripping from me when I said, "So, I told LT to go ahead and tell you, then kicked her out of the shop, hoping she'd want to hold it over my head instead. Hoping it would give me time to figure out what to do."

"Why didn't you just tell me?" Scarlet asked, voice shaking as her eyes shone with tears. "I—" She gestured between Samantha and me. "Didn't I walk in that day? I did!" Her head moved in a chaotic mess of nods and shakes. "No one said anything to me. *You* said Chase was complaining about LT." She threw the last accusation at Samantha, glaring at her friend as all that pain and doubt bled from her.

And that doubt . . .

Fuck, I didn't know who it was directed at, but it terrified me more than anything had in my entire life because I couldn't lose Scarlet.

"We weren't ready for you—"

"There's no *we*," I snapped, cutting Samantha off as my body trembled with the adrenaline and fear pumping through my veins. "There has never been anything between us. I don't know how you deluded yourself into believing everything in the first place, and to pull all the shit you have been? Not just before, but recently? What were you trying to do? Scare your best friend on top of trying to make her leave me?"

"I wanted you to remember."

"Get out," Scarlet said, voice weighed down with all that confusion and pain, and those two simple words had my heart faltering.

But when I finally managed to look at her, Scarlet's hatred was focused on the girl near me. "You've been there for me through everything," she began, voice thick with emotion and grief. "I always thought you were trying to be a voice of reason. Wanting me to see both sides because you'd be fully in support of Chase one minute, and the next, you'd make it sound like you've always doubted him. And I never—*God*," she cried out.

"You were just gushing over the news that Chase asked me to marry him again," Scarlet went on. "You *just* asked me how we were going to celebrate, and all this time—" She swiped angrily at the tears that slipped down her cheeks, eyes narrowed in a lethal mixture of rage and devastation when she said, "You're a delusional sociopath. You need help. But I won't be there when you get it. Get the fuck out of my house."

I glanced over when I felt eyes on me and found Samantha

looking up at me as if she expected me to stand by her side. Defend her.

Leave with her.

A sneering laugh left me as I jerked my chin toward the entryway. "You heard her."

"Chase—"

"Out," I said through clenched teeth. "We're going to have a massive fucking problem if you try to contact us in any way again. Understand?"

If it hadn't been for the flash of anger in her eyes, I wouldn't have known if she'd actually heard a word I'd said—took them as *truth*. Then again, I wasn't sure what to think with Samantha anymore. She'd played a role so well for so long. Never letting anything leak out until she wanted people to see it.

"Take your cousin with you," Konrad called out when Samantha finally turned to leave, never bothering to even meet Scarlet's devastated and infuriated stare.

"You're going to miss me," Litany said with a dramatic sigh as she started following Samantha toward the entryway and came to a staggering stop when Scarlet grabbed her shoulder.

"I haven't begun to fully grasp what Samantha was doing," Scarlet began, voice a destructive mixture of hatred and sorrow, "but I know exactly what you did and what you tried to do." Steeling her jaw when it trembled, she narrowed her eyes at LT. Head slanting slightly when she continued. "If you ever come near my fiancé or say anything suggestive to him again, I will remember that you tried to blackmail him into fucking you, and I won't hold back. If I were you, I would stay far away from all of us. Take your fucking pink box too."

Litany's eyes were rolling when she turned from Scarlet's grasp and headed for where the pastries sat at the edge of the counter. For once, she didn't look at—or say anything to—Brandon, Konrad, or me as she grabbed the box and left.

The silence that filled the house once they were both gone was something in itself.

Relieving and guilt-ridden.

Thick and light.

Swirling with all that confusion and pain.

"I'm sorry," I said, finally breaking it just as Brandon murmured, "We should probably go."

I didn't look in his direction, just gave a single dip of my head as I kept my focus on the girl standing on the opposite side of the kitchen. Back straight. Arms wrapped tightly around her waist. Beautiful face creased with disbelief and devastation.

"Why didn't you tell me?" she asked once the guys had left as well.

"I didn't know how."

"But you didn't do anything," she said as if that should've taken away the fear I'd been living under.

As if it wasn't still there, lingering just beneath the surface.

"She was convinced we were together, Scar," I reasoned. "LT was coming up with shit like she didn't have a problem with taking me down. I was terrified that, even if you didn't believe them, it'd still put that doubt in your head, and it would destroy us anyway."

"You still should've told me," she said, voice shaky from her lingering emotion. "When I walked in that day or after she left. That night—*anything*."

"I panicked," I admitted, pressing a hand to my chest. "I was still reeling from the insanity of the entire thing, and I panicked. But then hours passed and a day and another, and I felt trapped by the entire thing because LT was trying to make it worse, and I'd already done that by not telling you right away."

A harsh breath scraped up my throat. "I remember being fucking terrified when you went to brunch that weekend and for what they would say the next time they were all here. I knew I needed to talk to you before then, and then . . ." I flung out my arm as a deprecating sound built in my chest. "I was distracted."

"What?" she asked, the word a little unsure.

"The morning of the accident." My head bobbed quickly before shaking. "I don't remember driving, but I remember that morning. I was . . . Jesus, I was so on edge. I kept thinking I needed to get back to you. That I needed to just talk to you. Everything Brandon did nearly set me off—it'd been like that all weekend."

"Brandon," she echoed, eyes wide as she took a couple steps toward me. "What did he do?"

"Nothing, but Samantha had gotten in my head," I admitted ruefully. "I get it now . . . why I woke up thinking I'd been in some sort of love triangle with Brandon and Harper. Because Sam was trying to get you to want Brandon. To fall for him and leave me for him."

"That isn't going to happen," she said without an ounce of hesitation. "You should've known that *then*."

"I know," I said quickly, even as my head listed hesitantly. "Just like you should've known that all I see is you. Not Harper. Still, when that gets in your head . . ."

Scarlet studied me for a few seconds, a crease forming between her eyebrows before she conceded with a nod.

A pained laugh wrenched from me. "And that's why I didn't know how to tell you what was happening. Because *that's* how easy Samantha could've gotten in your head."

"No," she said resolutely. "No, *you* were convinced you were in love with Harper. *You* had memories with Harper. That's what got in my head. Someone else trying to convince me they're with you isn't going to do anything because *I know you*."

Shame pushed into my veins when I realized I'd been so gripped by my fear of Scarlet potentially doubting me that I hadn't noticed I'd doubted *her*.

I'd doubted the strength of her love for me and let it mix with my need for her until it had filled me with a fear so consuming that it'd ruled every thought and decision that weekend.

"I should've trusted you," I murmured, head nodding. "I should've told you. But that weekend . . . I remember watching you and Brandon. Listening to every conversation the two of you had while we were surfing and at family night. Looking for any signs and getting irrationally jealous if you so much as laughed at anything he said."

"Chase—"

"I know," I repeated, hands raised placatingly. "Scar, I know. Like I said, Samantha had gotten in my head with that. And it only made me worry more that she'd get in yours. But that last morning, I nearly punched him so many times for literally nothing. All I could focus on was getting home to you. All I could think about was getting everything out in the open. I was distracted as hell."

Scarlet's expression fell when she finally realized what I was saying. "I've heard Brandon and Konrad describe what happened that morning," she said softly, slowly, as if making sure I was listening. Making sure I *believed* her. "There was no way you could've prevented that wreck."

I lifted a shoulder because she couldn't know that.

No one could.

"I'm sorry," I whispered, bringing us back to the beginning. "I'm sorry for what she did and what she's been doing. I'm sorry you're losing your best friend. I'm sorry for not telling you the second you walked in."

A shaky smile tugged at one side of Scarlet's mouth. "You did this time." At the slant of my head, she explained, "The second I walked in, you told me everything."

"Remembered that feeling," I said as I held out a hand toward her, giving her a choice in coming to me, and felt some of that strain ease when she moved toward me.

Sliding her hand into mine and pressing against my side without hesitation.

"That same heartbreaking pain and gut-wrenching worry because I knew there was a *chance* you'd believe them. Knew there was a *chance* I could lose you. But I knew exactly what would happen if I kept it from you, and I wasn't going through that again."

Her fingers tightened around mine for a moment as if in gratitude, but she didn't say anything. Just let me hold her there in the kitchen as she tried to absorb everything while I did the same . . . all over again.

Letting my memories that had been unlocked consume me and mix with the ones that had been a constant this past month. Finally seeing them the way Scarlet had from the beginning.

My life fully twisted around to create another one so similar and different at the same time.

And at the center of it was the girl in my arms, even if my mind had tried to erase her.

"What do we do now?" Scarlet asked a while later.

"Chinese?"

"*Chase*." My name rushed from her on a saddened laugh as she pushed at my stomach. But instead of moving away, she wrapped her arms around my waist and looked up at me, giving me the perfect view of her.

Those dark, hypnotic eyes.

Those full lips.

That smile that had captured my attention from the very first night. Slow, sensual, fucking breathtaking.

She pushed up on her toes to press her mouth to mine. The kiss soft and unhurried before she settled on her feet, as if she just needed that connection again after the shit we'd gone through. "I can see you're thinking about something. Talk to me."

I held her closer as I studied this girl who was all wicked temptation and the brightest light. This girl who had taken my heart and refused to give it back from the moment she'd walked into the tattoo shop. This girl who had been through Hell and back with me so many times already and was still there in my arms.

Letting my fingers trail along her jaw, I tipped her head up and slanted my mouth over hers. Hovering there for a moment as more of our life raced through my mind. "Just remembering."

TWENTY-FIVE

SCARLET

Anna slowed as she neared the table in our favorite brunch spot the next morning, eyebrows bunching together as she pointedly took in the only other chair at the table opposite me.

"Where is everyone?" she asked as she slid into the seat, still holding onto her bag like she might have to get right back up and leave.

I pushed a mimosa her way and watched as her eyebrows rose.

"Oh, it's one of those mornings?"

"I already have an entire carafe on the way," I informed her as I drained the rest of my first one.

"Well, hold on, friend. Let me catch up." She unceremoniously dropped her bag to the floor and hurriedly grabbed the champagne flute. "What are we celebrating?"

"We aren't."

She paused with the flute halfway to her lips before leveling me with a look. "I already have my alcohol, so start spilling."

I drew in a slow breath and did exactly that.

———

"I think I'm in actual shock," Anna said after we'd polished off the carafe of mimosas. "Like *literal* shock. I would've understood if it'd been LT—she'd make sense. But *Samantha*?"

"I know," I muttered as I played with the remainder of my food, my shoulders lifting heavily. "I still don't know how to wrap my head around it."

"What are you going to do?" She waved half a strip of bacon at me. "Are you going to press charges for everything she did?"

"No." My head shook as I explained, "Chase and I already talked about it. If she does anything else, we'll do something then. Get a trespass warning or a restraining order against her —something, I don't know how it all works." An incredulous breath fled from me. "Just so crazy to even be talking about things like that for her. She was going to be my maid of honor."

"I know, friend. I'm sorry," Anna said sadly. "So unreal. Honestly, no offense or anything, but if she wouldn't have confessed to it, I wouldn't believe that any of it had been her."

"No, none taken," I said quickly, waving off her words. "I'm right there with you."

"Not entirely sad LT's gone though," she murmured, making a face as if she wasn't sure if she was saying too much too soon.

I tried to voice one of my go-to reprimands, all while fighting the urge to laugh.

When the laugh slipped free, Anna pointed at me. "See? You agree."

"I don't *dis*agree."

"Knew you didn't like her either," she said victoriously.

"It wasn't that," I said in LT's defense, even though I had absolutely no reason to defend her. "I just didn't love that she was always hitting on Chase, even if I knew there was nothing to worry about." When Anna continued watching me, waiting because she knew that wasn't all, I conceded, "Fine, I never liked her."

Anna smacked her hand on the table. "I knew it!"

"She made really good pastries though," I added, my mouth falling into a pout because I was going to miss getting free bread and other baked goods on the regular.

"Ugh, she did," Anna said on a groan, then scooted her chair back and gave me a sarcastic look as she stood. "And in the words of LT, *'I have to pee.'* I might also need an Uber because *whoa.*" She gave me a knowing look as she took a second to make sure she was steady before leaving me there.

Fighting another laugh.

Feeling lighter than I had since the bomb had been dropped and capable of getting past the shocking betrayal and loss of my best friends.

———

"That isn't your car," Chase said when the Uber pulled away from our house a while later. Expression all adoring bemusement as he wrapped an arm around my waist and pulled me close for a kiss that was slow, lingering perfection and had me swaying into him even more.

"Mimosas," I said in way of explanation as I pushed up on my toes to steal another kiss.

A confirming sound rolled up his throat as a smile hinted at the edges of his mouth. "That right?"

"Anna had most of them," I said as he turned, leading us up the driveway. "But I still had maybe three . . ." I drew out the number, smiling mischievously as I did and laughing when he playfully dug his fingers into my side.

"And how'd it go? Telling her everything."

"She was shocked, obviously," I said with a shrug. "Wanted to make sure I was okay and asked what we were going to do, but it was good. You know how Anna is, she finds a way to laugh at every situation, and she did the same with this. It made me feel better overall. Made me feel ready to mentally deal with it and move past it."

"Good," Chase murmured, but I could still see that worry lingering in his eyes. See that whisper of his misinterpreted guilt. As if he'd had any hand in it . . . as if he'd been the cause of everything Samantha had done.

And I hated that those false memories still had that pull on him.

"You're still trying to work around what you thought happened and what actually happened, aren't you?" I asked when he brought us to a stop in the garage, where he'd been when I'd gotten home.

"Feels like both are real sometimes," he admitted as he pulled me close again, one of his hands lifting to gently trail across my jaw and down my neck and sending a shiver of heat through me. "I can remember what happened, but then I'll get this drop in my stomach like I'm still fucking terrified because I've done something. Like I'm terrified for when we find out."

"But you didn't do anything," I reminded him, and he subtly nodded.

"I know." His shoulder lifted. "Might take time to go away the same as it took time to remember."

I clenched my hands in his shirt, my fingers grazing the hard muscles of his stomach when I asked, "And do you?" I asked, uncertainly easing into the topic we'd avoided yesterday. "Remember *everything*?"

His eyes skated over my face again and again before he admitted, "No," on a hushed breath. "I don't know what all I'm missing, but it felt like everything slammed into me at once yesterday morning. And then later, I realized I didn't remember certain things like your family or graduating. But this morning, I woke up to a memory I hadn't realized I'd still been missing, and I've been getting little pieces back all morning."

I pressed my fist against his stomach as excitement wound through my veins. "It'll all come back," I whispered encouragingly, my smile matching the one slowly creeping across his face. "What'd you wake up to?"

"You," he said as that smile shifted. Turned soft and made my heart do the craziest things. "The first time we went to the beach and spent hours talking and getting to know each other like we had any reason to be out there when you were still taken. Pretending we weren't already falling in love with each other."

"I love that beach," I said as those memories danced through my mind. Our story that was complicated and painful and so beautiful.

"That *spot*," he corrected gently. "I remember kissing you there. I remember not being able to let you go. I remember getting so lost in each other that we forgot the entire world because nothing mattered more in that moment than us."

A storm of wings took flight in my stomach as he quickly

took me through our life, all while his fingers continued making feather-soft designs along my skin.

"I remember asking you to marry me *there* because that's where I fell in love with you." Tenderly curling his hand around my neck, he tilted my head back so he could search my eyes before both of his hands dropped to mine. "I remember all those things, but I fell in love with you again *right here*."

My chest shook with the impact of my next breath when he pressed a small, hard object against my left palm.

"I already asked you because there was no waiting at that moment, and that's how it's always been with us—getting caught up in a moment and acting then. But I want to give this back to you," he said as he twisted my hand so my palm was facing up, my engagement ring cradled inside.

And the sight of it there rocked me. Overwhelming me with the significance of it.

This wasn't just a promise—we'd already made that long before. This was a mountain filled with heartbreak and uncertainties that had been placed in front of us.

And we'd overcome it.

"Every version of me has fallen in love with you," he said as he gently picked up the ring and grabbed my hand in his. "Every version of me will love you until time ends. Marry me, Scarlet."

A breath that was equal parts joy and emotion tumbled past my lips as I nodded. "I will marry every version of you," I said unwaveringly and tipped my head up to press my mouth to his when he slid the ring onto my finger, where it belonged.

Where it would stay.

In every version of our lives.

EPILOGUE

CHASE
One Year Later

M y stare drifted around my parents' living room, taking in all the holiday decorations and love flowing through the room. The piles of opened presents stacked by everyone because my parents didn't know how to do anything *small*.

Then again, nearly all the presents were forgotten once Konrad proposed to Bree.

Nearly because Brandon and Harper's son, Liam, was squealing at pitches only dogs should be able to hear from his new sit-and-play, having the time of his life. All while my family and friends doted on him between conversations of their own about McGowan's, Brandon and Harper's news that they were expecting again, and, of course, Bree wanting to get married *yesterday*.

But I just watched. Taking it all in. Afraid to miss a thing.

Because as absurd as it was, I still had moments where this overwhelming sensation would grip my chest, warning me that my entire life could disappear if I so much as closed my eyes.

And with how perfect life was, I'd been having those moments more and more often—this morning included.

Then again, I still had moments where it would hit me—a flash of something that never happened. Stronger than a dream. Weaker than a memory.

And it always took a second too long to remember that was never my life. A second too long to realize that rush of anger with Erin or sliver of jealousy with Brandon were completely unwarranted.

But they all knew. They understood.

Of everyone, Scarlet understood because she'd been there through it all. She knew exactly how my mind had twisted things around, and she knew she'd been at the center of every altered memory.

For our family and friends, *"the other Chase"* was now something of a joke whenever anyone noticed me with an expression that wasn't what they considered *me*.

But for the most part, our lives had finally gone back to normal.

Surfing in the morning. Gym and breakfast with the guys after. Scarlet in the garage with her training sessions. Me in the shop, doing what I loved. And Chinese food whenever I irritated my girl, which was often enough.

"You're quiet," Scarlet said from where she sat between my legs, voice low to keep from drifting and filled with understanding when she asked, "Are you trapped between lives?"

"Thinking."

She squeezed my arm comfortingly before her fingers returned to their mindless task of slowly spinning my wedding band around and around my finger. "What about?"

"Chinese food." A coughing laugh punched from my lungs

when she jammed her elbow into my stomach. "Kidding," I rasped.

"Ass," she murmured lightheartedly.

"I was thinking about *this*," I said seriously, then caught her fingers between mine and placed our hands on her six-month pregnant belly. "How it feels like we got to this place exactly when we were supposed to. How, in every life, you're my world."

She rested her head against my chest as a contented sigh pushed from her lips. "Trying to make me fall in love with you, Chase Grayson?"

"Thought I'd already done that?"

I felt her amused hum vibrate against my chest before she shifted enough to be able to look up at me. A soft, teasing smile lighting up her face that fell into a perfect, sensual *o* when I continued.

"You consume me," I whispered, voice low and rough and dripping with honesty. "Then. Now. In every life."

Those eyes I loved so much danced when she echoed, "Every life."

THE END

Look for more *Taking Chances* novels from Molly McAdams!
Taking Chances (available now)
Stealing Harper (available now)
Trusting Liam (available now)

Coming soon . . .

It's been years since we've seen the blended Rebel family. But while they've been living *moderately* normal lives for the first time in generations, their enemies have been gathering— waiting for the perfect time to pay back past sins.

Because as we already know, no one ever truly escapes the mafia . . .

So, it's time to go back to Wake Forest.

It's time to recruit new blood into the family.

Prepare for Diggs's story!
Read the Redemption and the Rebel series today!

ACKNOWLEDGMENTS

Cory—As always, thank you for being my constant support. Everything I do is possible because of you. I love you!

Kelly—I wouldn't have written this without the push from you! Thank you so, so much. Peas and carrots.

Molly, Amy, and Nicole—A massive thank you for the never-ending support and encouragement. Your friendships mean the world to me. I don't know what I would do without y'all.

Molly's Monsters—Y'all are literally the best group on Facebook. Thank you for all your support, encouragement, and the amazing, uplifting spirit y'all have created in there.

My readers—I'm so lucky to have the best readers in the world. Thank you for *ten* amazing years of publishing, and thank you for loving Chase, Harper, and Brandon so much that I had no choice but to tell this story.

Letitia—Thank you, thank you, thank you for the gorgeous cover. You're such a rock star!

ABOUT THE AUTHOR

Molly grew up in California but now lives in the oh-so-amazing state of Texas with her husband, daughter, and fur baby. When she's not diving into the world of her characters, some of her hobbies include hiking, snowboarding, traveling, and long walks on the beach . . . which roughly translates to being a homebody and dishing out movie quotes with her hubby. She has a weakness for crude-humored movies and loves curling up in a fluffy blanket during a thunderstorm . . . or under one in a bathtub if there are tornados. That way she can pretend they aren't really happening.

Made in the USA
Las Vegas, NV
13 September 2022

55193134R00187